Sign up for our newsletter to hear
about new and upcoming releases.

www.ylva-publishing.com

Other Books by KL Hughes

The Art of Us
Popcorn Love

the Wrong McElroy

KL HUGHES

Acknowledgments

Thank you to my wife for supporting and loving me, for encouraging me every day to keep pursuing my dreams and to be brave enough to always wear my heart on my sleeve. No love story has ever moved me as ours has. I know we will continue writing it even long after we run out of ink and words.

Thank you to my editor, Michelle Aguilar, for your dedication to making each story I tell as effective as it can be. I so appreciate your advice and guidance every step of the way, even when you ask me to slaughter my darlings.

Thank you to the Ylva team for continuing to champion queer writers and our stories, and for your hard work and dedication in making sure those stories are available to anyone seeking them (there are so many of us).

Finally, thank you to all my readers, those of you who've been with me for years and those of you who are picking up the work for the first time. Your enduring support, your enthusiasm for the work, and your continued return to the page to relive old stories or dive into new, inspires and motivates me and allows me to keep doing what I love.

Dedication

For my family – the giant, boisterous mess of laughter, banter, love, and tradition that largely informed and inspired the McElroy family. I love and miss you all, even when you annoy me.

Chapter 1

"I CAN'T BELIEVE I'M DOING this." Fiona Ng watched her reflection in the passenger-side window. Her face glowed bright against the shadowy background of the car's interior. She could just make out Michael's smile as he resituated himself in the driver's seat. "I really can't believe I'm doing this."

"What's so hard to believe? You're doing it because you're my best friend."

"I'm seriously rethinking that job position."

"Oh, so now being my friend is a job?" Michael reached over the console and yanked on a handful of her long black hair.

Fiona faced him. His dark orange curls frizzed out above his ears and appeared brown in the low light, but his freckles were still visible. They splashed across his face in varying sizes, eating up the bridge of his nose and dotting down the length of his neck. "It is when you make me be your beard for your family's four-day Christmas weekend."

"Only because I get tired of my mom and grandma nagging me about when I'm going to settle down. I'm twenty-nine, but they act like I'm halfway to the grave and should already have a two-story house and four kids and, like, a 401K or something."

"I'm not having kids with you," Fiona said. "That's taking it way too far."

"Our kids would be cute, like little ginger Mulans."

"Mulan was Chinese."

"I know, but I don't know any Chinese-Malaysian-Singaporean Disney princesses. Do you?"

"Mulan wasn't a princess." Fiona took a sip of her Starbucks iced coffee and smiled around the straw. "You realize your old Southern grandma's going to have a heart attack, right? Like, I'm going to say my last name, and her brain's probably going to short-circuit."

"Probably," Michael said, "but she at least has enough decency to keep her short-circuiting on the inside."

"Sure she does," Fiona said. "I give it twenty minutes, max, before she asks me if I know the man who runs the Chinese restaurant down the street."

"Nah. There isn't a Chinese restaurant down the street."

Fiona leveled him with a glare.

"I'm kidding," he said. "Look, it'll be fine. Just relax."

"When have you ever known me to relax?"

"True. You've got the anxiety bug."

"Incurable, unfortunately."

"Well, I still love you."

Fiona snorted. "How generous of you."

"You're welcome," he said with a shit-eating grin. "But seriously. I know you're kind of sensitive about your heritage and culture and stuff—"

"Aren't most people sensitive about their identities?"

"You know what I mean," he said. "Just that, you know, it took a long time for you to love yourself as you are and want to learn about your family and stuff."

"This pep talk is giving me a rash, Michael."

"Shut up." He laughed and poked her knee. "I'm just saying that if my grandma—or anyone, for that matter—says anything shitty, I'll put a stop to it. I've got your back."

Fiona lay back in her seat and huffed out a sigh. "You promise?"

"Promise," he said. "That is, if Lizzie doesn't beat me to it. She hasn't attended a single family function in the last five years that hasn't resulted in her lecturing someone about equality or racism or the benefits of flushing the Republican party down the toilet."

"Yeah, well, some people *need* lectures."

"No argument there." He grabbed Fiona's coffee and took a drink. "Is Lizzie the youngest? The one who just graduated high school?"

"No, that's Jessie." He passed her coffee back. "Lizzie's the one who lives in Los Angeles."

"Oh, right, the med student."

"No, that's Grace. She lives in Seattle. Lizzie's the film student, though 'student' might be stretching it a bit far. She's taking, like, *one* online workshop thing."

"You have way too many siblings."

"It's true."

"I mean, your mom really should have banished your dad to the garage or something after the first three."

"After the first *four*. Otherwise, I wouldn't have been born, and you would be miserable without me."

"That's debatable."

"Ouch, woman. Break my heart, why don't you?"

Fiona flashed a smile and pulled her feet up under her. She reclined her seat and stretched her arms above her head. "It feels like we've been driving for hours."

"We have."

"Oh, well, that would explain it, then."

"Only about an hour left now, though, so you'll get to stretch your tiny legs soon."

"My legs are glorious."

"And tiny."

"So is your—"

"Don't you dare."

Fiona let out a wild burst of laughter, then sighed. "How the hell am I going to remember everyone's names? A girlfriend would know your family's names ahead of time, right? Aren't straight girls always trying to win over their boyfriends' moms or something?"

"Lesbians don't try to win over their girlfriends' moms?"

"I wouldn't know. I've only had two relationships serious enough to warrant meeting the parents, and with one of them there were no parents. With the other, the parents lived in a different country, so potential disaster avoided."

"Well, how did they act around *your* parents?"

Fiona cut him a look. "Really?"

"Yeah. I don't even know why I asked that. There's no way you'd take a girl home to meet your parents."

"They're still convinced that if I spend enough time with you, I'll change my mind about being a lesbian."

"They seriously overestimate my swag."

"They overestimate the entire male population," Fiona said. "Also, don't say 'swag.'"

Michael snorted and shoved her shoulder. "All right. Get the pic."

"Where is it?"

"On my phone." He motioned toward the console. "It's in the family album."

Fiona scrolled through the image gallery until she found it, the same photo from his apartment back in St. Louis. Staring at her from the screen were all thirteen members of the McElroy family. Orange-red hair blazed from left to right, and freckles surrounded bright, toothy smiles. Michael, his four sisters, three brothers, mom, dad, grandma, grandpa, and, of course, the family cat, Otis, also a ginger, sat against a fake snowy backdrop in bulky Christmas sweaters that appeared itchier than they did festive. "Jesus, this is worse than the family photo my mom made us get when I was six and we all had matching bowl cuts."

"I've seen that picture, and there's no way this one is worse than that."

"Your cat is wearing an ugly Christmas sweater. Your *cat*, Michael."

"Even your grandma had a bowl cut in that picture, though."

"God, I know. You're right. Mine's worse." Fiona shook her head and used her thumbs to zoom in on the picture. "You know my grandmother has a massive print of it hanging in her house, right? Like, *why*, Gran? Why? She's proud of it."

"Honestly, I kind of want a massive print of it hanging in my apartment, too."

"I will die before I allow you to display my forced bowl cut on your corkboard."

"Might be worth it."

"Rude."

Michael laughed. "All right, so McElroy Family rundown. You ready?"

She zoomed back out with a quick tap of her thumb. "Ready."

4

"Okay, so, left to right, starting in the back. You've got my grandpa, Charlie. He died four years ago, so on to my grandma, Sophia. She's my dad's mom. My mom's parents both died when she was a teenager."

"I think you've told me that before. Car crash, right?"

"Yeah, so then it goes down to my dad, also named Charlie, and my mom, Rose, but everyone calls her Rosie."

"I'm already lost."

"No, you're not. If you can remember seven billion drugs *and* their side effects in your Pharmacology class, you can remember these names."

"I mean, seven billion is a bit of a stretch. More like 150, maybe 175."

"I saw your study guide. It was definitely seven billion."

"Your mom is cute."

"Please, no."

"She's got those sweet little wrinkles around her eyes."

"*Stop.*"

"And let's just say she's not lacking in the curves department, either. I mean, were your sisters blessed with the same—"

"I swear to God, Fiona." He reached across the car, trying to cover Fiona's mouth with his hand without taking his eyes off the road. Fiona dodged, laughing, and refreshed the phone screen.

"All right, fine. I'm stopping. So, your siblings?" She pointed to the first in line, a guy who looked nearly identical to Michael, though older around the eyes and with an abundance of gray sprinkled about his otherwise orange hair. "That's Charlie, right?"

"Yeah." He didn't look at the photo, focusing instead on the road, but Fiona knew he didn't need to. He knew where every person sat and who wore which ridiculous sweater.

"He's the one with kids?"

"Two girls, Lucy and Madison. They're still pretty little. His wife's name is Paige, but they're kind of on the rocks right now, so I don't even think she's coming."

"Oh."

"Yeah, no one really knows what's going on there, just that they're separated and she hasn't come to any family functions in a while now. Mom thinks she might be seeing someone else, which of course makes her want to throttle her, but Charlie keeps telling her to stay out of it and mind her own, which is ridiculous, because I don't think she's minded her own business a day in her life."

"It's a Mom thing."

"It's a Rosie McElroy thing for sure," he said. "Anyway, Charlie was the first boy in the family, so named after Dad and Grandpa. Next to him is Sophie, named after Grandma, and they're thirty-five."

"Both of them?"

"Yeah, they're twins."

"Oh yeah, I remember now."

"They act like twins too. Finishing each other's sentences, reading each other's minds. The whole nine yards. It's really annoying."

"I can read *your* mind sometimes."

"No, you can't."

"I always know what you want to eat."

"Okay, fine. I'll give you that."

"Though, admittedly, it's pretty easy when you only ever want pizza or sushi."

"And yet you always know exactly which one."

"Skills," Fiona said. "Okay, so, what about the rest of them?" She looked down at the picture and followed along as Michael spoke, matching each face to its given name, and trying to burn the information into her mind so she wouldn't mess up when she finally met them all. If she was going to do this whole fake-girlfriend thing, she was determined to do it right. She hadn't majored in musical theater for one semester freshman year for nothing.

"After Sophie is Jack. He's thirty-two."

"He's the one in the Marines?"

"Right. He's stationed in Bahrain right now, though, so he won't be there. And then there's me, of course, the handsome one right there in the middle."

"Right. Yeah. The smug one there. I see him. Next."

"Then Brian and Grace, who are also twins, but they don't really act like it. I mean, they're close but not—"

"Not psychically in tune?"

"Right."

"How old are they?"

"Twenty-eight."

"So, your mom must have had them pretty soon after you."

"Yeah, they were almost two months premature, too, so we're actually only ten months apart," Michael said. "Brian likes to joke that me, him, and Grace are actually triplets."

"Damn. Two sets of twins. Your mom's poor vagina."

"Ew. Stop."

"I'm just saying."

Michael shuddered.

"Oh, grow up. It's a body part, not the creature from *The Black Lagoon*."

"Says *you*."

"Well, if it wasn't for that creature, you wouldn't exist."

"So, *anyway*," Michael said, "after Brian and Grace is Lizzie. She's twenty-six, then last is Jessie, and you know she's eighteen. Just graduated high school in May."

Fiona laughed and pointed at Jessie's face. "She's the only one in this picture that looks more annoyed than happy to be there."

"Yeah, Jessie's never been great at swallowing her feelings. Well, feelings of hatred, at least."

Fiona slid her finger back to the woman right before Jessie, who was sporting a cheesy, wide grin and long hair that was a dark shade of orange like Michael's. She had two different-colored eyes, one blue and the other green. "Lizzie has heterochromia?"

"Heterochromia? Seriously?"

"That's what it's called."

"Weird-ass eyes is fine," he said. "No need to get all technical about it."

"Right, because being an ass is better than being technical."

"Sometimes." He shrugged. "Anyway, makes her easy to spot, so that should help you out. Plus, Lizzie's always the loudest, which means she's also always the one Mom is yelling at. Charlie's easy, too, because his hair is more gray than red now, and Grace is the one with the nose ring, so no trouble there either."

"Sure."

"I'm serious. It's going to be fine."

Fiona clicked off the screen and put Michael's phone back in the console. "You know you're paying for every pizza we eat for the next year."

"Well, I—"

"That wasn't a question."

He laughed. "Fine."

Fiona lay her head back and closed her eyes. "Sophia, Charlie, Rosie, Charlie, Sophie, Jack, Brian, Grace, Lizzie, Jessie."

"Otis," Michael added, and Fiona let out a long groan.

The McElroy family home was more of a country mansion than anything, which didn't surprise Fiona. She knew Michael's parents were well off. His mom was a caterer, and his dad, though now retired, had owned a hugely successful chain of farm-supply stores that spanned three states. And well, they definitely would have needed the space. Raising eight kids and a cat required ample square footage. Still, standing in the snow ten feet from the McElroy's massive wrap-around porch and staring up at the towering columns intimidated her.

"I feel microscopic next to this house," Fiona said as Michael grabbed their bags from the trunk. "I mean, am I suddenly the size of an ant, or is that just my imagination?"

Michael slammed the trunk closed and handed her one of the suitcases. "What do you mean 'suddenly?'"

"Please don't make me hit you with my suitcase. It's heavy, and I don't want to have to lift it that high."

"You wouldn't even if you could."

"Your parents are going to be really sad when they discover your body in the snow tomorrow morning, frozen like a popsicle, while I sleep soundly and warmly in your childhood bed."

"Good luck," Michael said. "I don't think anyone ever died from blunt force trauma to the *knees*."

Fiona shoved him. The snow shifted under his feet, and down he went, tumbling to the ground and pulling Fiona down with him. She landed on top of him with a grunt, and her loud laugh transformed into a cloud of fog. He smashed a handful of snow in her hair, then tried to scramble away from her before she could retaliate. "Hold still," she said, "or it'll be worse when I finally catch you."

"Oh, honey, see! I told you I heard something outside."

Both Fiona and Michael froze in place, Fiona on top of Michael and Michael wedged down into the snow. They turned toward the porch. Fiona recognized Michael's parents standing inside the open front door, the light from the house haloing around them. They wore matching forest-green bathrobes over pajamas, and Charlie Sr.'s thinning orange hair stuck up on one side. He was tall and lean. His wife was the opposite. The top of her head barely reached his upper arm, and despite her thick robe, it was easy to see her body was curved like a country road.

"Oh, hey!" Michael looked up at Fiona, still perched on top of him, then back to his parents. "Uh, hey, Mom, Dad. What are you guys doing up so late?"

"I told you we were going to stay up until you got home, honey," Rosie said as she smoothed down her coarse hair. "You didn't tell us you were bringing a...a friend with you."

"Oh, right. Yeah." He looked at Fiona again, but neither of them moved. It was as if the snow had melted through their skin and into their brains.

"Uh, son," Charlie Sr. said, clearing his throat, "what are you two *doing* out here, exactly?"

Reality snapped into place, and Fiona shot off Michael as if he'd suddenly caught fire and she was afraid of getting burned. They jumped to their feet and brushed snow off their clothes as they mumbled about how they were "just playing around" and tripped over a snow...man, or something.

"Right," Charlie Sr. said as he and Rosie both visibly fought smiles. "Tripped over a snowman. Seems plausible."

"Shut up." The words chirped out of Michael in the tiniest squeak Fiona had ever heard. He cleared his throat and wiped his hands on his pants. "So, uh, anyway, Mom, Dad, this is Fiona. She's my, um, girlfriend."

"Girlfriend," Fiona repeated with an awkward nod. The smile she plastered on felt as uncomfortable as it likely looked. "Super excited to finally meet you both."

⁌∽↝◦⧫◦↜∽⁌

The walk up the grand staircase and down the first hall went on forever. Fiona aged a year with each rapid-fire question Mrs. McElroy hurled their way. It seemed never-ending.

"Since when do you have a girlfriend, Michael? Why didn't you tell us you had a girlfriend? She's beautiful, honey. Oh, silly me. Fiona. Fiona, isn't it? Fiona, you're just beautiful. Isn't she beautiful, Michael?"

"Yes, Mom."

"Fiona, will you be staying the whole weekend with us?"

"Yes, Mrs. McElroy, if that's all right."

"Call me Rosie, and of course it's all right. It's wonderful. I've been hoping Michael would settle down now for ages. I always worry about him up there in St. Louis on his own. Don't I, Charlie? Don't I worry?"

Charlie Sr. hummed in agreement from down the hall, trailing along behind them, and Rosie let out a sweet laugh. "Oh, Michael, honey, Charlie's girls wanted to stay in your room, so you'll have to stay in Jack's."

"That's fine."

"He face-called us just the other day, you know, and he practically has no hair at all now," she said. "He just keeps cutting it shorter and shorter."

"It's FaceTime, Mom," Michael said. "And I'm pretty sure he has to keep his hair short."

"Well, I know that, honey, but *that* short?" She stopped at a door somewhat hidden in a nook at the end of the hall and opened it. "Here we are." She heaved their suitcases, which she'd insisted on carrying, onto the bed. "If you need any extra clothes, I brought in some of your things from your room. They're in the closet, and there are spare socks and underpants in the dresser for you, too."

Michael's cheeks turned the same color as his hair. "Uh, thanks, Mom. I'm good, though."

"Okay, but you know you always say that, and then you never have enough."

"Yeah, I know, but I'm good. Really, Mom. Thanks. I'll just do some laundry if I need to."

"Well, they're perfectly good underpants, honey. I don't see why you don't just wear what's already—"

"He's fine, Rosie," Charlie Sr. said from the doorway, and Rosie sighed.

"All right, fine," she said. "I know when I'm being hushed." She patted Michael's cheek, then turned toward Fiona. "Now, do I need to set you up in another room, Fiona, or did you two want to stay together?" She looked at Michael and dropped her voice to a whisper. "You know your father and

I don't have any rules against your girlfriend staying in your room with you, honey. You're a grown man. We just ask that you keep the volume down and be safe."

Fiona had only seen Michael so embarrassed one other time, and it was when he'd gotten food poisoning sophomore year and hadn't made it to the cafeteria bathroom in time. He hadn't even bothered washing his clothes after, because he'd refused to acknowledge what happened. Instead, he'd thrown it all away—his pants, underwear, socks, and even his shoes. She felt his pain this time around, though. Heat made the skin of her chest and neck itch, and she imagined she looked nearly as red and splotchy under her shirt as Michael appeared from the chin up.

"Mom, really? Come *on*."

"It's nothing to be embarrassed about, Michael. You know, Charlie and his wife used to—"

"I'll take my own room," Fiona cut in, "if that's all right, Mrs. McElroy. I mean, Rosie."

"Really, Fiona. You're welcome to stay here with Michael. Don't feel like you have to separate."

"She said she wants her own room, Mom."

"I heard her, honey. I'm just making sure you two aren't—"

"You know what?" Fiona clapped her hands together. "I'll just stay here. If you're sure it's all right, then I'll stay with Michael."

Michael bugged his eyes out at her, and Fiona mimicked the expression. They stared at one another until Rosie interrupted the showdown by yanking them both by their necks into a tight hug.

"Okay, well, you kids settle in, then, and we'll see you in the morning." She released them and kissed Michael's cheek. "I'm so happy you're home. Lizzie will be here in the morning. She's excited to see you since you two missed each other last year."

"Okay, cool," Michael said, still red in the face. "Night, Mom."

Fiona felt her face stretch again into that same pained smile as before. She nodded. "Good night, Rosie."

"Good night, you two." She shooed her husband down the hall, then closed the door behind her.

The moment she left, Michael turned on Fiona. "Stay *here*? What were you thinking?"

"I was thinking your mom was never going to leave until we made it clear that we love each other so much we can't stand to sleep in separate beds. I was giving her what she wanted."

"You never give my mother what she wants. I *told* you this. If you give her what she wants every time she wants something, she'll keep wanting things until you give her your freaking soul."

"Oh, Christ, Michael. The woman's your mother, not the Grim Reaper."

"But she's like the mother of all mothers. She could probably literally mother you to death."

"Fine. Next time, I'll try to be more adamant in *letting her down* and *disappointing her*, then. I mean, what's the big deal? It's not like we haven't slept in the same bed before."

"I know that." He shoved his suitcase onto the floor and collapsed on the bed. "That's not the problem."

Fiona grabbed a few empty hangers from the open closet and began taking her clothes out of her own suitcase, hanging them piece by piece. "Then what is it?"

"It's that my parents and all my siblings and my freaking *grandma* are now going to think we're in here *boning* every night."

The shudder that worked its way up Fiona's spine couldn't be helped. She tried to fight it, but there was no use.

"See!"

"Yeah, all right, that's weird, but it's not like we actually are in here boning, so who cares what they think? I mean, you wanted everyone to think I'm your girlfriend, right? So, there you go." She stretched out beside him. "At least your mom gets excited for you. I texted my mom that I aced my Physiology exam, and she said, 'Not bad. Your father bought lemon trees on sale for the garden. Buy one, get one half off.'"

Michael laughed. "I love your mom." He wrapped his arm around Fiona's shoulders and sighed. "It's going to be a long weekend, isn't it?"

"Definitely."

Chapter 2

"WAKEY, WAKEY, EGGS AND BAKEY, loser!"

The words thumped through the haze of sleep mere seconds before the weight of a body slamming into hers jolted Fiona awake. She let out a horrendous scream as the person landed directly on top of her and yanked the comforter off her head. Her arms flailed helplessly as her hair clouded her vision.

"Oh, holy shit! You are *not* my brother."

Fiona's heart raced. Her eyes were sticky with sleep and blinded by hair, and all the oxygen in the room seemed to be evading her lungs. She quickly swiped her hair away and blinked up at the petite but curvy young woman straddling her and slowly calmed as she took in each feature: frizzy dark-orange hair, a toothy grin, one blue eye, and one green.

"Lizzie, what the hell are you doing?"

Fiona leaned up to see Michael standing in the open doorway of the bathroom, mouth covered in toothpaste foam and a towel wrapped around his waist. Clearly, he'd been up for a while.

"Uh, apparently making a complete jackass of myself," Lizzie said with an awkward laugh. She looked down at Fiona, red-cheeked. "Sorry. I'm Lizzie."

"Fiona."

"Oh, Fiona! Hey, yeah, Michael's talked about you before. Nice to finally meet you."

Fiona pressed a hand to her heart and took a deep breath. "You scared the hell out of me."

"Yeah, the bloodcurdling scream sort of gave that away."

"Do you always introduce yourself by jumping on people?"

Lizzie smiled, her entire face crinkling. Freckles spotted her face like a game of connect-the-dots, and Fiona suddenly found herself thinking of connecting them, one by one, with the tip of her finger. She used the sleeve of her dark-green flannel shirt to swipe a bit of hair from her face. "Only the cute ones."

A jolt sparked low in Fiona's gut. She squirmed, surprised. They stared at one another for a long moment, unmoving, with Lizzie still straddling her and Fiona wondering where she should put her hands. She felt flushed and confused and entirely unwilling to contemplate the fact that the weight of Michael's sister on top of her felt so much more pleasant than burdensome.

"Uh, Liz?" Michael said.

"Yeah?" Lizzie didn't look at Michael. Her gaze was fixed on Fiona.

"You can get off my girlfriend now."

Fiona blinked hard. *Shit.* For a moment, she'd forgotten she was there to be Michael's Christmas girlfriend. Lizzie slid off her so quickly that she landed on her ass on the floor. She sprang up a second later, hair flying around her face and her thin sweater wrinkled up on one side.

"Girlfriend?" she said. "Huh. Wow."

"Yeah." Michael slung an arm around his sister. "Girlfriend."

Lizzie patted his back and ducked when he tried to kiss her forehead with toothpaste-covered lips. He laughed and went back to the bathroom to spit.

"So, uh, how did you manage to convince someone to date you?" she called after him, her gaze returning to Fiona. "I mean, she's a real girl, Mike, not the inflatable kind. I'm so proud."

"Ha." The porcelain and tile made his voice echo. "Very funny."

"It definitely took some convincing," Fiona said as she pulled the blanket up a bit higher to cover herself. It was silly since she was fully clothed, but she couldn't help it. She felt uncomfortable and slightly aroused, which made zero sense. The lingering haze of sleep, paired with waking to a cute girl on top of her, had clearly caused her brain to short-circuit. *Michael's sister*, she scolded herself. *She's Michael's sister.* The scolding didn't stop her from tracing Lizzie's curves with her eyes. She had her mother's figure—full breasts, wide hips, and, like Fiona, barely passed the five-foot mark.

Lizzie's boisterous laugh was surprising for her size. The sound of it sent the same jolt through Fiona as before. *Oh no.*

"See," Lizzie said. "Even your girlfriend knows you've got no game."

Michael reappeared in sweatpants and a T-shirt, mouth clean of foam. He grabbed his sister before she could jump away. "Is that right?" He managed to get her in a headlock and knuckled the top of her head until her coarse hair was a frazzled mess of tangles. "Two years you don't see me, and this is the treatment I get?"

"Just telling it like it is, Big Brother," she grunted from his armpit. She then managed to knee him in the back of the leg hard enough to break his balance. He stumbled, releasing her, and she smacked him on the back of the head before taking off out of the room. "I'm telling Mom!"

"Big baby!" Michael called after her, then turned toward Fiona. "Still wish you had siblings?"

The bathroom served as her safe haven for thirty minutes before Michael finally knocked on the door and said, "I hope you're using the air freshener."

"Gross. Shut up."

"I'm just saying. I've known you for three years now, and I've never seen you take more than fifteen minutes to get ready."

"I'm preparing for my soul to depart from my body."

"I thought you said she was just my mom, not the Grim Reaper."

"After meeting her *and* your sister, I'm rethinking my position." Fiona stared at herself in the mirror, her freshly showered face and damp black hair gleaming back at her. The brown skin of her face was bare and shiny from a wash and a tad paler than usual. Sun had become a foreign thing to her, as she'd spent her summer bopping back and forth between the university library and the hospital. She hated the way makeup clogged up her pores, so it never bothered her not to wear it. Not until now. She hadn't expected to feel nervous, yet she found herself hiding in Jack's bathroom, overthinking her natural amount of cuteness and wondering if she should, in fact, be considerably cuter. She couldn't stop smoothing her hands down her plain white sweater and black leggings. *I am a bland breakfast date. What if they don't like me?*

15

"Let me in."

She popped the latch, and Michael squeezed in behind her, wearing a red St. Louis Cardinals T-shirt and gray sweatpants. At the sight, Fiona instantly felt better. His nose wrinkled as he closed the door behind him. "You could have at least lit a match or something." Fiona smacked his shoulder, eliciting a laugh. "Everybody likes you, Fi."

"You have a point."

"I always have a point."

"And occasionally, it's a good one." She grabbed her brush from the sink and held it over her shoulder. "Braid my hair?"

"Fine. But you can't tell anyone it was me."

"I won't."

"Sit down."

Fiona settled down on the closed toilet seat and turned her back to Michael. She propped her feet up on the side of the tub and slouched her shoulders. Instantly, she heard her mother's voice in her head telling her to sit up straight or else she would end up a hunchback like her great-great grandmother who she'd never actually met. Fiona scoffed at the internal scolding and slouched even more. Behind her, Michael began to work the hairbrush through her hair, snagging a few times on tangles he then gently worked out.

"Mike?"

"Hm?"

Fiona closed her eyes at the bristles scratching across her scalp. It was soothing. "What kind of couple do you think we'd be if we actually were one?"

"That's easy. We'd be the hermit couple."

Fiona snorted. "The *what* couple?"

"You know." He separated her hair with the brush and gathered up three thin sections to weave together. "We'd be the couple no one ever sees because all we do is sit at home together and watch our favorite shows and order takeout and fight over *Mario Kart* and whether Batman is really a superhero or not."

"Not," Fiona said at the same time Michael added, "Which he totally is."

"You realize we're never going to agree on this, right?"

"Definitely not."

Fiona shifted on the toilet and sighed. "You really don't think we'd be one of those fun couples everyone wants to hang out with?"

"Sit still."

"Well, this toilet seat isn't exactly comfortable, and you're taking forever."

"Do you want a good braid or a sloppy one?" Michael thumped the back of her ear. "It's not my fault you've got a bony ass."

"Just hurry up."

"I'm going as fast as I can. And no, I don't think we'd be one of those fun couples. Not to say we aren't fun. We just never go anywhere."

"We go places."

"The grocery store, each other's apartments, and the movie theater on seven-dollar Sunday don't count, Fi."

Fiona deflated. "I've become a fossil," she said, "a sad, lesbian fossil whose longest relationship is with a ginger man, and I haven't even finished graduate school yet."

Michael secured her braid with a rubber band from the countertop and said, "People love fossils. There are whole museums dedicated to them."

"You realize I haven't had a girlfriend in more than two years, right?"

"You've been busy with school."

"My vagina is a stone."

Michael quietly began to hum a familiar tune. It took a moment for Fiona to recognize the well-known score of Chopin's "Funeral March," and as soon as she did, she whirled on the toilet seat and sucker-punched Michael in the gut. "Hate you."

A grunt escaped as he clutched his stomach. He then wrapped an arm around her and grinned as he led her out of the bathroom, laughing. "Hate you, too, kid."

⁂

The McElroys' kitchen was the size of her whole apartment back in St. Louis, and once Fiona saw the entire family stuffed into the space, she understood why. Michael's siblings crowded around the kitchen island while Rosie cooked breakfast. Together, they made the enormous space appear much smaller, more like a walk-in closet with a stove than an actual kitchen. The room smelled divine, like smoky, sizzling pork and fresh-baked bread. The sheer goodness of it was overwhelming, and Fiona's mouth began to water. Her stomach rumbled. She imagined it had always been like this in their house—redheaded kids screeching and squealing and scrambling about while the divine scents of a Southern smorgasbord wafted around, room by room. She smiled as an image of a tiny Michael stuffing his face popped into her mind.

"Mike!"

The eldest sibling, Charlie, stood from his stool. He was tall and lean-muscled, though not as tall as Michael, and sported short hair that was mainly gray and a smile Fiona could only describe as contagious. The green John Deere T-shirt he wore was weathered and so faded that the large logo in its center had nearly disappeared.

"Hey, man, get in here." He yanked Michael into a hug and clapped him on the back. "Good to see you."

"Yeah, Mom told us all about your new girlfriend, Mikey."

Another brother, whom Fiona assumed had to be Brian since Jack couldn't be there, stayed seated. He was stockier than his brothers, shorter overall, and thicker around the middle and in the face. His buzz cut appeared in sharp contrast to the shaggy, short styles of the other two, and his face was further distinguished by a dense cluster of freckles just under his right eye. "We thought you might be too *busy* to come down to breakfast, if you know what I mean."

Fiona snorted when Rosie smacked Brian on the back of the head with a dish towel. She wore the same forest-green robe she'd donned the night before. "Stop teasing your brother."

"You're right, Mom. I should respect my *elders*."

"Watch it," Michael said, then tugged Brian into a quick embrace. He kissed the top of Grace's messy head where she sat beside her twin. Fiona could tell it was Grace by the small rose-gold hoop in her slightly upturned nose. She kept her hair short, a pixie cut that had yet to be tamed for the day, and wore a purple T-shirt with *University of Washington* printed across the front in gold lettering.

Grace patted the side of Michael's face as he leaned over her. "Hey, Mike." Her voice was low and sweet until he stole a sip of her mimosa. Her tone flattened as she waved toward a glass carafe full of spiked orange juice in front of her. "Oh, yes, please drink *my* drink instead of pouring your own. It's not like there's an entire pitcher on the counter or anything."

It was only then that Fiona noticed what sat beside the carafe: a massive, almost perfectly round orange ball of fur occupied a good portion of the island countertop. Fiona frowned and stared, but no one else in the room seemed even the slightest bit bothered by its presence, so she did her best to ignore it. When Michael patted it, however, the giant ball suddenly unfurled itself to reveal a fat, angry-looking cat with a flat, punched-in face.

"Hey, big guy," Michael said, but the cat didn't seem interested in responding. He stretched out his front legs, tiny sharp nails popping out momentarily, then put his butt to Michael and jumped off. He hit the floor soundlessly and curled around Rosie's leg as Michael scoffed. "Fine, then, Otis. Be like that. I didn't want to pet you anyway."

"Oh, he's just sleepy," Rosie said, adopting the most ridiculous baby voice Fiona had ever heard. She bent, lugged Otis up into her arms, and squashed his flat face against hers. "Isn't that right, little Oti-pootykins? Yes, he's just tired. Yes, he is." She blew on his face, then kissed him, loudly. "You love your bubby, don't you? Yes, you do. Yes. Yes, you love all your bubbies and sissies, don't you?" Another loud, smacking kiss, then she sat him back on the floor and squirted a dollop of hand sanitizer into her palm from a pump bottle on the counter. "He'll let you love on him later."

"Yeah, right. He hates everyone but you and Grandma." Michael took another sip of Grace's mimosa, then set the glass back on the table. "Where's Soph? And Lizzie?"

Charlie waved a hand to indicate the rest of the house. "Somewhere wrangling my children, most likely."

"Because he can't do it himself," Brian said.

"Incoming!" The familiar voice drew Fiona's attention toward the door a second before one tiny strawberry-blonde girl in pink leggings and a green sweater zipped by her. A second later, another, dressed in what appeared to be a cross between an elf costume and a pair of footy pajamas, barreled into Fiona's legs. The little girl stumbled, teetered over, then got up and took off again as if nothing had happened at all. Lizzie was on the latter's heels. Her hair flew out from her head as she gave chase, and her goofy smile made Fiona's stomach stir.

"Sorry," she said, nearly knocking into Fiona as well. She steadied herself by latching onto Fiona's arm, and the two of them were suddenly sharing the same thin space again. They stared for one tense moment, then Lizzie dropped her hand and carried on after the girls, disappearing into another room.

"Girls, say hi to your Uncle Mike," Charlie called after them, but they were already gone. He looked at Michael. "Sorry, man. They like Lizzie better than you."

"So do I," Brian teased, and Michael whacked them both on the backs of their heads.

A sudden presence behind Fiona startled her. She turned to find a woman with eyes the muted color of a cloudy sky and the same contagious smile as Charlie. She was taller than the other McElroy women, closer to her twin's height, and her long, auburn hair was pulled back in a low bun. "You must be Fiona," she said and held out a hand. Fiona shook it gently. "I'm—"

"Sophie." Fiona hadn't memorized their names and faces for nothing. "Yeah, I recognize you from Michael's family picture."

"Oh God. It wasn't the one with the awful Christmas sweaters, was it?"

"Actually, it was exactly that one, yeah."

Sophie groaned. "Well, plus side is you've now seen us at our fashion worst, so we can only improve from there, right?"

"Says the thirty-five-year-old woman wearing pajama pants covered in cartoon frogs," Brian said.

Sophie looked down at her pants and shrugged. "If you can resist Maddi and Lily's faces, then you tell them you don't want to wear whatever cartoon-themed clothes they probably got *you* for Christmas this year."

"Who says they got me anything cartoon-themed?"

"Have you met my kids?" Charlie downed the last of his mimosa and poured himself a bit more. "I mean, if you think cartoon frogs are bad, you're in for a rude awakening."

"Anyway." Sophie rested a hand on Fiona's arm. "It's nice to meet you."

"Yeah, Fiona, it's nice to meet—Oh, wait! I haven't actually met you yet," Brian said, then elbowed Michael in the ribs.

Michael bent over, clutching his side, and grimaced. "All right, all right."

"You make it so easy, man."

"Really, Michael," Rosie said as she set a cover over a pan of sizzling bacon, "don't just leave her standing in the doorway." She smiled at Fiona over her shoulder. "Come on in, hon. No need to be shy."

Fiona took a few steps into the room, and Michael awkwardly wound their hands together. "Uh, well, guys, this is Fiona Ng. Fiona, this is my family."

"Who have no names, apparently," Grace said with a kind smile.

"I know all your names, actually."

"Yeah, she made me quiz her on the way here."

Heat flooded Fiona's face. "You weren't supposed to tell them that part."

Michael quickly called out the names of his siblings, and one by one, they waved, except for Jessie, who didn't even bother looking up from her phone. She sat with her thick, curly orange hair crowding her face, her rail-thin body swallowed by a sweatshirt three sizes too big for her, and grunted in acknowledgment. Only when the others threw napkins at her did she put her phone down long enough to say, "Michael's got a girlfriend. Cool. What do you want, a trophy?"

"And, of course, you've already met—"

The bang of body to table echoed through the room as Lizzie suddenly slid into the kitchen on her socked feet. "Son of a—"

"Lizzie," Michael said.

Lizzie rubbed her side. "What *about* Lizzie?"

"I was just saying you and Fiona have already met."

"Oh yeah." Lizzie squeezed past Charlie to snatch a piece of bacon from a paper-towel-covered plate on the counter. She crunched it down quickly while dodging her mother's swatting towel. "Sorry again about tackling you in bed this morning."

Jessie's eyebrows shot up over her phone. "Whoa."

At the same time, Rosie exclaimed, "Elizabeth Dawn, you did *what*?!"

"Relax, people," Lizzie said. "It's not what it sounds like."

"It's actually exactly what it sounds like," Fiona said, and Lizzie bit her lip to fight a smile. The sight made Fiona's face hot again. She ignored the feeling and turned toward Michael, releasing his hand to lay hers, instead, on his upper arm. It wasn't exactly intimate, but Fiona figured it looked endearing enough. "Apparently, Michael and I make similar-looking bed lumps."

Rosie huffed out a laugh. "Elizabeth, I swear." She thrust a basket of silverware toward her daughter. "Go set the table up." A stack of empty plates went to Brian next. "Come on, now, all of you. Time to eat."

"Where's Dad?" Michael asked as he took a plate piled high with bulging, grease-speckled sausage links from his mother.

"Oh, he ran down the road to pick up Grandma, but you know it takes her a while to get up and out since her hip surgery." Rosie handed the fried potatoes to Fiona and patted her shoulder. The act made Fiona smile. She hated all the awkward hovering that usually accompanied the experience of not knowing anyone. Thankfully, Michael's family wasn't the type to let anyone linger in that space for too long. They were the kind to pull you in and make you one of them. It felt almost familiar, as if Fiona had been a part of their family for years.

A heavy, handcrafted oak table occupied the center of the formal dining room and ran nearly its entire length to accommodate the McElroy clan. Seats were squashed together with barely enough room for elbows, and the chattering began before a single one was filled. Fiona followed Michael in with the last of the breakfast dishes and took the seat beside him. She was surprised when Lizzie plopped down next to her, close enough that their arms touched and Fiona could smell the lingering scent of conditioner in Lizzie's hair. Apricots.

"Hey." She snatched a yeast roll from a basket and took a huge bite, chewed once, then stored the bread in her cheek so that she looked like a redheaded chipmunk. "Mind if I sit here?"

Fiona shook her head. "It's your house."

"Correction." She swallowed the bite of roll and choked. "*Used* to be my house." The instant the words were out, she began to gag and cough.

"For God's sake, Elizabeth!" Rosie reached over and whacked Lizzie's back hard enough for the thud to echo around the dining room. "If you'd take the time to actually chew your food before swallowing it, you wouldn't risk killing yourself every time we have a meal. Put your arms up."

Lizzie threw her arms up over her head as Rosie whacked her on the back again. When the coughing fit passed, Lizzie took a drink of orange juice, then stuffed another massive bite of roll into her mouth. "Can't help it, Mom," she said around the bite, ducking under Rosie's stern glare. "It's too good, and I'm a starving artist, remember?"

"Your baby-fat cheeks say otherwise," Brian teased.

Lizzie curled her top lip at him. "That's the *roll*, jackass!"

"Language, please."

"Yeah, yeah, Mom. *He* started it."

"He's mean as a striped-tail bug, I know, but there's no help for it. He's the Devil's child, that one."

Brian snorted and bit off the end of a fat sausage link. His fingers were already coated in grease. "Ah Mom, you're going by The Devil now? It's so formal."

"She doesn't claim you, Beelzebub." Lizzie held her fingers up in a cross formation and hissed at him. "No one does."

Fiona couldn't hold her laugh in any longer. Her shoulders shook as she turned to Michael. "Is it always like this?"

"Unfailingly."

"What did your mom say? Mean as a what kind of bug?"

"Oh, the rare striped-tail bug, hailing from the seventh circle of Hell. You haven't heard of it?" He laughed. "The imaginary kind, Fi." He then dropped a couple spoonfuls of scrambled eggs onto his plate. "You want eggs?"

"Of course she does, honey." Rosie passed a heavy bowl of thick white gravy to Charlie. "She's thin as a pole. We need to fatten you up a bit, Fiona. Little meat on your bones is good for you."

"Oh, I've always been small," Fiona said. "It kind of runs in my family."

"Well, this one's that way, too." Rosie pointed her fork at Jessie. "Though for the life of me, I don't know how. She's eaten enough for four since she hit puberty. Her daddy's downright convinced she's got a hollow leg."

"There's nothing wrong with being thin, Mom," Michael said.

"I know that, silly. I just think a woman ought to have a bit of cushion on her. Keeps her warm."

"Just in case you're planning on hibernating and living off your stored fat anytime soon," Sophie said, causing an uproar of laughter around the table. "Right, Mom?"

"Oh hush, you," Rosie said, though she wore a wide smile of her own. She waved a hand at Jessie impatiently. "Lizzie, hon, pass down that plate of potatoes, will you?"

"I will if you get my name, right," Jessie said as she held the plate of fried potatoes hostage.

Rosie closed her eyes for a moment and shook her head. "Jessie. Good grief. You knew what I meant."

"Sure, *Dad*."

"Hush, you rotten egg." Rosie picked up her napkin and swatted at her youngest. Jessie, however, was out of her reach, so she only managed to hit the table. "Hand me the damned plate already."

"Language," Lizzie chirped at her, only to receive an identical napkin swat a second later. This one successfully nailed its target.

Brian shoved a huge forkful of syrup-laden pancake into his mouth. "Well, I don't know about you guys, but I fully plan on hibernating for at least an hour after this breakfast."

"Guess that would explain the ten sausage links you've eaten in the time it's taken the rest of us to pass the plates around," Jessie said from Michael's other side. She sipped orange juice through a bendy straw and casually clapped Grace's hand in a quick high five.

Brian's response was lost to Fiona as a nudging elbow distracted her. She turned toward an insistent Lizzie and found two interested eyes pinned on her, one blue and one green. "So," Lizzie said, "how are you liking your first McElroy family meal?"

But Fiona had just taken her first bite of food, a mouthful of gravy-covered biscuits, and Lizzie's words seemed like a distant memory as she closed her eyes and moaned. She opened them again when the entire room went quiet. The moment she did, however, every single person at the table burst into a fit of snickering.

"It's the gravy," Michael said. "Every time, without fail."

"This is not gravy." Fiona greedily licked her lips. "This is the nectar of the gods."

Rosie beamed and nudged the gravy bowl, which had made its way around to her again, back toward Michael. "Give her some more, hon."

"What's in this?"

"Oh, little of this, little of that." Rosie winked at her. "Recipe's been in my family for generations."

The warm press of a leg against hers distracted Fiona. She leaned back just enough to cast a subtle glance under the table. Lizzie's leg rubbed slowly up and down against hers, though deliberately or by accident, she didn't know. She looked up at Lizzie but was greeted with an eyeful of frizzy hair. Lizzie was leaning over the table, focused on Jessie, the two of them trading barbs about their musical tastes across the space Michael and Fiona both occupied. It was as if neither were there at all. No lusty glances sent Fiona's way. No cute little lip-nibbling as if to say, "Oops. Is *my* leg brushing *your* leg? Gee, how awful." There wasn't a wink in sight. No way had it been intentional.

The voice in Fiona's head scolded her. *Of course it wasn't intentional. That girl doesn't want you, Fiona. This is an innocent family breakfast, to which you were kindly invited by the best friend you're supposed to be helplessly in love with, remember?*

"Get it together," Fiona muttered under her breath.

"Hm? You say something, babe?"

Fiona tried not to frown as she turned toward Michael. *Babe? Really?* Once she saw his strained expression, however, her effort to keep from frowning became one to keep from laughing. "No, just, um, a song stuck in my head or whatever," she said. "Can't stop singing it. You know how it is. Right, *babe?*"

They stared one another down, barely suppressed laughter pulling at their lips. When Fiona snorted before she could stop herself, however, neither could restrain themselves any longer. They roared in each other's faces, shoulders shaking and eyes clenched closed. Fiona tossed her head back. Her mouth hung open, but no sound escaped behind the tiny grunts of someone catching their breath every few seconds.

"Stop," Michael said, between fits of his own. "Stop. You know I can't handle the quiet laugh. Stop it."

Fiona forced in a deep breath and blew it out slow. "Because your donkey laugh is so much better?"

"I can't *breathe*," he defended himself. "Stop it."

"You telling me to stop makes it ten times harder to stop." Fiona wheezed between the words. The laughter lost any semblance of purpose. They didn't even know why they were laughing anymore, but they couldn't make themselves quit. "Okay. Okay. Okay. We're stopping now."

She drew in a huge breath and held it. He did the same. "Don't look at me," she said, though she didn't quite say it at all. It was more what she *meant* to say, because her lips were rolled under and pinched closed, so the best she could do was hum the words and hope he understood. Of course, they'd been in this predicament enough times that he did, and he quickly turned away.

Fiona clapped a hand over her mouth and closed her eyes. She counted to ten in her head, the last of the laughter's tremors vibrating their way out of her shoulders. When she felt calm enough, she dropped her hand and let out her breath. She heard Michael do the same and glanced over. He was looking at her again, grinning.

"You're so annoying," she said, to which Michael winked and stabbed one of her gravy-laden biscuits with his knife. "Hey!" He popped half the thing into his mouth before she could stop him, the other half falling haphazardly onto his plate, and pumped his fist victoriously as he chewed it down.

It was only then that Fiona became aware of the complete absence of sound. Michael noticed, too, given the way his fast, messy chewing quickly ended in a painful gulp. They looked around the table at the now silent family, then at each other.

"Well, that was probably the most sickeningly cute thing I've ever seen you do, Mike," Grace said.

Michael suddenly seemed rather captivated by the table's wood grain. He pursed his lips and dragged his finger over one dark section. "Don't know what you're talking about."

"Oh, please." Charlie scrunched his face up and let out an obnoxious laugh, hee-hawing like a donkey with every breath. Beside him, Sophie threw her head back, mouth open, and pretended to laugh. Her shoulders shook so intensely, she appeared to be seizing. They pushed at each other's arms as they did so, and Charlie said, "Stop it. No, stop. I can't handle your adorable silent laugh!"

"No, you stop." Sophie pushed his shoulder. "You know I can't withstand your donkey sounds. They're too ridiculous and cute!"

"Stop."

"No, you stop."

"No, *you* st—"

"Okay!" Michael chucked a yeast roll across the table. It smacked into Charlie's shoulder and nearly rolled to the floor, caught by Brian in the nick of time. "We get it. That was gross."

Grace agreed with a nod. "Totally gross."

"Gross," Lizzie chimed and popped the last bit of a scrambled egg into her mouth.

"Grossest thing I've ever seen," Brian said. "Right, Jess?"

"Huh?" Jessie's head popped up from where she was subtly checking her phone under the table. "What? Oh, yeah, totally threw up in my mouth. Gag."

The rapid thudding sound of Rosie's fork knocking against the table drew everyone's attention. "Oh hush, all of you," she said. "Jessie Lynn, off your phone right now. Don't make me tell you again. And the rest of you, stop teasing your brother and Fiona. They can't help that they're in love."

"Whoa, Mom." Michael shook his head, cheeks pinking up as fast as it took him to say the words. "Let's not get crazy, okay? We've, uh, we've only been together a little while. Right, Fi?"

"Right. Yeah. Early stages, Mrs. McElroy. I mean, Rosie. But we'll see where it goes."

"Well, I just think you two are adorable together," she said after a sip from her coffee mug. A smudge of peach-colored lipstick remained on the rim when she returned it to the table. "Tell us more. How'd you two meet? When did you get together?" She smiled at Michael. "I've been trying to convince this one to get himself a nice girlfriend for years now, and all the other kids have brought someone home to meet us at one point or another, though we like to pretend Jessie never did, given how all that mess turned out."

"You said we'd never talk about it again, Mom," Jessie snapped.

"I'm not talking about it." Rosie sipped her coffee. "Then there's Lizzie, of course. She's never brought a boyfriend home, not even in high school, but then she's always been a bit of a homebody. Always had her nose stuck in her books in school, though where all that ambition went after graduation, you've got me."

"Gee, thanks, Mom." Lizzie stuck her tongue out and made a sound similar to that of a goat. It didn't make the slightest bit of sense to Fiona, but she laughed anyway.

Charlie propped his youngest, Madison, up on his knee and took a thick cloth napkin to her gravy-covered mouth. "So, what's the story, Mike?" Madison squirmed under his cleaning hand, but he kept a firm grip on her. "Sit still, Maddi. It'll be over faster if you just let me do it."

"Uh, well, we met at school sophomore year, and I guess we just hit it off."

"Ah, college hookups," Lizzie said with a dreamy look in her eye.

"Excuse me, Miss?" Rosie leaned across the table to poke her daughter. "Do you have a beau you've been hiding from us, too?"

Lizzie perked up as if someone had just jabbed her in the back with a cattle prod. Her spine went rigid, and her eyes bugged like those of a deer caught in headlights. Fiona couldn't tell if it was a look of fear, guilt, or something else. Maybe Lizzie just didn't like talking about her private life and relationships. Or maybe she was hiding something. Either way, Fiona found herself leaning toward her, as if she could possibly miss a thing from less than two feet away. She was painfully curious and didn't want to miss whatever was about to pop out of Lizzie's mouth.

"Ew, Mom. Stop." Jessie grimaced as she chewed the remainder of her biscuit, sounding as if the taste had suddenly gone bitter.

"What?"

"Don't say 'beau.'"

Lizzie's frozen spine thawed, and she relaxed as the new topic took hold—quite clearly saved by her sister's undying disapproval of, well, *everything*.

"Why not?"

"Because it's gross and old-fashioned. You might as well call yourself dad's 'little lady' or whatever." Jessie vibrated with a full-body shudder. "I gave myself chills just saying that. Ew."

"*Anyway*," Michael said, "where was I before I was so *rudely* interrupted?"

"You and Fiona met in college." Lizzie leaned back and stretched her arms up over her head. Her plate was scraped clean, the yolk-covered fork lying in its center like a bloody sword discarded on a battlefield. She'd faced a giant made of food and slayed it with fervor. "And she took pity on you because you're a sad little ginger who's been in college for, like, seventeen years now and still haven't gotten a degree. Am I warm?"

Fiona snickered. "Eh, he's not so little."

"It's true. He's gargantuan."

"Okay, first off," Michael said, "I didn't even start college until I was twenty-four, and then, you know, it takes time to figure out what you want to do. So, shut it. And second, I can't help that I'm tall. Besides, you're one to talk, Liz. You might only come up to my belly-button, but you're plenty wide."

"Damn right, I am," Lizzie said, "and every last bit of me is perfection."

"That's right," Rosie said with a chuckle. "All my girls are perfect just the way they are." Brian cleared his throat pointedly, and Rosie gave him a look. "All my boys are, too, you ornery thing." She turned her focus back to Fiona. "So, where did you and Michael meet exactly? Did you have a class together?"

Fiona wiped her mouth, having finished her last bite. She was so full, she was in physical pain, but she did her best not to show it. "Yeah. Yes, we had Calculus together, actually." She glanced at Michael. Maybe they should have come up with some special sort of story to tell about an awkward meet-cute kicking off their soon-to-be epic love story. Then again, it wasn't like the truth proved she wasn't his girlfriend. Plenty of people met their significant others in college. Besides, Michael was smiling as if he didn't mind, and it was too late to backtrack now anyway.

"Oh, are you a math major, too?"

"No, I'm actually working toward becoming a nurse practitioner. It's just a long road, and I've had a few light semesters along the way. Michael and I actually bonded over the fact that we were the oldest people in that class. Everyone else was, like, nineteen."

"Well," Rosie said, "I always say it doesn't matter when you start, just that you do."

"What if I start drinking?" Brian asked.

Beside him, Grace snorted. "A little late for what-ifs on that front, little brother. Didn't you start when we were, what, sixteen?"

"Stop calling me 'little brother.' You're literally three minutes older than me."

"And every second of those three minutes counts."

"It'll count when you *die* three minutes before me, too."

"Yeah, three minutes of having Heaven all to myself before my ignorant twin brother arrives."

"Statistically speaking," Fiona said and pointed at Brian, "you're more likely to die first."

Brian balked. "What statistics? That say what? Girl twins live longer than guy ones?"

"That women live longer than men. So, yes, I guess that would probably apply to twins as well."

"How much longer?"

"Around three years on average, I think."

"Listen, Mike," Brian said, "your girlfriend, here, is really bringing me down with her so-called 'statistics.'"

"She's a medical student, idiot."

"So?"

"So, I'm guessing she's studied a lot more statistics than you with your general-studies major that you never actually completed since you dropped out."

"Hey! General studies means I studied a lot of things, in general, and I *had* to drop out to take over the stores with Charlie."

"Honestly, it doesn't matter who's studied what statistics," Fiona said. "You can verify what I said yourself. Google is your friend."

Brian narrowed his eyes at her, then pulled his phone from his pocket. "Mom, I'm sorry, but I'm going to have to break the no-phones rule for a second."

"No, you don't. Put that away."

"Mom, it's a matter of life or death, literally."

"Well, you're not going to die right now, son," Rosie said. "You can look up your expected lifespan after breakfast."

"It's already after breakfast." He stuffed one last huge piece of biscuit in his mouth and held up his hands. His voice muffled around the bite. "I'm done. See?"

"Uh-huh. Swallow first."

As if on command, Brian immediately swallowed down his mouthful of biscuit. He winced as if it hurt, then choked. His eyes watered as he dissolved into a fit of coughing, as the rest of the table laughed and Rosie rolled her eyes.

"Grace, clap him on the back," she said, just as Charlie Sr. shuffled into the dining room from the kitchen. The tip of his nose beamed as red as Rudolph's, beat from the cold. A few strands of his gray hair were specked with fresh snow that hadn't yet melted. He frowned at Brian.

"What'd I miss?"

"Oh, nothing much," Rosie said. "Brian's concerned about dying."

"Huh," he said, then shrugged. "Well, does seem like he's well on his way, don't it?" He kissed the top of Rosie's head and took a biscuit off her plate. "Arms in the air, son." He tore a bite off the biscuit and chewed it with his mouth open. "Pass me some of that gravy, will you, hon?"

Chapter 3

Grandma Sophia was everything Fiona imagined she would be: older than dirt, adorable, and lacking entirely in the filter department. Her thick red hair was peppered with gray, and she had the same dense cluster of freckles under her right eye as Brian, magnified by one thick lens of her oversized square glasses. Her festive red Christmas sweater, featuring a jovial Mrs. Claus, clashed with the royal-purple cotton slacks she wore and the gold oxford shoes adorning her tiny feet. To top off the look, an unlit Virginia Slim cigarette sat poised like a toothpick between her lips. It bounced as she spoke but never once fell. She hobbled into the family sitting room at an angle, leaning on a cane that looked more like a gnarled limb she'd hacked from a tree than anything store-bought. One by one, she loved on her grandkids, squishing their cheeks and hugging their necks, until she finally reached Michael, who hovered at the edge of the room with his fingers laced through Fiona's.

"Hey Grandma," he said as she approached. He stooped to embrace her with one arm and let her pat his back. "How've you been?"

"Oh, I'm gettin' by, hon." Her grainy, weathered voice was the clear opposite of Fiona's own grandmother's voice, whose speech could be described more as a series of mouse squeaks than as actual words. "Come down here. Let me see your face." She adjusted her glasses, then cupped his cheek. "You're just growin' on up, aren't you?"

"Yes, ma'am." He placed his free hand over hers. "Looks that way."

Fiona smiled as she watched them together. She noticed that the more Michael was around his family, the more he was starting to sound like the fresh-faced country boy she'd met years earlier. Her smile fell, however, when Sophia's blue eyes suddenly landed on her. They dropped briefly to her hand, where it was entangled with Michael's, then crawled back up again.

"Oh, Grandma," Michael said, "this is Fiona Ng. She's my girlfriend."

Sophia's eyes narrowed a moment, then her wrinkled face split into a smile. Fiona couldn't tell if it was genuine or manufactured. Old people were always either the best liars or the worst. They'd had decades to practice their poker faces or decades to stop caring if people knew how they truly felt or not. It felt a little like Russian roulette; you never quite knew what was hidden in the chamber—disapproval or joy, loathing or acceptance. Fiona sincerely hoped that whatever was lurking behind Grandma Sophia's smile was more the latter.

"Finally got tired of us asking, huh?" Sophie waved Fiona down to her level and held out her hand. It was smooth and soft to the touch. Her bright-blue veins bulged and sprawled like spider legs under her thin, pale skin, but her handshake was firm. "Well, she's a pretty one, ain't she?"

"Thank you," Fiona said, breathing her in. The scent of stale cigarettes mingled with the overwhelming odor of menthol. She imagined Michael's father helping her rub Bengay on her joints right before heading over. "It's nice to finally meet you, Mrs. McElroy."

Sophia chuckled. "And such good English, too."

"Oh, Christ." Lizzie scoffed from where she stood leaning against the opposite wall. Fiona realized, in that moment, that everyone in the room was watching them. "Really, Grandma? You couldn't just say 'Nice to meet you, too?'"

"What?" Sophia wobbled around to look at Lizzie, keeping hold of Fiona's hand in the process. "It was a compliment."

"Mom," Charlie Sr. said and shook his head at her.

"Oh, don't 'Mom' me." She waved a dismissive hand at him. "You kids are so sensitive these days. Can't even give my own grandson's girlfriend a kind word."

Fiona didn't want the situation to spiral, so she said, "Actually, Mrs. McElroy, English is my first language."

"Well, is that right?"

"Yes, ma'am."

"Oh, enough with this *ma'am* nonsense." She patted Fiona's hand. "Call me Sophia."

"All right, then, Sophia."

"I meant no offense, hon," she said. "Back in my day, all the Chinese was immigrants."

"Grandma!" Lizzie's outcry nearly brought a wave of laughter up Fiona's throat and out. The sheer discomfort of the moment stirred in her belly, and Fiona's response to being uncomfortable had always been to laugh. She'd never been able to attend funerals because of it. She always just sent flowers or a card instead.

"What?" Sophia snapped at her granddaughter again. "What'd I do now?"

"Not all Asian people are Chinese," Lizzie said. "You shouldn't just assume where someone's from based on how they look."

"Well, excuse me, Elizabeth. I didn't realize Chinese was an insult now."

"I actually am Chinese," Fiona said, still awkwardly holding Sophia's hand, "but only part." She didn't have the slightest clue why she felt the need to elaborate or explain, but the words barreled out anyway. "My dad's Chinese. My mom is Malaysian. They both grew up in Singapore, though."

"Oh, is that right?" Sophia's eyes glazed.

Fiona still felt the need to clarify. "I was born in Los Angeles," she said. "I lived there all my life until I moved to St. Louis for college."

"Well, that's nice, isn't it?" Sophia patted Fiona's hand, then wandered off toward the kitchen, leaning on her cane. "Rosie, is there any bacon left, hon?"

As she shuffled away, Rosie gave Fiona a smile that made her look constipated and uncomfortable and followed after. Fiona turned toward Michael and raised a brow. She could sense every eye in the room on her, stares boring into the side of her face. Her stomach felt like it was trying to fold itself in half.

Michael looped an arm around her and pulled her into his side. "Hey, at least she didn't mention any Chinese restaurants, right?"

"Oh yeah, because what she *did* say was so much better." Lizzie appeared at Fiona's other side. "Sorry about her. *Her* grandparents emigrated here and pretty much spoke only Scottish Gaelic, but for some reason, she still thinks she's more American than anyone with a skin tone two shades darker than hers." She looked down at the pale skin of her own arm and laughed. "Which includes just about everyone outside this family."

When Lizzie looked up again, her different-colored eyes caught Fiona and held her. She offered up an easy smile that made Fiona suddenly wish Michael's arm wasn't around her. It became the elephant in the room, a weight knocking her down a size or two as she tried to decipher the weird energy bouncing between Lizzie and her and figure out why she felt so comforted by her presence.

"I guess that's just the South for you," Michael said. "It pretty much stays the same while the rest of the country evolves."

"That's *most* old white Americans, actually," Fiona said, "no matter where they're from. Missouri isn't any better, and you know it."

"True," Lizzie said. "She'll probably die before she changes her views."

"Who's dying?" Charlie Sr. had made his way over, shoulders hunched up awkwardly toward his ears, the same constipated expression on his face that Rosie had worn. Fiona had seen that look so many times in her life. It was nearly as uncomfortable as the conversations that always inspired it.

Jessie, who passed by them toward the foyer, said, "Everyone this afternoon."

"You wish," Brian called after her from the living-room couch.

"Oh, I don't have to wish." She paused at the intersection of the two rooms. "It's a scientific certainty, Brian. You need to come to terms with that. In fact, you all do." She pointed at her own eyes then at everyone else in the room. "Prepare yourselves."

Fiona looked up at Michael. "What are we preparing ourselves for, exactly?"

"You'll just have to wait and see."

"That sounds ominous."

Charlie Sr. chuckled at his daughter. "That's a lot of big talk, Jess."

"I can back it up," she said, then disappeared into the foyer.

Once she was gone, Charlie Sr. focused on Michael and Fiona. He glanced between them, tucked his hands into his jean pockets, and shrugged. "Listen, hon," he said to Fiona, "I just want to apologize for my mom. She means well. It's just, she's from a different time, you know."

The familiar compulsion to comfort him hit Fiona like a tidal wave. She felt obliged to tell him it was all right, to tell him that he didn't need to apologize. She'd struggled with that compulsion for as long as she could remember. It sprung up like a weed in every similar situation she'd ever found herself in. She was driven to assuage guilt she wasn't responsible for rather than stand up for herself, rather than comfort herself, rather than address the issues of offering an excuse dressed up as an apology. It should've been easy, as easy as saying, "Hey, so that's not the best way to go about this. Try this instead." But it wasn't. It wasn't easy, and it never had been, because no one liked to hear that they were in the wrong, that they'd done something offensive, that they needed to change. It invited controversy and, as Fiona had learned in the past, opened her up to worse issues than the ones she'd started out with.

"That's really not an excuse, Dad," Lizzie said, stepping up to the bat before Fiona could even work out what she wanted to say. Michael, on the other hand, only shuffled in place, quiet and apparently content to let the issue die unaddressed. "We all grow up in different times. That doesn't mean we can't learn to adapt or change the way we look at things. People do it all the time."

"Well, I know that." Charlie Sr.'s shoulders hunched even higher toward his ears so that his neck rapidly began to disappear under the rising collar of his flannel button-up. "But you just got to acknowledge that these things take time, you know? She didn't grow up the same way all you kids did."

"We grew up right here, in friggin' rural Arkansas, with the same outdated ideas as everyone else who grows up here. You think we had anything but white Christian kids at our school?"

"Well, I'm not going to argue with you about it, Lizzie, so…"

"I'm not trying to argue," Lizzie said. "I'm just saying that if she can learn to use the iPad you and Mom got her, she can learn not to be a racist. That's not an argument, Dad. It's a fact."

"Oh my God, Lizzie, we get it," Brian groaned from the couch. "You live in L.A, so now you're super 'woke' or whatever. What do you want? A pat on the back? Let it go already."

"That's exactly the attitude that keeps things the way they are, though," Lizzie said, and the room went silent, so silent that the air seemed to vibrate. It pulsed in and out around Fiona as if the walls were trying to decide whether to close in on her or not. Her throat tightened, making it hard to breathe. The longer she stood in the feeling, the more desperate she became to escape it. The longer Michael stood beside her, silent in the middle of it, the more upset she became.

She barely managed another two minutes before she shrugged Michael's arm off her shoulders and said, "I think I'm just going to run upstairs for a bit."

"Hey," Michael said, stepping after her. "You don't have to go anywhere."

"No, it's fine." She shook her head and backed toward the foyer. "I just remembered I told my mom I'd call her when we got here, and I never did. So, I should. I'm going to go do that now."

As she turned to go, Lizzie reached for her. Their hands brushed, then caught. Fiona squeezed Lizzie's fingers as hard as she could manage in the moment, her own silent way of thanking her for caring enough to occupy the uncomfortable space so few others, even Fiona's own best friend, were willing to occupy.

"Are you okay?"

"Yeah, of course. I'm fine." She shook her head again. It felt like the movement of a robot trained how to respond. She didn't care. All she wanted was to get out of that room before the space got smaller, before the conversation went deeper, or totally superficial, which might be even worse, and before she grew so uncomfortable that she wouldn't be able to choke back the awkward giggles she was prone to. Those giggles had, on more than one occasion, been mistaken as acceptance or forgiveness. She was no longer willing to offer them up in situations where neither were warranted.

As she left the room, crossing through the foyer to the stairs that would lead to her freedom, she heard the conversation carry on without her. She paused briefly to listen.

"You see what you done now, Lizzie?" Charlie Sr. said. "You ran her off."

"*I* ran her off?"

"Now she's going to think the whole family's a bunch of racists, thanks to you," Brian said. "Good going, Liz."

"Well, maybe she wouldn't think that if y'all wouldn't just let Grandma say stuff like that and not even call her out on it," Lizzie said. "Everybody just makes excuses for her because she's old."

Brian laughed. "Jesus, Lizzie. It's not like she spit on her or something. Every time you come back now, you've got some new issue you think you need to educate us all on. You're not better than us just because you voted for Hillary and bought a Black Lives Matter T-shirt. Just drop it already and get over yourself."

"All I'm saying is if the girl was uncomfortable, she could've just said so," Charlie Sr. said.

"Or maybe," Lizzie said, "we could try to be more self-aware, instead of expecting everyone else to make allowances for us and tell us when we're being assholes."

"Now, Elizabeth, I won't be talked to like—"

Fiona didn't stick around to hear the rest. She could predict well enough where it was headed, a circular battle in which Lizzie would end up repeating herself a dozen times to dismissive remarks and *well, but,* and *so,* arguments as thick as brick walls. Fiona had found herself in the same cycle countless times. This one wasn't hers to endure. The McElroy family could run the circuit on their own, in their own time, in their own way. She could only hope it eventually got them somewhere and that, along the way, Michael might join Lizzie in trying to steer them out of the loop and onto a path forward.

She ran up the stairs and down the hall to the room designated as her weekend home and collapsed on the bed. She'd never actually told her mother that she would call, but in that moment, she found that there was nothing in the world she'd rather do more. Her mother's voice, clear as day in her mind, was exactly what she needed to hear.

On the bed, limbs spread wide, Fiona stared at the ceiling. Classical music sung quietly from her phone, which lay beside her head. She'd never much cared for music without lyrics until she'd dated her last girlfriend, a music-history major and Taylor Swift-bashing enthusiast. It had only lasted a couple of months, but the short-lived relationship had left its mark. Fiona had since significantly reduced her daily allowance of repeats on Swift's "Bad Blood" and added five different classical stations to her Pandora playlists.

It soothed in a way that music with lyrics couldn't. She would lie back and let herself be carried off into the notes until it felt as if she was floating, drifting, dissolving into nothingness. Classical music had become a sort of meditation for her, a way for her to clear her head and release all the tension trapped in her body. Michael, who rarely missed Friday nights' Vino & Vinyasa sessions in Forest Park with Yogini Lauren, had tried more than once to convince Fiona that yoga achieved the same result and was "better for your body." But after he'd successfully talked her into one session, she'd refused to go back for another, and Michael had never really forgiven her for saying that drinking cheap wine and sticking their asses in the air was more ridiculous than relaxing.

"I don't recognize this one."

Fiona sighed at the sound of Michael's voice and kept her eyes on the ceiling. "Did you become a classical-music aficionado on the long walk up the stairs?"

"Not a chance." He laughed. "Guess I've just gotten used to the things you usually play."

"It's Thomas Bergersen."

"Oh. What happened to Beethoven?"

"If I recall, you said my phone was going to mysteriously find its way into the garbage disposal if I played *The Moonlight Sonata* one more time."

"It's so depressing."

"So is your face."

"Ouch." The bed dipped with Michael's weight as he sat on the edge. "Guess I don't need to ask if you're mad at me." He gently pushed her leg aside and raised her arm long enough to position himself under it. He lay down beside her, let her arm rest across his chest, and slung one leg over hers. "I'm sorry Lizzie made things uncomfortable."

They stared at the ceiling together, at ease with one another's warmth and touch. Fiona fingered the edge of Michael's shirt sleeve, rubbing the material between index and thumb.

"Is that what you think happened?"

"Am I wrong?"

"Completely."

"Oh."

The music filled up the space between their words, and Fiona pondered how she should go about explaining how she felt. It had always been simple enough with Michael. Their relationship had never demanded she walk on eggshells. She could blurt out her feelings, no filter, no thought, and he would navigate his way through them with ease. If he was confused, he would ask her to clarify. If he was hurt, he would tell her, and if he didn't agree, he'd never had any trouble explaining why. That was part of the wonder of who they'd become together over the years of their friendship—they'd learned to ride each other's waves with trust. There was no need for walls between them, no need for defensiveness or word-mincing. At the end of the day, no matter what they said to one another, there was genuine love and respect between them, and it kept their relationship steady, healthy, and honest.

This time, however, she was unsure of how to go about it. She didn't want to babble about how she felt. She wanted to be clear and concise. She wanted him to understand without her having to elaborate or talk herself in circles, because no matter how she chose to address it, it was going to be uncomfortable. The less time she had to occupy that discomfort, the better. She had had enough for one day already.

Michael said nothing, content to let her marinate however long she needed. Instead, he lay still beside her, his thumb slowly rubbing back and forth along the underside of her arm. The soft touch soothed her. Fiona closed her eyes and let herself enjoy the sensation of touch, the rise and fall of the music, and the reassuring familiarity of being close to Michael, close to someone who loved her.

"Lizzie didn't make things uncomfortable," she said after some time. "Things were already uncomfortable. They may not have been for *you*, because you weren't the one having racially charged assumptions made about you, but they were for me. Unfortunately, that's something *I'm* used to. I don't like it, and yeah, it makes my skin crawl, but it's something I've had to learn to navigate."

She took a deep breath and released it in another long sigh. "What I'm not so used to is someone stepping in to challenge those assumptions the way your sister did. It made you guys uncomfortable when she did that because, up until that point, you were all content to just stand there and let your grandma say what she wanted to say and pretend like it wasn't a problem, or make excuses for her and expect me to smile and laugh it off so none of you would have to feel guilty about it."

Michael continued to keep quiet, though she could see in her peripheral vision that he had turned to look at her. She didn't want to look back, because she was afraid to see his discomfort. She didn't want it to sway her or shake her or make her feel obligated to comfort him. She wanted to be firm and resolute, and that was hard to do when staring at a scorned puppy-dog face. But he was also her favorite person, and she wanted to comfort him, even when she *didn't* want to. So, she rolled onto her side and looked at him anyway.

The frown tugging his features down appeared more contemplative than upset. Fiona pressed the pad of her thumb between his eyebrows and pulled the skin upward.

"You promised you would put an end to it if your grandma said anything shitty." His skin turned whiter around the edges of her thumb as she slid it down his nose and over to one corner of his mouth. Her eyes burned and watered as she pulled that side of his frown upward. "You didn't."

He wormed his way closer, laying one large hand over the top of Fiona's where it now rested on his cheek. "I should've done what Lizzie did," he whispered, the words nearly lost beneath a sudden swell in the music enveloping the both of them.

"Yeah." She pinched his cheek then flipped over and put her back to him. "You should have." He lay silently behind her, nothing touching her but the warmth emanating off his long body. The morning winter sun, shining in through the sheer window curtains, didn't offer the same comfort. The contrast of her cool chest and arms and warm back made her shiver, so she inched back a bit. "Hold me."

He did. His pale, freckled arm, decorated with white-blond downy hair, circled her torso and slid her back against him. Warm breath puffed against the back of her neck as he rested his forehead against her loosened braid.

"Michael?"

"Yeah?"

"Do better."

"I will."

Chapter 4

"Don't stress." Michael fluffed up the thick scarf Fiona wore. The plush plaid material pushed up over her cold chin as he tugged and batted it about, making sure it covered all the exposed skin of her neck. "You've got this."

Fiona fidgeted under Michael's reassuring pats. Each pat made a whoosh-and-pop sound as his big hands smacked against the puffy material of the coat Rosie had conjured from the hall closet and insisted Fiona wear. The brown material was soft and fat and bulging, and her earlier glance in the foyer mirror had confirmed Fiona's suspicions. She had indeed transformed into a walking toasted marshmallow. "I am a tiny person."

"Yes, you are."

The cold curled around them like angry hands, digging at the skin as if attempting to burrow under and freeze them from the inside out. It had been nice at first, a blast of cool air after hours inside a hearth-warmed house, but now it was biting. It seemed to grow colder the longer they stood in the snow, and Fiona's bones were beginning to hurt. "What if I get buried in a pile of snow and no one can find me because I'm so tiny? What if I die a slow, painful, freezing death? What if all that's left of me is a pathetically small block of Fiona-shaped ice?"

He smiled. "My parents have always wanted an ice sculpture in the yard."

"Michael."

He laughed. "You'd thaw out in spring."

A poke to the gut did nothing. His coat was as fluffy as hers. His scarf was just as thick. His fiery hair frizzed out in all directions, riddled with the static of piling on too many layers. Fiona would have teased him if she wasn't so busy worrying about her impending doom. There was bloodlust on the McElroy's faces. This wasn't just some family game to them. It wasn't a fun holiday sport they indulged in once a year.

It was *war*.

The maniacal grin on Jessie's face as she hid behind a self-made wall of snow and created an armory of snowballs faster than should have been humanly possible was all Fiona needed to see to know that she would likely never see her parents again. She would never again walk in the warm sun. She would never finish school and become a nurse practitioner or fulfill her lifelong dream of opening a lesbian coffee shop and naming it The Les Bean. Today, she feared, would be her final day on earth, for a rabid clan of country-bred redheads had drafted her into battle, and she was woefully unprepared.

"I knew Jessie's weird rant in the living room sounded ominous," she said. "You should have told me this was part of the deal when you asked me to come down here with you."

"Would you have still come?"

"Would I have had the option to opt out?"

"That's not really a thing here."

"Then no. I wouldn't have come, and I'm currently considering stealing your car keys and fleeing back to downtown St. Louis, where they diligently scrape all the snow off the streets into big, dirty piles and no one has to play, or *die*, in it."

"Relax." He bopped her frozen nose with the tip of a gloved finger. "I told you. You've got this."

"I grew up in Los Angeles, Michael." Each word produced a tiny puff of fog. "The closest thing I ever had to a snowball fight was when Heidi Burch threw one of those Hostess Sno Ball cakes at me in fifth grade because I didn't send her a valentine."

Michael roared with laughter. "That's brutal. What'd you do?"

"I ate it," Fiona said, not even looking at him. Her eyes were fixed on Jessie, who was still churning out snowballs behind her little white wall like a rage-powered, automated assembly line.

"The fact that your sister, who I was almost certain was a robot you guys kept around for comedic relief, keeps laughing like the Wicked Witch of the West is making me feel like I should get back on my old anxiety meds."

"Oh, she's definitely a robot. She mostly just grunts and stares at her phone and, you know, occasionally threatens someone, but the Christmas snowball fight is like her crack. She loves it more than she loves any of us. Maybe even more than social media, Candy Crush, and making fun of people." He looked over at her. "And she's totally cheating! What the hell?" He cupped his hands around his mouth and shouted. "You're not allowed to start building your arsenal until Mom blows the whistle!"

"Mind your business, Ginger!"

Michael snorted. "Why are you yelling at yourself?"

"Better yet, why are you yelling at the whole family?" Brian called from his own little corner, shared with Grace, where the two of them were working on a protective wall. It wasn't very tall, but they could hide behind it well enough if they kept to their knees.

Michael patted Fiona's marshmallow arms again. "Look, all you have to do is duck most of the time. I'll do all the throwing, if you want. Just stay behind me, and if I say run, run."

"*Run*? Seriously? What if I can't keep up? Look at me in this coat! I feel like a penguin raised on a diet of jumbo shrimp and blubber, not to mention the fact that these giant boots your mom made me wear keep sinking into the snow. How does anyone run in all this stuff."

"Hey, we got lucky this year," he said. "We hardly ever get the good, deep, powdery stuff. It's usually more sludge or ice, and not very much at that, so we have to improvise. One year, Dad got one of those fake snowmakers. Didn't really do so great with the snowballs, but it was still pretty fun. Another year we did hot-water balloons. Now, that was awesome."

"I'm sure."

"If you get hit, it's really not a big deal. I mean, nothing to be scared of or anything. Like I said, it's good soft snow this year, so it shouldn't hurt unless you take it to the face, and even then, it only stings for a second."

"Oh, great." She wasn't inspired. "Well, as long as it only stings for a *second*, then, you're right. Sure. No big deal."

"Stop being such a wuss, Fi. You'll love it. I promise."

Fiona grumbled and waddled along behind him as he led her to the trunk of a dogwood tree. It was gray and barren from the effects of winter, and each branch was blanketed by a layer of fresh snow, but, to Fiona, it was beautiful all the same. She had always had a thing for trees in winter—something about their nakedness and how it made them seem so lonely yet so resilient. It wasn't something she got to enjoy in Southern California, but in Missouri, there were trees aplenty. Clearly, it was the same for Arkansas.

"I'm telling you," Michael said as he quickly began building up a miniature protective wall beside the tree, "this is the best spot. I've won four different Christmases at it. It's lucky."

"Good." Fiona crouched down beside him to help with the wall. "'Cause I'm not taking any snowballs to the face."

"I make no promises." Michael grinned at her, his cheeks and nose a bright pink from the cold. "We have to leave the base if we want to get any hits."

"Why do we need hits?"

"It's like dodgeball. If you get hit, you're out, though Mom usually lets us take two hits before calling us out. She's the ref. Dad's the scorekeeper. Anyway, if you get hit, you're out, so we want to hit as many as we can, and we've got to leave base to do that. We just come back here when we need to replenish our arsenal or take quick cover. Got it?"

"What if someone takes our spot while we aren't here?"

"Not allowed. Once you set up base, it's yours. No one's allowed to steal any of your snowballs or take cover behind someone else's wall. It's cheating. You gotta make your own ammo and shelter. It's every McElroy for himself out here, unless you're on a team, but even then, if your teammate gets out, you're still in until you get hit."

Fiona patted the last bit of snow onto the top of the short wall while Michael began making snowballs beside her.

"Can you please stop using words like *arsenal* and *ammo*? It's a snowball fight, not World War III." She sounded as disbelieving of her own words as she felt. She knew from her own observations and from the look Michael was giving her that it absolutely *was* World War III: The McElroy Family Christmas Edition. *Shit.*

"Didn't you just get on your sister about *that* being against the rules?" She nodded toward the pile of snowballs Michael had already completed. "Don't we have to wait for the whistle?"

He shushed her. "Everyone else is cheating, so we gotta keep up."

"I can't take part in such tactics, Michael. I'm an honest woman."

"Sure you are, *girlfriend*."

She cackled and shoved him over in the snow as the loud sound of a throat clearing echoed about the yard. Fiona popped her head up over the wall to see Rosie standing in the middle of the yard, holding a bullhorn to her mouth. No wonder the throat-clearing was so loud. She wore a coat that was striped like a referee's shirt, and a silver pipe whistle dangled from a thin black rope around her neck. At the sight of both, Fiona snorted so hard she choked. "Where the hell did your mom get that coat?"

"I'm pretty sure she made it."

"All right, kids," Rosie announced into her bullhorn, "I want a clean fight. You know the rules. No stealing bases or ammunition. No tree climbing or getting on top of the shed. No tackling. Two hits and you're out. Winner takes all."

"No tackling?" Charlie stood from behind the lopsided snow wall he was building with his two daughters. The little girls sat on each side of him, the oldest smacking blobs of snow onto the top of the wall while the youngest ignored the wall altogether. She plopped onto her back instead and raked her arms and legs through the snow to make a snow angel. "Since when?"

"Since always," Sophie called out as she exited the back door of the house with a stack of winter clothes and accessories. She shoved a beanie onto Brian's head as she passed his and Grace's base. "Just because you and Brian don't follow the rules doesn't mean they don't exist." She then tossed a pair of thick gloves to Lizzie, who, until that point, had been completely silent. When Fiona followed the flight of the gloves with her eyes, she saw why.

Lizzie was almost completely hidden behind a massive wall of perfectly sculpted snow bricks. How she'd managed to build it in such a short time was beyond Fiona, and all she could do was sit and gawk at the gleaming wall.

Michael, on the other hand, was annoyed. "Lizzie, what the hell is that?!"

She stepped to the side of her wall and, with a cocky grin, held her arms out toward the work as if revealing a prize or piece of art.

"Like that, do you? Living near the beach has its perks. I've been practicing with sandcastles."

"That's cheating!"

"No, it's not," Rosie said. "There's no rule against practice."

"Yeah!" Charlie Sr. hollered from his cushioned chair on the back porch where he sat beside a large dry-erase board for keeping score. "So quit your bellyaching, all of you, and focus on the game. Countdown's 'bout to start, and, like your mom said, winner takes all, so get ready."

Fiona looked to Michael. "There are prizes?"

"Heck yeah, there are prizes. You think Jessie, of all people, would willingly get cold, wet, and potentially smacked in the face with a ball of ice for *nothing*?"

"Ten!"

A spark of panic ignited in Fiona's gut as Charlie Sr. began to shout out the countdown. "Oh shit," she said. "Oh shit. Oh shit. I'm not ready. Michael, I'm not ready."

"Nine!"

"Yes, you are. Just stay behind me. If we get separated, try not to get hit."

"Eight!"

"Uh, yeah. Okay." Fiona glanced over the wall, her gaze hopping from base to base and passing over each determined face of all Michael's excited siblings. The only faces not riddled with rabid glee were those of Charlie's youngest, Maddi, who was still making snow angels, and Sophie and Grace, who wore only soft, amused smiles as if happy just to be with their family, no matter the circumstances.

"Oh," Michael added, "and stay the hell away from Charlie and Brian, if you can."

"What? Why?"

"Five!"

"They like to tackle, then pretend they didn't."

"Even me? But I'm tiny and a *girl*. I'm practically the same size as your nieces!"

"Yeah, they don't care." Michael laughed. "And what's with the 'I'm a girl' crap? Lizzie would tackle you just as soon as Charlie or Brian would."

"Three!"

Fiona ignored the feel of her eyebrow ticking up, of the flutter in her lower stomach and the rush of heat in her chest at the image conjured to mind. "Well, then, why didn't you say to stay away from her, too?"

"'Cause there's no staying away from Lizzie. If she wants to, she'll get you, one way or another. For the most part, though, she sticks to her base."

"One!"

Michael jumped up from behind the wall, three snowballs balanced in one hand like a tennis player ready to serve and one ready to throw in the other. "Go!" he shouted as Rosie blew the whistle, and Fiona instantly gave a hair-raising scream. She didn't look around but simply ran, eyes fixed to Michael's back, her short legs doing their best to keep up with his leaping steps. She didn't even bother grabbing a single snowball.

The McElroy's massive backyard became a blur of shining white and the shifting, bouncing material of Michael's coat. Squeals and shouts and laughter rung out left and right, mixed with the crunching sounds of heavy boots plowing through settled snow.

"Take cover! Take cover!"

Fiona didn't know who shouted out the command, nor did she know to whom it was directed, but she listened all the same. She threw her body to the ground, squashing herself against the snow in a pile of puff and anxiety, and threw her arms over the back of her head. The next sound she heard was Michael's delighted laugh as he jerked her by her arm back to her feet.

"Not you, you big dork. Brian was shouting at Grace. I got her anyway."

Fiona clutched the back of his coat as he barreled through the snow. "Already?"

"Yeah, she never lasts long. It was only her first out, so she could've stayed, but she always sits out after the first. We're pretty sure she does it on purpose because she doesn't really wanna play."

"Can't imagine why."

He led her quickly toward the side of a large metal barn, rusted in some places but otherwise standing firm and solid. He lowered his voice a bit as they slunk along the side toward the back of the barn. "If you'd stop covering your eyes and screaming, and actually *play*, you'd like it." He peeked around the corner when they reached the edge. "Clear." He turned back toward her, his shoulders dropping. The tension eased from his brow. "You know how much you like to win."

Fiona inclined her head. "True, but I also know how much I hate being cold or wet, especially at the same time."

"So don't get hit," he said as if she hadn't just been thrust into battle with experienced competitors who knew the game, knew each other, and likely also knew a hundred different ways to knock her on her ass using nothing more than powdery white rain.

"Sure. 'Cause it's so easy not to get hit."

"It's not *easy*," Michael said, "but it's not hard either. You just have to pay attention. You do that, and you can dodge a lot." As he spoke, Fiona caught a flicker of movement out of the corner of her eye. A flash of red hair. A retracted arm, ready to throw. Her stomach dropped, and she knew they were doomed.

"Duck!" The word leaped up her throat almost of its own accord, though she knew it was too late. Any second now, a fat ball of snow would smash into the side of Michael's face like a cold, angry fist, and down he would go. Then, it would be only Fiona, and there was no way she could survive on her own.

Michael, however, was fast on his feet. His reflexes had him on the ground in an instant, as if dropping to do pushups at Fiona's command. Fiona shrieked as the snowball whizzed by his head and smashed with a near-silent whoosh into the back wall of the barn. A second later, Michael was on his feet again, whirling around just in time to catch Jessie skittering away like a cockroach caught in the light.

"Yeah, you better run," he shouted after her, then turned back to Fiona. "See! Like that! That was awesome. Just pay attention like that, and we'll take the game, easy." He motioned for her to follow him as he inched toward the opposite side of the barn. "Ready?"

"Ready for what?"

"Let's go," he said, without answering, and Fiona had to fight back the urge to scream again. He darted out from behind the cover of the barn and sprinted across the yard, chucking a snowball as he went. Fiona had no idea where it flew or who it hit or if it hit anyone at all. She was too busy trying to keep up with Michael's long strides, which wasn't easy to do on flat pavement, let alone when plowing through thick snow. They'd nearly reached their base to gather more ammunition when Fiona's boot snagged on something in the snow—a stick, maybe—and down, down, down she went.

It felt like something out of a movie, as if the entire world slowed to watch her embarrassing descent, and all Fiona could do was watch the ground fly up to meet her. Her knees hit first, followed quickly by her pelvis, stomach, chest, and, finally, her chin. She barely had time to register being face-first on the ground before a snowball smacked into the space right beside her face, missing her by an inch, no more.

"Damn!" Fiona rolled onto her knees just in time to see Charlie squatted nearby, quickly patting together another snowball to finish the job he started. She knew she was done for, but before Charlie could launch another one her way, a softball-sized snowball exploded in his face. Fiona gaped as Charlie spluttered, spit out snow, wiped his eyes clean, and shouted.

"Dammit, Jessie!"

Jessie stood at the side of the barn, partly covered, partly exposed, with a ridiculous number of snowballs clutched in one arm and the other readying another to throw. She cackled as she had done earlier, the sound still just as unsettling in its wicked glee. Fiona couldn't help but laugh as well, though. Jessie was just enjoying herself so much. It was terrifying but infectious.

"That's your second one, Charlie," Rosie called from near the house, bullhorn positioned in front of her mouth. "You're out."

"That wasn't my second, Mom. I've still got one more."

"Brian hit you earlier."

"It didn't hit me," Charlie said. "I swear."

"Like hell it didn't," Brian's disembodied voice echoed from the far side of the yard. His hiding spot was truly effective.

"I saw it hit you," Charlie Sr. said from behind his coat and scarf. The coffee cup in his right hand steamed in the cold air. His left hand held a fat, black marker, which he used to cross out his eldest son's name. "I didn't raise you to be a sore loser, son." He motioned toward a large carafe on the small table beside his chair. "Come on now. There's coffee. Come join your sisters and warm up."

On the other side of the table sat Grace and Sophie, both bundled in a single shared blanket and swaying slightly on a white wicker porch swing.

"Give it up, Charlie," Sophie yelled and patted the space to the side of her. "There's a spot for you here on the losers' swing."

While Charlie was grumbling his way to the porch, Fiona ran as fast as she could to Michael's side.

He put an arm around her. "You okay?"

"Yeah, I'm fine."

"You sure?" His attempt at keeping a straight face failed horribly. His cheeks bloated so severely that he looked like a puffer fish. "That was just, you know, *quite* a fall."

"I swear to God if you laugh, I'll—"

The obnoxious laugh that burst free reverberated around the entire yard as if the snow had turned to rubber and sent the harsh melody bouncing about in all directions, back and forth with no end. Fiona set her jaw. "All right," she said. "You asked for it."

She swooped down, plucked up a previously rolled snowball from their base, and hurled it like a pie right into his laughing face. He was so shocked that, for a moment, he couldn't move. All he could do was stand there, mouth gaping open and full of snow while Fiona dissolved into a fit of giggles. The revenge high was short-lived, however.

"Mutiny!"

Fiona frowned and turned toward Rosie, who held up her bullhorn and pointed it right at her. "We've got a mutiny!"

The three eliminated McElroys on the porch all jumped to their feet, throwing their hands up. "Mutiny!" Charlie hollered, pumping a fist in the air. "That hasn't happened in years. Go, Fiona!"

"What?" Fiona looked at Michael. He wiped the snow from his face. "What does that mean?"

"A mutiny," he said, shrugging. "It means you turned on your teammate, so now there's nothing I can do."

"Nothing you can do about what?"

"About protecting you. You committed mutiny, Fi. So now we're enemies."

"What? No! No, I was just playing."

"Too bad, kid. You should've thought about that. You're on your own now."

They stared at each other, Fiona gaping and Michael grinning, the sudden twist in events sinking rapidly in. Then, at the same time, they both launched into action. Michael squatted and grabbed a snowball while Fiona took off as fast as her short legs could carry her. She screamed like a banshee with every crunching step.

"I didn't know the rules," she squeaked as she ducked just in time to miss the snowball whizzing overhead.

"Now you do." Another snowball shot by her, nearly grazing her puffy shoulder, and she heard his shout behind her. "Ow!"

Fiona turned back just in time to see the snow sliding off the side of Michael's face. He growled and threw down the rest of his arsenal as Rosie declared that he was officially out of the game. Fiona didn't know who'd hit him, but she was grateful, because he wouldn't be after her any longer. But that feeling lasted only about a second before the realization sank in: She had no one left to protect her. She didn't even know who was still in the game.

"Okay." She made it to the barn and slowed to a near crawl, crouched low, and inched along its side. "Grace and Sophie are on the porch," she muttered to herself, "and Charlie. Now Michael. Okay, so that just leaves Brian, Jessie, and—" She edged around the back of the barn and collided with someone's back. "Fuck," she hissed as the person whirled around.

"Trying to sneak up on me, huh?" A snowball sat securely in Lizzie's hand, and Fiona didn't understand why it wasn't already smashed against her own face. Instead, Lizzie simply held it and looked at her.

"No, I was just trying to get away from everyone else. I swear. Please don't hit me in the face with that." She nodded toward the snowball. "I mean, at least just throw it at my chest or something."

Lizzie laughed, quiet, melodic. Her breath fogged out in front of her. "Where's the fun in that?"

With a groan, Fiona closed her eyes and said, "I knew that wouldn't work. Fine, go ahead. Do what you must."

"Brian, you're out!" The sound of Rosie's voice cutting through the crisp air had Fiona opening her eyes again.

"Just the three of us now," Lizzie said. "You, me, and my feral little sister."

"*Feral* is an understatement."

"True. She's completely unhinged. It happens every Christmas. I don't know. It's like some kind of demon takes over, and suddenly she has an attention span that applies to something other than her phone. It's miraculous and also highly disturbing."

"It's a little scary, yeah." She calmed, the tension seeping from her body as a laugh worked its way up. She and Lizzie stood together comfortably, just looking at one another. Fiona didn't know what was happening, but suddenly, it was like they were somewhere else entirely. The cold air wasn't so cold anymore. It didn't bite at her. In fact, she felt warm, and the longer Lizzie looked at her like that, like she was content to just hide away with her behind the barn all day, the warmer she became.

When Lizzie took a small step toward her, that warm air disappeared. All the oxygen in the world zapped out of the atmosphere, and Fiona was trapped in a breathless sort of suspension. She watched as Lizzie took another step, her toothy smile widening as she did. She reached up, startling her, but Fiona didn't move as Lizzie's fingers brushed over her face, just over her left eye.

"You've got snow on your forehead."

Fiona's lips parted, and words came out, much to her surprise. Her throat was a wasteland. "Yeah, I fell."

"I saw." Her hand lingered on Fiona's face—her fingers sliding down, tracing the length from Fiona's jaw to her chin—then finally fell. "It was pretty great."

The spell was broken, and Fiona could breathe again. "Maybe for *you*. Not so much for me, though."

The sound of fast, crunching footsteps jarred them both from the strange pull between them. Lizzie whipped around. Jessie had just rounded the back of the barn with a snowball at the ready, but Lizzie was faster. She sent her own snowball soaring before Jessie could launch hers. Her aim was true. The ball landed smack in the center of Jessie's chest.

Fiona took her chance. While the other two were focused on one another, she sprang back around the side of the barn and took off running. She could hear Jessie shouting over her shoulder as she ran.

"That's only one hit, Liz! I'm still in the game."

"Not for long."

Footsteps echoed around and behind Fiona, crunching, crunching, crunching. But she didn't look back. She could only assume it was the sound of Jessie and Lizzie running away from one another, rather than one of them chasing *her* down. She could only *hope*.

"Run, Fi!" Michael screeched from the porch, dashing every ounce of hope Fiona had. She *was* being chased—by Jessie or Lizzie or *both*, she didn't know. She figured it out a moment later when a heavy weight rammed into the back of her knees and sent her crashing to the ground.

"Gotcha!"

Fiona struggled to roll over, the weight of her coat and another body pressing her into the ground. She finally got herself turned, only to immediately have her hands pinned above her head.

"No tackling, Lizzie!" Rosie called from the sidelines.

Lizzie laughed. "I tripped!"

Staring up into Lizzie's face was like a sudden bout of déjà vu. Fiona blew a strand of hair from her eyes. Her hat was gone, and the careful braid Michael had made for her had come entirely undone after being tousled about one too many times. "I'm starting to think you like being on top of me," she said with a grunt, then immediately regretted it. Heat spread through her chest, crawled up her neck, and pooled in her cheeks. She was shocked when the snow didn't begin to melt beneath her.

Lizzie tightened her hold on Fiona's wrists. "Maybe I do," she said, then turned just as red as Fiona imagined herself to be.

They sat like that for what felt like ages, Fiona struggling against Lizzie's grip and Lizzie adamantly refusing to budge.

"What is this? A staredown?" Brian yelled from the porch. "Somebody smack somebody with a snowball already. Let's go, Liz. Finish her!"

Lizzie sat back, still on top of her, and relaxed. "Sorry," she said, "but this is war." She scooped up a handful of snow, rounded it out, and held it over her head. She winked down at Fiona. "Don't worry. I'll avoid that pretty face of yours."

A cloud of white suddenly exploded at the back of Lizzie's head, powder flying out around them in a cloud. She threw herself down, fully on top of Fiona. Their cheeks rubbed together, hot breath puffing against Fiona's earlobe. "Wait here," she growled as if it was the most reasonable thing in the world to ask someone to wait to be metaphorically killed. Her hands dug into the ground for more snow. "My sister is a freaking pain in the ass." The next second, she was on her feet, and the enticing warmth that had devoured Fiona's every inch was gone.

Jessie howled with laughter as she stood across the yard from Lizzie, one snowball in her right hand and two in her left. "Told you I was still in the game," she said. "Shoulda kept your eye out."

"You think you're so slick, don't you?"

"Oh no. I don't think it. I know it."

"You and me, then. Showdown. You ready?"

"Was I born ready?" Jessie threw one tightly packed snowball up in the air and caught it. It remained perfectly intact. "Yup. Sure was."

Fiona sat up to watch the showdown, the two youngest McElroy children standing twenty paces apart as if preparing for a good old-fashioned Wild West duel. Any second now, they would draw back. Any second now, they would fire, someone would be eliminated, and the game would be down to Fiona and whomever was left standing. The thought was enough to make Fiona want to burrow down into the snow like a tundra shrew and live out the rest of winter in hiding.

Unless...

As quietly as she could, she scraped together a handful of snow and formed it into a tight, firm ball. Slowly, she crawled to her knees, then her feet, trying to stir as little as possible so as not to alert either of the other two to her movement.

For the longest time, Lizzie and Jessie stood frozen and tense, staring each other down while Fiona lingered behind Lizzie, seemingly unnoticed. When they finally moved, it was as one. Both exploded into action as if prompted by some invisible, inaudible trigger, and Fiona was jarred into motion as well. She jerked her arm back as the other two did and launched the snowball, closing her eyes despite knowing she should keep them open. Proper aim was kind of dependent upon seeing the target, after all.

For a split second, the yard was silent. Only the sound of the cold breeze whistling through cracks in the barn's exterior disturbed the quiet stillness. It was as if they were suspended in time, waiting, and Fiona could feel the collectively held breath around her.

The ringing "Ha!" that broke the air was followed quickly by a gasp that instantly drew Fiona's eyes open. She was greeted with the shocked faces of her only two opponents: Jessie stood across the yard, a snowball still sliding off the thick material of her coat, just at her left shoulder; clearly, Lizzie's aim had once again been true.

Jessie's, however, had not; Lizzie didn't have a speck of snow on the front of her body when she turned around to face Fiona. Her elbow, however, pointed up toward the gray sky as she reached to touch the back of her head, and a moment later, she revealed a handful of white. "You hit me," she said as if in a stupor, and all Fiona could do was gawk at her.

The next second, the observing gallery on the back porch erupted, clearly as astonished as both Fiona and Lizzie by what had just occurred.

Michael leapt off the porch and dashed across the yard, a few of the others jogging behind him. He hurled himself onto Fiona, nearly knocking her to the ground, then picked her up and bounced her around as he repeated himself over and over again. "Oh my God. Oh my God. I can't believe you just did that. Oh my God. I can't believe it."

"Okay, we get it," Jessie snapped as she marched toward the house, surrounded by cheers sent Fiona's way and taunts sent hers. "You can't believe it. Get over it already."

"Oh, now, hon," Charlie Sr. said as his youngest tramped onto the porch. "Don't be that way. You know it's just a game."

"Whatever." She crossed her arms over her chest. "I'm fine."

"Jessie Lynn, you better stop being a sore loser," Rosie barked through her bullhorn.

"Well, Mom, that's just the only kind of loser I know how to be." She trudged right by her father and disappeared through the front door.

"All right, well, while some of us are being Debbie Downers over the game," Rosie announced, voice booming, "the rest of us are going to celebrate. For the first time in—"

"Ever!"

The collective shout of her children made Rosie laugh. She held the bullhorn back to her mouth. "For the first time in ever, yes, a McElroy has *not* come out on top in the annual Christmas snowball fight."

"Yeah, so that means it shouldn't count, right?" Lizzie stood as Jessie had, with her arms defiantly crossed. She wore a tight smile, though she kept her eyes downcast.

The others quickly wrapped their arms around her and ruffled the top of her head until her hat fell to the ground.

"It's all right, Liz," Charlie said, knuckling her neck so that she squirmed and tried to scoot away. "We won't hold it against you."

"Speak for yourself," Brian said.

Lizzie shot him a glare. "Hold it against yourself, then. If you'd still been in the game, maybe you could've done something about it, but oh, wait, you weren't in the game because you were out—because you completely sucked ass."

"Elizabeth Dawn!"

Lizzie laughed and leaned into Charlie's hug. She yanked Brian into the fold, hugging him as well. "I'll get you back for that," he said.

"Yeah, yeah."

Fiona smiled as she watched the scene unfold. So this was what it was like to have siblings. She imagined them as kids, growing up in such close proximity, racing the same hallways, cycling through the same toys, learning by way of the same books and verbal cues, comforted by the same sounds and sights and aromas, and being swaddled in the same blankets by the same arms. It wasn't something Fiona could relate to, and it left a pit in her stomach she recognized from her own childhood: the hollow cast of loneliness.

Lizzie was squashed between her siblings, but she managed to poke her head out enough to catch her breath. Her smile was as bright as the untouched parts of the frozen ground, and Fiona couldn't look away from her. They caught each other's gazes. Lizzie stuck her tongue out at Fiona as if to say it was all a silly game, no hard feelings, but there was a glint in her eye that gave her away. It spoke to the contrary, telling Fiona all she needed to know. *Enjoy it while you can. I'm coming for you.* At some point, Lizzie would get her revenge. Tackle her in the hallway when Fiona least expected. Leave her to wake up to a mustache and beard made of whipped cream. Fiona had seen countless movies showcasing pranks between siblings and friends. She could only imagine what Lizzie had in store for her, and it all sucked. Still, she couldn't help grinning. She'd won, and damn, winning felt good.

She was nearly shocked off her feet when Lizzie's arm suddenly shot forward and latched onto her coat. Fiona stumbled into the hoard of

McElroys, smothered by their arms, and laughed. All the tension from earlier had gone, all the awkwardness dispelled, and in that moment, she was just another part of the family. Another McElroy.

"Right, Fi?"

Fiona blinked, only just realizing that Michael had spoken to her. "Huh?" She struggled to stick her head out from under Brian's arm so she could see him. "Sorry. What did you say?"

"The cold starting to get to your head, or did you breathe in Brian's armpit too long?"

"Hey. My pits are minty fresh, dude."

"Sure, they are." Michael looked back at Fiona. "I said, you're gonna share your winnings with me, right?"

"Oh yeah. Winner takes all. I forgot." She squeezed out of the pack and tried to brush her hair down with her hands. It was hopeless. "But you never told me what exactly I'm supposed to be taking."

"Only the rarest, most precious trophy in all the world," Brian said. "I'm so jealous right now, I could hate you. I'm trying really hard to like you anyway, though."

"Wow. That's quite the endorsement. So, what is this trophy? Can I see it?"

"See it?" Brian scoffed. "You'd better do more than just look at it, or else, I will."

Rosie walked over to the group. "You kids and that darn pie, I swear."

"Pie?" Fiona's brow shot up. "The trophy is a pie?"

"No, it's not *a* pie," Brian said.

Michael finished for him. "It's *the* pie. Mom only makes it once a year. Once. And the only person who gets to eat *any* of it is the person who wins the snowball fight. And anyone they choose to share it with—hint hint." He wagged his brows at her. "Just saying. You wouldn't even be here, winning a pie, if I hadn't brought you."

"Hey," Lizzie said. "Let's also not forget that you wouldn't be winning anything if I hadn't so graciously offered my head as a target for you, okay? So, I mean, I think that deserves a little appreciation. Am I right?"

They all stared at her, then burst out laughing. "Sure, Lizzie," Charlie said. "If that was the case, we'd all deserve pie."

Lizzie tossed up her hands. "Well, maybe we do!"

"Come on." Michael swooped down to hoist Fiona off the ground. "We can argue about pie later. Let's get inside by the fire."

Fiona slung her arms around Michael's neck and held on. "Is this my victory lap?"

"Yup." He jogged toward the house, carrying her bridal style. "You won us the war. That makes you the queen. Queens get carried, don't they?"

"Ha! I don't know, but I'm not complaining. I'm freezing."

"Me, too." Michael readjusted his hold on her as he took the stairs up the porch two at a time. Two big strides and they were at the door. "But now we can cozy up by the fire and gorge ourselves on pie."

"Well, *I* can. I don't know about you."

"I will drop you."

"What I meant to say was 'Yeah, of course we can.'"

"That's what I thought."

⁂

The hallway leading to the den was like a visual timeline. Photographs of various sizes bedecked the walls in clusters, and as Fiona slowly made her way from frame to frame, she was able to watch the McElroy family evolve. She carried a small, messy plate and popped forkfuls of pie into her mouth as she stepped from one to the next, observing with care. Strawberry-blonde infants turned to toddlers and those toddlers to fire-headed, gap-toothed kids. Awkward school photos showcased unfortunate tween acne and even more unfortunate bangs, not to mention a few unforgiveable perms. Baby-fat faces evolved into hard-angled jaws and peach-fuzz facial hair. Girls turned to women and boys to men, and the young, smiling parents of each and every one grew gray around the temples and lined around the eyes and became grandparents in photographs that made Fiona's heart feel swollen and heavy. She couldn't stop smiling as she took it all in—Michael's family history.

Her own family was scattered around the world. She knew her mother's parents but not her father's. She'd never met her uncles or cousins who lived in China, and the one time she'd been to Singapore to see the place where her parents grew up and fell in love, she'd been so young she hadn't cared to take any of it in. So much of her life growing up in the United States had been spent ignoring the rich array of cultures that decorated her family history. She hadn't much wanted to learn, and every time she'd been made to endure jokes about her eyes or her parents' accents, she'd wanted to even less. Distance had felt good when she was a kid. It wasn't until she was an adult that the distance had begun to ache, and playing the game of catch-up, trying to learn everything she could as quickly as she could, hadn't made it ache any less.

She'd had to slow herself down, give herself time to absorb it all, one precious piece of family history at a time. Embracing all she'd been encouraged to push away, however, was worth it. It was worth the time to learn, because it was a part of her, and the value in loving oneself and respecting oneself enough to truly *know* oneself was something she quickly realized she couldn't put a number to.

She didn't have photos like this, a long, visual timeline to trace the moments and the years and the connections going back generations. She had only her own memories and photos, the short timeline of her less-than-thirty years and a few great shots of her parents from before they came to America. So it was nice to see a family so thoroughly documented, so many moments of sheer joy captured and immortalized on film. She was glad Michael had that, that he could point to an image and say, "This was the day my great-grandpa took me fishing for the first time." It was a precious privilege not everyone had.

An older photograph caught her attention, its color washed out and edges a little weathered. It appeared as if it'd been wrinkled up and tossed from box to box before finding its way to a frame. A large group of people filled in the space. An elderly man and woman stood at the back, posed solemnly in front of a large wooden barn. He wore a long-sleeved, button-up shirt with suspenders and she a floral-patterned sundress. Arranged before them were three rows of children—four teenagers, five kids, a toddler, and an infant. The boys wore denim overalls with no shirts, their pant legs rolled up at the ankles to reveal bare feet, and the girls each wore a plain, simple, short-sleeved dress suitable for presentation as well as play. The baby lay lopsided in the toddler's arms, who sat on the ground in the same overalls and no shirt. His belly stuck out on both sides of the denim, and he stared at the baby instead of the camera.

"Dad's family." Lizzie stood at the end of the hallway, leaning against the wall, watching her. "Bigger even than ours."

"Hey." Fiona smiled. "How long have you been there?"

"Not long."

"You guys have so many photos."

"Yeah." She sighed and moved toward her, arms crossed comfortably over her chest. "Mom's a bit of a picture whore. She probably took a good fifty or sixty during the fight today. If you've got Facebook, just wait. She'll be adding you just so she can tag you in every one."

Fiona laughed and scraped off another piece of pie. "I didn't notice a camera."

"Oh, she finally joined the rest of us in the twenty-first century and started using her phone." She tapped the faded photo with her index finger. "Grandma and Grandpa had this one done professionally in, like, 1970 or something. I don't know. That's Dad there." She pointed again, this time laying the tip of her finger over one of the teen boys standing in front of the elderly couple at the back of the shot. The boy was young, mottled with freckles, and had his face scrunched up as if staring into a bright sun. "I think he was fifteen when they took this."

Fiona tried to imagine the boy evolving into the man she'd met, the one with the tired but happy smile and the wrinkles around his eyes. It didn't seem possible. She stepped toward the photo and squinted at the woman in the back. "So, that's Grandma Sophia?"

"Yup, before the Arkansas sun turned her into an old prune. Well, that and the two packs of Virginia Slims she smokes a day."

"She looks..."

"Miserable, yeah. None of them look happy in that picture. We make jokes about it all the time, but Dad says that's how the photographer told them to pose."

"They definitely don't seem overjoyed."

"Maybe they were wishing they had shirts on."

A smile touched Fiona's lips. She shook her head. "That's a lot of kids."

"Yeah, eleven altogether." She tapped another kid in the photo, a teen girl with long, frizzy hair standing next to Charlie. "That's my aunt Charlotte, Dad's twin." She grinned. "Michael didn't tell you Dad was a twin, did he?"

"No."

"Oh yeah. It runs in the family. His grandma was a twin, too."

"Wow. Do they come and visit ever? Or do you guys go visit them? Where do they all live?"

"Well, most of them live in Texas. That's where Dad was born. But, yeah, we see them every few years. We go there. They come here. It's been a while since the last time, though, now that I think about it. We used to see them a lot when we were kids."

"So, your dad's twin sister doesn't live nearby? I always imagined twins being kind of inseparable."

"Oh, Charlie and Sophie are for sure. They literally live right next door to each other and hang out all the time. But Dad and Aunt Charlotte are more like Brian and Grace. They don't need to be around each other all the time. I think Grace and Brian talk on the phone like once a week maybe, but that's pretty much it. Grace is *a lot* like Dad, actually. Doesn't talk much to anyone. Is kind of shy. She's always been that way."

"Yeah, I noticed she didn't talk nearly as much as everyone else. I was wondering how that was going to go over with her becoming a doctor. Lots of interaction."

"She's in pathology, actually, so unless corpses start talking, I think she'll be okay." She straightened one of the crooked photographs on the wall. "What about you? Any sisters or brothers? A freakishly large amount, perhaps? We like that here."

Fiona laughed and shook her head. "Not a single one, actually. Sorry."

"Ah, well, you can have a few of mine, if you want. I'll even give you Brian half-price."

"How generous."

"What about your parents? You said they were from Singapore, right? Do they have any family there still?"

"My mom does," Fiona said. "An aunt and a few cousins. The rest of her family lives in Malaysia; well, except my grandparents. They live in Los Angeles, just a few blocks down from my parents, actually."

"Oh, I bet that's really nice for your mom, having them so close."

"As long as Gran's not getting on her nerves, yeah, it is."

"Can totally relate," Lizzie said with a smile. "What about your dad's family? Do they live in LA, too?"

"In China."

"Oh wow. That's far. Do you ever get to visit?"

Fiona shook her head and shuffled a bit on her feet. She'd never had an easy time talking about her dad's family, because *he'd* never had an easy time talking about them. "He doesn't really speak to them anymore."

Lizzie frowned but didn't push. "That sucks."

"Yeah." She could have left it at that, and part of her wanted to, but Lizzie's smile was so welcoming, so warm. Her presence made Fiona feel safe and welcome and, in a weird but wonderful way, understood. They were worlds apart as people—who they were, where they came from, what their families were like—but Fiona felt comfort in Lizzie. She felt connection. "I've never met any of them either. They had a big falling out when my dad decided to marry my mom. His family's apparently really traditional, and my mom's not Chinese, so... He kind of left all of that behind when he and Mom moved here, and I guess that was the end of it. I think he misses his younger brother the most. I've caught him a few times looking at a picture in his wallet, but it's not something we talk about. Like, ever."

Lizzie didn't say anything for a long time. Instead, she shifted the slightest bit closer and let the warmth of her shoulder against Fiona's be her answer. After a short silence, she looked down at the last lingering pieces of the pie on Fiona's plate and asked, "How many pieces of pie is that now, by the way?"

"One too many," Fiona said with a laugh and a sheepish smile. She scooped off another tiny piece and ate it. There were only a few bits of filling left, then the crust. "I can feel it in my gut, but I can't stop."

"We tried to warn you."

"I don't even know what this yellow melty blob is, but I'm in love with it."

"Didn't Mom tell you? It's Ooey Gooey Butter Pecan Pie."

"Okay, I know, but that doesn't sound like a real thing to me."

"Well, you're eating it, aren't you?" She looked at the disappearing pie, eyes wide with longing. It was pathetic and adorable, and Fiona couldn't help but draw even nearer.

"Okay, fine." She dipped the fork into the last bit of filling. "You want a bite?"

Lizzie didn't say a word, just immediately opened her mouth like a baby bird in a nest, waiting to have its lunch dropped into its open beak. The second her lips wrapped around the fork, a moan that set Fiona's teeth on edge slithered up and out.

That seductive snake of a sound wrapped around Fiona's body and squeezed, making every muscle tense and ache. Her thighs clamped roughly together as she watched ecstasy flood Lizzie's freckled, beautiful face. "Wow," she said, throat suddenly parched. "You really love this pie."

Another moan nearly made Fiona drop the plate. Her sweaty fingers actually did slide off the fork when Lizzie said, "I could kiss you right now." Thankfully, Lizzie's hand was already around the utensil. She smiled and licked between the tines.

Fiona's brow ticked up of its own accord. She could feel it, popping up there like an unsolicited email invitation: *RSVP for one pie-flavored kiss!* She tried to lower it back down, but it refused to listen.

"Michael and Sophie are the only ones who ever share, and neither of them has won in a while."

"When was the last time you won?"

"I don't know. Three years ago? Four? Something like that."

"That's a long time to go without this pie."

"Hence the kissing." Lizzie stepped toward her, and the voice in Fiona's head started to scream. Nothing clear, just loud, panicked screams that vibrated through her entire body, the kind that used to echo in her head when she was still in the closet and a pretty girl decided to exist within a fifty-foot radius of wherever she was standing. Fiona knew she should make a break for it but found she couldn't move a muscle. Lizzie had gone full Medusa, her intense gaze turning Fiona to stone.

"Hey, you guys are missing the movie."

Panic and relief made for a strange mixture. They tangled together and swirled about Fiona's gut as Michael hovered at the end of the hall, waving them toward him. It was a familiar feeling, one she'd experienced several times as a teen—the feeling of *almost* being caught doing something she shouldn't. Her stomach teetered on the edge of bottoming out, as if unsure of whether to feel guilty about what had almost happened or satisfied by the fortune of good timing.

Lizzie didn't seem to be experiencing any of it. In fact, she didn't seem the slightest bit conflicted. She appeared, instead, to be rather annoyed by the intrusion. "Yeah, we're coming," she said, shooing him off.

He disappeared around the end of the hall, back to the den where the home's biggest television was kept, and Fiona and Lizzie were left alone again. "Here," Lizzie said once he was gone. "I'll take your plate back to the kitchen."

"Oh, you don't have to do that. I can take it."

"No, go on." She took the plate from Fiona, their fingers slowly brushing together and lingering under the porcelain. "You don't want to miss the movie."

"Guess not." Fiona started around her but stopped again almost immediately. Lizzie's hand gripped her upper arm, and with a gentle tug, pulled her back. Close. Lizzie leaned in, the tip of her nose rubbing through the baby hairs near Fiona's temple. All the blood in Fiona's body began to heat, working its way toward a boil the longer they stood there, lingering in that space, in that quiet, in all that delicious tension.

Then, Lizzie kissed her. It was simple, short, a warm touch of her lips to Fiona's cheek, just in front of her ear. "Thanks for the pie," she said, her voice low and velvety, as rich as the dessert had been, and then she was gone.

She headed off in the opposite direction toward the kitchen, and Fiona was left paralyzed. How this one woman had such an effect on her, she didn't know, but it was undeniable. Lizzie McElroy was like lesbian catnip, or perhaps just Fiona Ng catnip. The smell of her, her touch, even just her presence made Fiona's nerves pop and spark like firecrackers. She felt dizzy and out of her mind, yet at the same time, there was an overwhelming sense of warmth and comfort as if she were always on the verge of drifting into a perfect sleep. It was confusing, maddening, and undeniably addictive.

A steadying breath quivered its way up and out as Fiona stood in Lizzie's wake. This one Christmas weekend had just transformed into the longest of her life, and she was still on the first day. *How the hell am I going to last three more?*

She shook her head and made for the den. A movie was a good distraction, this movie in particular. Fiona had seen *Frozen* at least five times since its release, twice in the theater. She practically had the whole thing memorized. As the sounds of singing grew louder, she cast one last glance over her shoulder, to the place where Lizzie had kissed her, a soft and sweet and innocent kiss. And at that point, more than ever, she knew she needed to make like Elsa and *let it go.*

"Why isn't there a TV in here?" Fiona rolled over for the tenth time in as many minutes. "How did your brother survive teenagedom with no TV?"

Michael, propped up beside her in bed with a book in hand, turned a page and smiled. "I told you to bring a book."

"We're only here for four days. Excuse me for not thinking I'd actually have time to read a book."

"You always have time to read a book, because you hardly ever go to sleep before two in the morning."

"It's not even ten o'clock yet. I'm going to die of boredom."

"Tragic. If only you'd brought a book like I did."

"Stop acting so superior. You're not some sage old wizard because you brought a used copy of..." She leaned up enough to peek at the front cover of his well-worn paperback. "Tell me you're not seriously sitting here reading *The Call of the Wild.*"

"What's wrong with *The Call of the Wild*?"

"Only that it's completely *not* you." Fiona thumped the book's back cover. "What? Did you google 'manliest books of manliness?' You're a YA guy, and you know it. I don't know why you don't just own that. You love *The Hunger Games* and *The Maze Runner* and *Legend.* And every time you've ever tried to read something else, you complain about how boring and hard to follow it is. You even read the *Twilight* books."

"Okay, yeah, but I didn't *like* them."

"Right. That must be why you flew through the entire series in less than two weeks. Because you just *hated* it so much."

"You know if I start something, I have to finish it." He held his book stubbornly, staring at the page as if determined to burn a hole through it with only his gaze. "You *know* that."

"And *you* know you're not actually reading anymore, so why don't you put the book down and talk to me instead?"

"I want to finish my chapter."

"Seriously?"

"Seriously."

"I'm going to pinch you with my toes."

"You better not."

"And they're freezing cold right now, too."

"Don't."

"I'm going to do it."

"Fiona, I swear to God."

The longest, most dramatic whine she could manage pierced the air. Fiona put as much misery as she could into the sound. "Michael, please." She wiggled up against him and stuck her face in the crook of his neck. She poked his jugular with the tip of her nose, hard, then poked him again. "Please. I'm so bored."

"Read on your phone."

"No. The screen is too tiny. It hurts my eyes."

"That wouldn't be a problem if you'd upgrade from the iPhone *Three*, or whatever version you've been using for the last six years, and get a bigger screen."

"Excuse you." Fiona jerked back and lay a hand on her chest, offended. "It is an iPhone *Four*, thank you very much. And why should I pay 600 dollars for a new phone when my old one still works fine?"

He shrugged. "Well, tough, then."

"You are really getting on my nerves right now. You know that?"

"Right, because you're not getting on mine at all."

Fiona knew he was trying to rile her. It was intentional. He liked to watch her squirm, and though she desperately wanted to resist, just to deny him the pleasure, she was too restless to care about caving. So, she whined again and rolled away from him, taking all the covers with her. She wrapped herself up in them like a burrito and sent him the winningest look she could manage.

"Really?"

"Until you learn how to treat your *guest*," she said, "your guest, might I add, who happens to be doing you an *enormous, gargantuan* favor out of the sheer goodness of her heart, you can freeze."

"Fine!" He slammed his book closed, not even bothering to mark the page, and tossed it onto the bedside table. "God, you're such a brat."

"So are you."

"I wasn't being a brat until you started being one."

"Are you mad?"

"No."

Fiona sat up and yanked the blankets up around her neck like a scarf. "Are you mad, Michael?"

"I said I wasn't."

"Wow. You're really mad."

"Fiona."

"Michael."

He stood and stomped to the other side of the bedroom. "I said I'm not mad."

"Then why are you stomping around like you're mad?"

"Because it sucks when you're right."

Fiona grinned. "You hate the book, don't you?"

"I fucking hate it so much."

They looked at each other and burst out laughing.

Michael pulled open the two doors of a tall dresser cabinet on the opposite wall. Fiona hadn't paid much mind to the piece of furniture, figuring it to be just another place to throw her clothes if need be. She hadn't ended up using it, so she put it out of her mind. When Michael opened the cabinet doors, however, she wished she'd given it more than just a passing glance. Inside the large cabinet at the top of the dresser was a moderately sized flat-screen TV. Fiona nearly cried. Michael waved his hand in front of the black screen as if he had conjured it with magic. "Wah-*la*!"

"Oh my God." Fiona pulled the blankets over her nose to quiet a tiny squeal. "I love you so much right now."

"You should."

She freed her mouth again. "But I still have to tell you, for the thousandth time, that it's *voilà*, not 'wah-la.'"

Michael released an exaggerated sigh. "You said 'teenagedom' earlier."

"Yeah, but teenagedom at least makes sense. *Wah-la* doesn't. At all."

"Oh, and *voilà* does?"

"Um, yes, because it's an actual word, Michael. It's French."

"Hey. You might speak three languages, but French isn't one of them."

"I don't have to speak French to know a French word. I don't speak Spanish either, but I still know what *gracias* means."

"Well, whatever." The TV remote landed on the bed with a plop. "Take that. I gotta use the bathroom. I think it's a smart TV, so if you want to sign in to Amazon, we can watch *Game of Thrones*."

"Ooh yeah." Fiona settled in at the headboard and switched on the TV while Michael disappeared into the bathroom. "What season are we on now?"

"Five."

"Okay." She went about the work of signing into her Amazon account on Jack's TV. "Shit. Mike! What's my password? Oh, wait. I think I remember it."

When Michael didn't return after a minute or two, however, she realized it was going to be a while, so she stole his phone off the bedside table and started a game of Candy Crush.

"So," she said as she thumbed away at the game, "your family is cool." She thought of Grandma Sophia's sweet, wrinkly smile and rude comments. "Well, most of them." Nice people who were also racist really confused her. It was a good thing she was playing at being straight for the weekend. A *gay* Asian would have been too much. The old bat might've keeled over right then, right into the Christmas tree.

"They have their moments," Michael answered from the bathroom. "I think they were all a little surprised when you kicked everyone's ass today."

"Trust me. No one was more surprised than me."

"You totally won by accident."

"No lie."

"It was fun, though," he said, "watching you get into it after running around like a terrified chicken the whole first half of the game."

"*Game* is a severely misguided word choice." She moved a blue candy piece into place and watched the tiles disappear. "*War* is more accurate. Your sisters don't mess around."

"Yeah, everyone gets really into it."

"Clearly." Fiona frowned. "I like them, though. Your brothers and sisters."

"Yeah. It's nice being able to spend time with them, but it's definitely best kept to a couple times a year. Otherwise, it's like being a kid again."

"What's wrong with that?"

"Nothing, except we all tend to revert back to the most immature versions of ourselves the longer we're together."

"Yeah, but that can be fun sometimes." Fiona growled as the Jelly Queen defeated her, then quickly started another round of the game. "So, your sister."

"Which one?"

Fiona chewed her bottom lip and glanced up at the closed bathroom door. "Lizzie."

"What about her?"

"You guys seem close."

"Yeah." The sound of the toilet flushing drowned everything else out for a minute. Michael cleared his throat. "We weren't really when we were kids. I was always closer to Brian and Grace since we were basically the same age, but I'm way closer to Lizzie now." Sink water rushed through pipes, then squeaked to silence, and the bathroom door finally opened again. Michael stood in the opening, drying his hands on a small towel. "Why do you ask?"

Fiona avoided his eyes and shrugged, trying to appear as casual as possible. "Technically, I didn't ask," she said. "Just made an observation is all."

"Right…" The partially damp towel soared across the room in a crumpled ball and hit Fiona's shoulder. "She tackled you pretty hard today."

"She's kind of a beast."

He laughed and leaned against the bathroom door frame. "She knows it, too."

"Your mom said she's the only other one of you guys who's never brought anyone home before. She's never been serious with anyone?"

"I don't know. She doesn't really date much, I don't guess. Why?" He looked at her hard, knowing. "She's not gay."

"Okay. I didn't say she was. I just, you know."

"No, I don't know. What?"

"I get a vibe is all."

"A gay vibe?"

"Maybe."

"Well, sorry to have to tell you, but you're seriously off your game."

"If you say so."

"You are."

"I mean, that plaid flannel shirt she had on today, though," she teased.

"That's a Southern thing, not a gay thing," he said. "I've told you before, gaydar doesn't work in the South. There are straight women down here who have mullets and chew tobacco and are as butch as it gets, and they still go home to their husbands every night."

Fiona laughed. "Hey, plenty of lesbians have husbands, especially in the Bible Belt. Compulsory heterosexuality is a thing, my guy."

"Lizzie's not gay, Fiona."

"Okay." She fiddled with the remote. "Have you ever gone to visit her in LA?"

"You'd have known if I had. Me and you have been friends as long as she's been in LA."

Fiona said nothing, keeping her eyes on the blank screen.

"Fi."

"Huh?"

"Why are you being weird about my sister?"

"What?" She shrugged again. "Who's being weird?" She turned the TV volume up, then down again—up, then down. The queued episode of *Game of Thrones* had yet to begin, so no sound actually played. She was free to fiddle without consequence. "I'm just making conversation."

"About my sister. Being *gay*."

"I mean, we can talk about your brothers if you'd rather." She glanced over as he crawled back into bed beside her. "Kind of got a vibe from Charlie, too, if I'm being honest. And I mean, he *is* having trouble with his wife, so." She smiled and hoped it would ease the rising tension. It did. Michael's shoulders relaxed even as he stuck his tongue out at her and mock-laughed. "No, I've just had the most interaction with Lizzie so far. That's all. Just thought I'd ask."

"Uh-huh," he said. "Well, asked and answered, yeah?"

"Yup." She let it drop, sensing his uneasiness. Clearly, the topic of his little sister's sexuality was not one he was willing to entertain. Or maybe it was just that it was *Fiona* who was broaching the subject. She wondered how he'd have responded if a straight girl had asked him the same question, but she didn't push it. His reaction had been enough to communicate that he considered his sister firmly off-limits. The whole idea didn't sit right with Fiona. Lizzie was a grown woman and could make her own choices.

At the same time, however, Michael was her best friend. She was supposed to be there for him, *with* him. She didn't want to risk doing anything that might screw everything up, or worse, might put them at odds with each other.

He stared at her a moment longer, gaze boring into the side of her face, but then his seeming curiosity passed, and he turned his focus to the TV. "We ready?"

Fiona swallowed the lump she hadn't realized had been building in her throat. "Just have to hit *play*."

Chapter 5

THE SECOND-FLOOR STORAGE CLOSET SMELLED odd, like mothballs and air freshener mixed together. It made Fiona's nose itch. She rubbed it on the sleeve of her shirt as she stood on guard duty under the old lightbulb's dim light, watching Lizzie's back like a hawk. Any sign of a tremble and she was ready to catch her. "Is your family's entire Christmas weekend going to be one competition after another?"

"Pretty much." Lizzie stood on her tiptoes on top of a small stepladder, poised under a shelf mounted atop a coat rack. With a bit of effort, she managed to pull down the first box of a tall stack of long, rectangular boxes. "When you've got eight kids to entertain, competitions are kind of a given. Mom's always found it easier to get us to do things if she made us compete with each other. It's effective, was *really* effective when we were kids. You know, as long as we don't bite each other's heads off."

"Is that something you're prone to do?"

"A few of us." She passed the first box to Fiona. "Got it?"

"Yeah, but I don't know how I'm supposed to catch you if you start filling my arms up with boxes."

"Well, if it comes down to me or the boxes, save the boxes." She reached for another. "Mom'll kill me if we present her with boxes full of smashed and crumbled gingerbread. It's Lucy and Maddi's favorite. She could totally live with me having a broken tailbone if it meant keeping them happy."

"Sounds painful."

"It is. Trust me."

"Ooh. How did you manage that? Don't spare the details."

"*I* didn't manage it. Grace did."

"Grace?! Sweet, quiet, shy Grace somehow broke your tailbone? No way."

Lizzie handed down another box. "Sweet, quiet, shy Grace was a little prone to tantrums when we were kids, and I made the mistake of falling on top of her carefully crafted dollhouse."

"Uh-oh."

"Yeah, uh-oh." Lizzie hung onto the coat rack and turned on the ladder to face her. "Dad had made the whole thing for her himself, then they built and painted every little piece of furniture together over the course of, like, two years. She loved that thing. Like, *loved*. Of course, I didn't *mean* to smash half of it to bits, but did that matter? Nope. Not a bit. I swear I thought fire was gonna shoot out her nose or something."

Fiona shifted under the boxes. They were just long enough to make holding them for more than a few moments uncomfortable. "So, what happened?"

"Well, first she hit me with a hairbrush," Lizzie said, grinning. "Pretty hard, too. I hit her back, then ran away so she couldn't get me back."

"Smart."

"Not really. She chased me down the hall, cornered me right in front of this very closet, and kicked me through the door."

Fiona's jaw dropped. "*Through* the door?"

"Through the door." She stared at Lizzie as if waiting for her to reveal that she was only kidding, but Lizzie just sighed. "Landed on my ass so hard it broke my tailbone. Mom was pissed. She made us apologize to each other every day for two weeks and pledge to stop every time we got mad and remember that we were sisters and were supposed to love each other. As if that would stop us from wailing on one another at the slightest inconvenience."

"Damn. Having siblings is apparently a life hazard."

Lizzie laughed. "It saves you as much as it endangers you, so I say it's worth it." She turned back to the shelf and grabbed down another box. "Anyway, now you have that story as evidence in case the snowball fight yesterday wasn't enough. We clearly get a little *too* competitive sometimes."

"You think?"

"But no one's ever accidentally killed anyone, so I'd say we're doing all right." She stretched as far as she could toward the back of the high shelf. "Jesus, Mom, did you have to put them so far back?"

"Why aren't we having the tall people do this? You realize Michael is here, right?"

Lizzie lowered back down. "Fiona, come on. Where's your short-people pride?"

"Oh, that? I left it in the grocery store like ten years ago after I tried climbing up the shelves to get a can of soup and brought the whole thing crashing down."

Lizzie stared at her a long moment, lips pinched tightly shut.

"You can laugh."

The sound jumped free, loud in the small space of the closet and infectious. Fiona felt it wiggle its way in, and the next thing she knew, she had cracked as well. "Please tell me someone got that on video and there's a meme of you trashing a grocery store floating around on the Internet somewhere?"

"If there is a God, then no," Fiona said. "So, anyway, I abandoned the anything-tall-people-can-do-I-can-do-too attitude that day, and whatever random kind giant happens to be lurking around the grocery store when I'm there gets me my soup now."

"That is a sad, hilarious story," Lizzie said. "I should make a movie about that."

"Short people would fill the theaters."

"Dabbing their eyes with tissues because it's just *too real.*"

"I smell an Academy Award."

"Mm, yeah. Smells like a lie." She handed down a couple more boxes. A merry little gingerbread man with purple gumdrop buttons and a red icing mouth beamed up at Fiona from the cover of the top box as he stood proudly next to his classic gingerbread house.

"How do you think gingerbread men avoid the temptation to eat themselves?"

The stepladder wobbled as Lizzie let out a loud bark of laughter. She latched onto a few old coats hanging on the closet rack to steady herself. "You can't say stuff like that when I'm trying to balance on my toes on a stepladder, okay? Unless you want to endanger my life."

Fiona smiled. "Sorry. It's a valid question, though."

"It is. I'm guessing it's probably the same as with humans."

"What do you mean?"

"Well, we don't eat ourselves either despite knowing how good it is to *be* eaten." She waggled her eyebrows at Fiona over her shoulder, who laughed despite the way the words made her stomach flip.

"That is *so* not how I meant that."

"But it applies." Lizzie popped down from her stepladder and blew a bit of hair out of her face. "How many kits is that?" She counted down the boxes in Fiona's hands with her index finger. "Okay, that's six, so we need at least four more. Mom always gets extras, but we can leave those until we know if we need them or not." She climbed back up the stepladder and strained on her toes to retrieve yet another box. "Anyway, so our anatomy won't let us eat ourselves, unless you're, I don't know, a contortionist or something, so I'm guessing it's the same for gingerbread men. I mean, think about it. If they bend over too far, they'd just break in half, right?"

"Okay, sure, but why can't they just pull off their little gumdrop buttons and eat those?"

"Because they've got no hands, Fiona," Lizzie said as if it was the most obvious thing in the world. "Brace yourself. This stack is about to get seriously tall." She turned on the ladder with four long boxes in her hands but lost her footing just as she was about to pass them over. The ladder wiggled and wobbled under her, then gave way entirely. It tipped and took Lizzie with it.

Fiona barely had time to curse before Lizzie's body crashed into hers. Her back hit the closet wall, knocking the wind out of her, and all she could do was wheeze and grunt, trying to refill her lungs, as the momentum took them down. The boxes cascaded around them. Some crashed to the floor while others were squashed and trapped between their chests. One of Lizzie's elbows dug into Fiona's gut as she tried to get her footing and failed. Finally, her legs gave out and she collapsed, her forehead smacking into Fiona's to add to the already overwhelming amount of discomfort.

The sound emanating from Fiona's empty, stinging lungs filled the small space, a cross between a whine, a growl, and some strange sort of goat bleat. Lizzie was off her in a second, pulling her up by the arms and digging a hand between her shoulder blades. "Breathe," she said, laughing around the word. Fiona held her gaze and gulped at the air like a fish out of water, but nothing would go in. Nothing would sink down to where she needed it most.

"Oh my God. *Breathe* already, woman." She massaged Fiona's back as if attempting to entice the frozen organs to do their damned job again. It worked. Fiona's lungs spasmed back into motion, and the air she had only just helplessly sucked at finally shot down into her body in a glorious rush of sweet relief.

"Holy shit," Fiona said, voice shredded and gritty. She coughed and took another deep breath, then leaned into Lizzie's shoulder before she even had time to process what she was doing. Lizzie didn't seem to mind. She pulled Fiona even closer, resting their heads together, and continued her rhythmic massage.

"You can say that again."

"Holy shit." Fiona released a long stream of breath and closed her eyes for a moment. "Michael should've warned me that I'd spend the weekend being tackled by his sister."

"Yeah, but then you wouldn't have agreed to come," Lizzie said, tilting back enough to look at her.

Fiona caught her gaze and found herself ensnared. *If you only knew*, she thought. Being repeatedly tackled by Michael's hilarious, adorable, sexy-as-sin sister would have been a much more enticing incentive than the "great food" and "my smiling face" he promised instead. She felt her tongue swipe over her bottom lip, felt her body rock her the slightest bit forward. She functioned without thought or choice as if she'd suddenly become a remote-controlled robot, and Lizzie McElroy held the remote.

They drew close enough that Fiona could feel Lizzie's breath on her face, smell the lingering traces of cinnamon on her tongue from the baked apples they'd had at breakfast. Her own breath hitched when she felt Lizzie's warm fingers rest against her sternum and then slide upward. They skated over Fiona's collarbone as their noses brushed, and Fiona's eyes fluttered closed. She didn't know what she was doing, only that it was foolish, foolish and perfect. She didn't want to stop.

"Liz? I heard a crash. You still alive?"

Fiona's eyes flew open again. She and Lizzie rocketed apart with such force that the back of Fiona's head smacked against a cardboard box shoved into a corner. She heard the thump of Lizzie's body against the opposite wall, followed by a loud curse. The next moment a tall shadow appeared in the doorway.

"Sweet Jesus, Mary, and Joseph. I told your momma not to send the shortest of the bunch."

Fiona blinked, eyes adjusting to the sudden change in light, and realized the shape in the doorway was Charlie Sr. She thought to what had only just *almost* occurred, what the man could have walked in on instead, and her stomach clenched in protest. Guilt washed through her like murky water, a cold omen.

"Thanks for stating the obvious, Dad," Lizzie said with a grunt. "Help me up, will ya?"

He bent and hauled his daughter up by the arm. Once she was on her feet, he brushed a bit of hair out of her face and dusted off her shirt. "You okay, hon? Didn't bust your tail again, did you?" He chuckled as he turned to help Fiona up as well. "Hate to have to spend Christmas in the ER."

"I'm glad my broken butt amused you so much, Dad, but I'll have to disappoint you this time. My tail's just fine." Lizzie looked around at the mess of boxes on the floor. "Don't know that I can say the same for the gingerbread kits, though."

"Ah." He waved a hand dismissively. "We'll make it work."

"Yeah, tell that to Mom. She's liable to break my tailbone for me."

He laughed, then looked at Fiona. "What about you, hon? You all right?"

"I'm all right, I think. I'll probably be sore in the morning, though."

"Well, you aren't a true McElroy 'til you've busted your ass a time or two." He nodded toward Lizzie. "This one's a testament to that." He bent and gathered up a couple of the boxes. "I'll take these down. You girls got the rest?"

"Yeah, we'll get 'em," Lizzie said. "Thanks for the help."

"Welcome." He shuffled out of the closet and down the hall, leaving them alone again. They stared at one another for only a moment before the silence ruptured around their laughter. They each threw their heads back and let the sound tear its way free until they hurt in new, better ways.

"Is your mom really going to be that mad?" Fiona asked once they calmed again.

"She's not going to be happy, but if we're lucky, all the gingerbread pieces will still be intact, and we'll get off scot-free. We should grab a few of the extras, though, just in case."

Fiona smiled as she listened to Lizzie talk. "You know, when I first met you, your accent wasn't super pronounced, but the longer we've been here—"

"The twangier it gets?" Lizzie resituated the stepladder and bounded up it again. She grabbed two more boxes and passed them down to Fiona, who set them to the side. "Yeah, it happens every time I come home. Even happens if I just have a particularly long phone call with my mom sometimes."

"Yeah, Michael's the same way. Since we've been here, his has gotten so much thicker. It reminds me of when I first met him. He sounded like a good old country boy back then, and he still does, but it's flattened out a bit since he's lived in St. Louis."

Once on the ground again, Lizzie began collecting the discarded boxes and restarted the stack she'd built in Fiona's arms before everything went topsy-turvy. "And let me guess which accent you like better."

"I actually like his true accent, *your* accent." Fiona shifted under the boxes and popped her chin over the top so she could see. "Really, I do. I think it's cute."

"Uh-huh," Lizzie said, her tone disbelieving. "Cute. Sure."

"I *do!*"

"You're from LA, so I don't believe you. When I moved to LA, I couldn't get people to leave me alone about my accent. I still can't. I swear I can't say a single word to a single person in LA without them immediately being like, 'Whoa, where are you from?'"

"Which is ridiculous considering LA is like the melting pot of accents."

"True." Lizzie paused at the end of the hall and turned to look back at her. "You good?"

"Yeah." The boxes' corners poked at her arms. "I can't really see anything without propping my chin on top and choking myself, but I'm good."

"Well, don't choke yourself. Just follow the sound of my voice."

"You're just as short as me and carrying the same number of boxes, though. How can you see?"

"I can't. I've just got this entire house memorized. Trust me. Come on." She continued onto the main hall that led to the staircase. "So, what part of LA are you from?"

"I mostly grew up in Culver City, until I was, I don't know, twelve or thirteen, I think. Then, we moved to Pasadena."

"Did you ever go to that huge flea market they're supposed to have there?"

"The Rose Bowl? Psh. Listen, if you knew my mom, you wouldn't even have to ask me to know that the answer to that question is yes."

"Hey, my mom would be eating that shit up, too. She loves a good flea market, though I feel like the California version is probably worlds apart from what we have here." She paused. "Okay, I'm stopping. Don't ram me."

Fiona quickly stopped and propped her chin on top of the boxes for a moment to make sure she wasn't on top of her. Then she noticed the stairs. "Oh my God. I forgot about the stairs."

"It's okay. We're just gonna do one at a time and not break our necks. Deal?"

"Considering I'd really like to keep my neck intact, yes. Deal."

"Okay, here we go." Lizzie took one step down, peeping around the side of her stack. "One down. Five million to go."

"Whoa, whoa, whoa. No." Michael's voice floated up from the bottom of the stairs. "This is a disaster waiting to happen."

"No way. We totally have it."

"Um, I know you, and I know Fiona, and neither one of you is going to make it to the bottom of these stairs alive." He hopped up to meet them. "So, just let me help you and be grateful. How about that?"

"Well, if you're so helpful," Fiona said, "why did we just spend the better part of fifteen minutes using a stepladder? Your tall ass could've done the whole thing for us."

"While we sat on the couch by the fire sipping hot chocolate," Lizzie said, handing two of her boxes to Michael.

Fiona passed off two of her boxes as well, and Michael stuffed them under each of his arms. "*Or* while we sat on the floor right outside the closet watching *you* do all the work and *not* falling on our asses."

"While sipping hot chocolate." Lizzie grinned over her shorter stack of boxes and followed Michael down the stairs. "Basically, I'm saying I don't care where we sit as long as there's hot chocolate."

"Win the House-Off, and Mom'll reward you with a huge hot chocolate." Michael jumped off the bottom part of the stairs like a hyper child and landed with ease. "*With* extra cool whip on top."

Lizzie carefully stepped off the last stair and trailed after him toward the kitchen, Fiona on her heels. "I told you to stop calling it a House-Off."

"And I told you I'll call it whatever I want."

"Okay, but *House-Off* sounds stupid. Fiona, tell him it sounds stupid."

Fiona set her boxes on the kitchen counter with a relieved sigh. She then rested her elbow on the top one and lay her head in her hand. "It sounds stupid, Michael."

He narrowed his eyes at her. "You're supposed to be on my side."

"I'm on the side of truth."

"Okay, but how is Gingerbread-House-Building Competition any better than House-Off?"

"Well, for one," Lizzie said, "the former is self-explanatory."

"And the latter sounds like some kind of pest repellant." Fiona picked up a napkin from the kitchen counter and chucked it at Michael. It caught in the air halfway to him and drifted back down to the surface, harmless.

"Oh, yeah?" He snatched the failed missile from the counter. "I'll show *you* a pest repellant." The napkin proved a rumpled but effective weapon once he rolled it into a ball between his palms and threw it back. It bopped Fiona's forehead, right between her eyes, then rolled down her face and chest. She barely had time to process the hit before Michael sprang around the end of the counter and tackled her. "How's this for pest repellant, huh?"

Fiona squirmed under Michael's tight hold as he encased her with his long, skinny arms, scooped her off the floor and swung her this way and that. "Help," she squeaked, pushing at his hands and kicking her legs wildly around. Both were pointless endeavors, as nothing she did could break his hold. He then tossed her over his shoulder, her ass pointing toward the ceiling while her head flopped at the base of his back, and shot toward the glass double doors leading from the kitchen to the backyard. "Lizzie!"

"No, stop," Lizzie droned, though she didn't move a muscle to help. She was clearly enjoying the show too much. She leaned against the counter and smiled as Michael toted Fiona off toward the wintry hell waiting outside the doors. "Help. Someone. Anyone."

The glare Fiona sent from where she limply hung, having given up the fight, was the best she could muster in her current state. "I thought we were friends," she called piteously as Michael jerked open the kitchen doors and ran into the cold. The humid, icy air hit her face like a thousand tiny needles pricking at her skin, and all she could do was brace herself for what she knew was coming.

With a grunt, Michael heaved her over his shoulder and tossed her into a snow drift that had gathered near the large trunk of a tree stripped nude by the season. It took only about ten seconds for the white, wet mound now cradling her to begin leeching through her thin clothes and soaking into her skin. Her teeth began to chatter almost instantly. "Oh," she said, voice shaky, "you're dead." She struggled to sit up, found it impossible, and collapsed back into the snow. "You're s-so dead."

Michael laughed, unthreatened, but at least did Fiona the courtesy of flinging himself down into the drift with her to share the miserable cold. "Ah, come on," he said, rolling toward her. He pitched an arm and leg over Fiona's body and squeezed her tight against his chest. "Don't be like that. It's not so bad."

Fiona snuggled up to him as close as she could, gripping the front of his shirt and burying her freezing face in his chest. He was so warm. "F-fuck off."

"She says as she cuddles me." He loudly breathed several hot puffs of air onto her ear. "Is that helping? Are you warm yet? No? Would it make you feel better if I threw Lizzie in the snow, too? She didn't even try to help you, after all." When Fiona nodded against his chest, he rolled off her and started to stand. Fiona's grip in his shirt stopped him. "Okay, you gotta let go, or I can't go anywhere."

"I'll die," Fiona said, though she uncurled her fingers and let him go anyway.

"Be right back. Don't die." He popped onto his feet and shivered. "Shit, it's cold." Fiona sent him the same glare she'd shot Lizzie's way and tried to conjure up a plan for sweet revenge. Her brain, however, was a block of ice, thus entirely uncooperative. All she could think was that if she closed her eyes the way she wanted to, she might fall asleep like all the people dying from hypothermia in the movies did. Only there was no one there with her to shake her shoulders and scream, *Stay awake, Fiona! Fight it! You have to or you'll die!*

God, she was dramatic. If she wasn't a popsicle incapable of anything beyond shivering, she'd roll her eyes at herself.

The creak of the kitchen door opening sounded like a distant echo. Lizzie's voice followed, a phantom vibration from another life. "Oh my God. Did you just leave her out th—What? No. Michael, I swear to God. No! I only have a T-shirt on!"

"So," he said. "So does Fi. Besides, this is what you get when you abandon new friends in their time of need."

"I will kill you for this."

"Shoulda been a better ally."

Michael's steps crunched heavily in the snow, then Lizzie landed with an *oomph* beside Fiona. "Oh, fuck me!" The words hissed through her teeth as she immediately rolled toward Fiona and wrapped around her like a koala bear clinging to a eucalyptus tree. Fiona didn't mind a bit. In fact, she welcomed the tight hold. As she'd done with Michael, she buried her face in Lizzie's chest, not caring a bit that the move effectively placed her right between Lizzie's ample breasts. Lizzie didn't seem to mind either. She shivered against Fiona and buried one hand under her hair. "It's cold as hell out here."

"You b-brought this upon yourself," Fiona said, voice muffled against the material of Lizzie's shirt.

"Goodbye, cruel world," Lizzie shouted toward the sky. "I hardly knew ye."

"Jesus, you two like to lay it on thick, don't you?"

Fiona felt Michael's hand clutch her arm like a life raft. The next thing she knew, she was being hauled out from between Lizzie's breasts and up from the icy depths of their shared three-foot-deep snow-drift grave. She hung like a rag doll over Michael's shoulder again as he ran her back in through the kitchen door. Warmth washed over her like a blessed rain, seeping through her frosty wet pants and T-shirt and into her chilled skin. Michael dropped her onto a stool at the kitchen island then headed back out for Lizzie.

"Warmth!" Lizzie sighed and held herself as she shimmied into the seat beside Fiona a minute later.

"Don't get your hopes up," Fiona said, drawing her legs up onto the chair, knees against her chest. "It could be a mirage."

"You're right. We're probably still outside, dying."

Michael dragged a chair over between them and sat. "Y'all realize I was laying in the same snow, right? And I'm fine."

"You're bigger," Lizzie said. "You have, like, two extra feet of body mass."

Fiona scooted her chair closer to the other two, leaning toward them for more warmth. "We're so tiny."

"Yeah," Lizzie said. "Why didn't you put us by the fire?"

"You try lugging two heavy bodies back and forth," Michael said with a laugh.

Lizzie shrugged. "Hey, you made that choice all on your own. If you're going to start something, see it through to the finish."

"All right." Michael hopped up from his chair and grabbed three coffee mugs from the living room. "Since I'm so nice, I'm going to make you guys some hot chocolate."

"That's not a courtesy." Fiona unfolded herself and stood. "It's an apology. Don't confuse the two."

"Yeah," Lizzie said. "You *owe* us."

"Fair enough." Michael took the cocoa mix down from a separate cabinet. "Where you going, Fi? Don't you want your apology chocolate?"

Fiona headed toward the hall. "Of course I do, but I'm going to die if I don't get out of these damp clothes. I'll be back down after I change."

"Oh, me, too." Lizzie stood from her chair. "Good idea."

"Weak," Michael said, "but fine. Don't take too long, though, or it'll get cold."

Cutting through the living room made for an unfortunate dilemma. Lizzie's parents, along with Lily, Madison, and Grandma Sophia, were all seated by the fire. As soon as Fiona and Lizzie entered the room, they became the center of everyone's attention.

"Hey, you two." Rosie waved them over. "What was all that hollering about? Michael giving you a hard time?"

As much as Fiona liked Rosie, she hadn't stopped shivering once since Michael brought her back inside. She was desperate to be out of her damp, cold clothes and into something dry, warm, and preferably long-sleeved. The goosebumps on her arms weren't likely to subside for a decade otherwise. Still, she was there to charm the family as Michael's darling new girlfriend, so she conceded a few steps, drawing closer to the couch, yet kept close enough to the foyer that she could make a break for the stairs at the first opportunity.

"Oh, you heard that, huh?"

"Well, of course," Grandma Sophia said. "Just because we're old doesn't mean we're deaf. Y'all *were* screaming like banshees, after all."

"And yet no one came to help us." Lizzie crossed her arms over her chest and leaned her hip against the arm of the couch. "Michael was just, you know, tossing us into the snow with no coats on or anything. Fiona has stage-three hypothermia, and one of my toes will probably fall off later tonight, but whatever. No big deal."

Rosie looked to her husband. "Does hypothermia come in stages?"

"Beats me," he said with a shrug. "But I know you can live without a toe or two. Ain't that right, Mom?"

Grandma Sophia swayed slowly back and forth in the rocking recliner closest to the fire. Madison lay lazily in her lap, shoes off and bare feet stuck out toward the warm glow. "Mhm. Your daddy only had two toes on his left foot, didn't he, hon?" She grabbed one of Madison's tiny feet and squeezed her last two toes, one by one. "This little piggy right here, and this little piggy right here."

Madison giggled, and her foot squirmed out of Grandma Sophia's hand. "But why'd he only have two toes, Grandma?"

"Oh, I don't know. You better ask Pop."

Madison slung herself over the side of the chair so she could see Charlie Sr. "Why'd Grandpa only have two toes, Pop?"

"Dad, no," Lizzie said before he could even begin. "Don't tell them that story."

"And why not?"

"Because it's terrifying." She moved back to Fiona's side, hovering near the foyer. "Not to mention gross. I had nightmares about that story for years."

"That's because you were the one who always mowed the lawn," Grandma Sophia said with a laugh. From her mouth, it sounded like the amusement of an old witch, cackling about the latest batch of children she'd turned into toads for her frog-leg soup.

Fiona leaned a bit closer to Lizzie, their shoulders brushing, and grinned at her. "Okay, I'll admit I'm interested in hearing this story now."

"I'll tell you upstairs," Lizzie said. "We can leave the theatrical version to Dad. Let him horrify the children on his own. Besides, you're still shivering, and we've got hot chocolate waiting."

"Oh, you two are no fun," Rosie said. She poked Lily's thigh. "Are they, Lily?"

Lily was stretched between her grandparents on the small sofa, head on Charlie's lap and feet on Rosie's. The iPad practically glued to her face didn't budge, and she didn't make a peep.

"Clearly, she disagrees," Lizzie said, then tugged Fiona's arm to lead her upstairs. "Let's go."

They were halfway up when Rosie called after them. "Don't take too long, girls. As soon as the others are back from the store with the stuff, we'll be getting started."

"'Kay, Mom!" Lizzie rolled her eyes at Fiona. "There's always *something* to be ready for in this house."

"You guys definitely like your activities," Fiona said, though her focus was less on the conversation and more on the warmth of Lizzie's hand still wrapped loosely around her forearm. She wasn't sure why Lizzie hadn't yet let go, but she couldn't deny the part of her that was glad she hadn't, the part that secretly hoped she wouldn't.

"Yeah, notice how the only people who seem to have time to relax are the old people and the kids." Lizzie tugged her over the last stair and down the hall. "Napping by the fire while everyone else gets a task."

"They all looked awake to me."

"Give it a minute. Grandma'll be asleep before anyone gets back from the store, and good luck waking her up once she's out." She stopped in the hallway and faced her. "Actually, it's not that hard to wake her. Just nobody likes to do it, because she's grumpy as hell if you wake her up unless you shove a cup of coffee under her nose before she has a chance to open her eyes."

"My dad's the same way about his coffee," Fiona said, "and his naps."

They stood in the hallway alone, smiling at each other but saying nothing. Lizzie's hand still held Fiona's wrist. She stroked her thumb back and forth over the smooth skin there, a strange kind of hypnosis. Fiona found herself falling into the feeling. Her eyelids grew heavy, and her feet felt as if they had somehow grown down into the floor. She couldn't move, could only feel and be and wonder what might come next.

Lizzie, on the other hand, didn't seem stuck to the ground at all. She was loose and liquid, flowing toward Fiona like a slow-rolling wave. She inched closer, then closer still. Her hand slid down from Fiona's wrist to her fingers. Their fingertips rubbed together, and Fiona felt the static and friction like lightning bolts. They zapped up the length of her fingers, up her arms, and over her shoulders. They sizzled down her spine, sparking along the way. Under Lizzie's touch, she was a live wire gutted and frayed. She was dangerous, combustible. With the right trigger, she would ignite, and there would be no going back from that.

"Are you...?"

The swipe of Lizzie's tongue over her bottom lip almost made Fiona miss the words. She was distracted by every little tick of movement, every vibration magnified. Every freckle was a destination as she mapped her way up from Lizzie's mouth to her unique, searching eyes, staring at Fiona as if they needed to find something, something specific.

Fiona took a slow breath through her nose and exhaled through her mouth, as if preparing for a leap. She was standing on the edge of something, though she wasn't sure what. The only thing she was sure of was that she ought to take a step back. She ought to retreat. She ought to know better. Her feet remained rooted to the floor regardless. She wasn't going anywhere as long as Lizzie was touching her this way, looking at her as if she needed something. Whatever it was, Fiona wanted to provide it. "Am I what?"

"Hot chocolate's getting cold!"

The call from downstairs seemed to jar Lizzie out of whatever searching reverie had entranced her. She shook her head and stepped back. "Guess we should hurry up."

Fiona's fingers tingled from the cold loss of touch. She itched to have Lizzie's hand on hers again but made no effort to reconnect them. The moment was lost, gone in a single blink of two different-colored eyes. "Yeah," she said, the word escaping in a weak rasp of sound. Her throat was a dust-blown desert, all the moisture in her body having flooded elsewhere. "I guess so."

"Okay." Lizzie lingered, shuffling in place as if waiting for something, anything, to keep her there a moment longer. When Fiona offered nothing, she shrugged and said, "Well, see you down there, then." She walked off, leaving Fiona alone in the hallway, staring at the wall with a million different thoughts swirling about her brain and feelings she couldn't name stirring in her gut.

※

Fiona sat on the floor of her and Michael's bathroom in nothing but her panties and bra. Her damp clothes lay strung over the side of the bathtub. Earlier, she'd been desperate to get out of the cold and into something warm and comforting. Now, the cold comforted her. It seeped into her back as she sat against the tub with her elbows propped on her knees. Her forehead rested in the palms of her hands as she stared down at the floor.

She'd barely managed to get herself undressed and changed into fresh, dry underwear before needing to sit down and think. Breathe. Heat washed through her like a sickening wave, making her stomach knot and roll. Part of her feared she might actually be coming down with something, an unfortunate consequence of being buried in the snow. The other part of her knew what really afflicted her.

"What the hell am I doing?" The whispered words bounced off the bathroom floor and back, hitting her in the face like a stinging hand. She repeated them again and again, reveling in that sting as it brought her back down to earth, to reality, to the hard-edged, bold, and underlined truth: that she needed to stop.

Stop thinking. Stop feeling. Stop wondering. Stop *wanting*.

Fiona closed her eyes and pounded her head against her hands. "Fuck," she croaked. "Fuck. Fuck. Fuck."

She couldn't stop, no matter how much she knew she *should*. Thoughts and feelings weren't things to be controlled. They were nature, wild. They would wander as they pleased, unafraid to be. At most, both could be ignored, avoided, but to do so was skirting the edge of danger. She could see the beast before her, and she needed to turn the other way, find another route, run in the opposite direction as if her life depended on it.

The thing was, she didn't know how to do that.

For two days now, she'd been stuck in the same house as Lizzie McElroy. Granted, it was a *big* house, and Fiona was fairly certain she could elude her, even if it meant locking herself in Michael's brother's childhood bedroom and not coming out again until it was time to leave. Such a tactic, however, wasn't tenable in her situation. She was there to show off to the family so his mother and grandmother would lay off Michael for once. She couldn't very well do that if no one ever actually saw her. His family would be convinced instead that he'd settled down with a socially inept troll who'd only come to take over one small bathroom of their massive house and charge a toll to anyone looking to shower there. So that meant being out and about, spending time with the rest of the family.

But to Fiona, it seemed as if Lizzie was everywhere, which wouldn't be a problem if Fiona's insides didn't catch fire every time she came around. But they did. It plagued her day and night. She had accompanied Michael for a specific purpose, to be *his* person for the weekend. His. Instead, she'd spent the entirety of the weekend thus far pining for the wrong damned McElroy.

That was the code: bros could date whomever they wanted, so long as they respected each other's families and boundaries. Mothers, daughters, sisters—they were all out of bounds, weren't they? Fiona wasn't a "bro," but she was pretty sure that the unwritten, unspoken rule applied in this situation anyway.

"Jesus," Fiona said to herself, "maybe I'm just over-fucking-thinking it." Maybe she'd misread Michael the night before, and he wouldn't actually be mad at all. No one could help how they felt, right? Maybe he'd understand that. Maybe since he had so many sisters, it would be ridiculous to assume they were all forbidden. She growled under her breath and dug her fingers into her hair. "*Maybe* girls aren't anyone's fucking property, and I can kiss whoever I want, dammit."

"That's right. You tell 'em, girl."

Her spine rammed against the side of the tub as she jolted up, but the pain barely fazed her. She was too concerned with the new presence in the room. Her mouth hung open as she stared. "I…uh…"

Lizzie stood in the bathroom's open doorway with an easy smile on her lips and a steaming mug of hot chocolate held in both hands. "You're not dressed."

Fiona looked down at herself, nothing but lanky, naked limbs and blue cotton panties that didn't match her maroon sports bra. She felt the redness in her cheeks, neck, and chest, burning with humiliation. "I literally want to die right now."

"Really?" Lizzie laughed. "I thought you wanted to kiss someone, dammit." She crossed the small room, sat on the floor in front of Fiona, and passed over the hot chocolate. "You were taking a while, so I figured I'd bring it up. I heated it up in the microwave, good as new."

Fiona didn't want to look at her. At the same time, she couldn't look away. The mug warmed her fingertips as she took it with a muttered thank-you. The scent wafted up and soothed her, calmed her racing heart. "Where's Michael?"

"Lily and Madison roped him into a game of Twister. He'll end up throwing his back out if the others don't return soon."

Fiona couldn't muster up much more than a half-hearted, lifeless laugh. Lizzie shuffled a bit closer. Her hand danced over Fiona's shin, as if ready to touch, then retracted. Lizzie smiled at her, but it was different. Sad, maybe. Worried.

"Listen. Are you okay?"

"Oh yeah." Fiona swallowed the lump Lizzie always seemed to inspire and stared down into her hot chocolate. She wished she could drown in it. "I'm *great*. I'm just sitting here in front of Michael's sister, basically naked."

"Having a crisis over wanting to kiss someone?"

Fiona looked sharply up at her.

"Should I go get my brother for you?"

It wasn't serious, the question. Fiona could tell by the look in Lizzie's eyes. That one look told her all she needed to know: Lizzie knew *exactly* who Fiona *really* wanted to kiss, and it damned well wasn't her brother. "Lizzie." She said it like a warning, a tone to ward off whatever was drawing them closer, weaving them together, tying them into a knot. Whatever it was, they needed to stop it before it became impossible to disentangle themselves, before they became such a mess together that there would be no hiding it, no going back. No retreat.

Lizzie's pale, freckled hands didn't hesitate another moment. They didn't hover. They found purchase on Fiona's shins, slid themselves up to her knees, and squeezed. "Hey," she whispered, inching closer. Her thumbs drew soothing circles into the sides of Fiona's kneecaps. "It's okay."

"It feels really not okay," Fiona said, the words barely more than breath. She expected another round of reassurance. Instead, Lizzie took Fiona's hot chocolate from her and set it aside on the floor. She then slowly, and one by one, straightened Fiona's legs out and inched them aside. Fiona wanted to ask what she was doing, but her voice was a useless clump in her throat, stuck, unmoving, as if afraid to interrupt whatever it was that was happening.

The silence had never seemed more alive than it did the moment Lizzie reached for her. It vibrated around them as she moved right into the space beside Fiona, with her denim-covered thigh rubbing against Fiona's bare one, and leaned in. Her eyes remained wide open, her lips a slightly upturned sign of confidence and comfort, of welcome. But she didn't greet Fiona with her lips, as expected. She didn't offer the kiss Fiona both dreaded and desired more than she cared to admit. Instead, she closed the gap between them by slinking her arms around Fiona's cold, naked back.

The embrace melted her. She liquefied in Lizzie's arms, all the tension leaking out and away so that all she could do was sink. The breath she didn't realize she'd been holding eased free as she closed her eyes and buried her face in Lizzie's neck. Gliding up the soft, fuzzy material of Lizzie's sweater, her arms returned the embrace.

A quiet hum buzzed in her throat, the sound of satisfaction, serenity. Lizzie's hair smelled like apricots and wood smoke, a strange combination that Fiona found inexplicably intoxicating. Her body was warm and inviting, like the feeling of lying in the sun or beside a hearth. "This is nice," she mumbled against Lizzie's skin, reveling in the rake of short fingernails up her back and under her hair.

Lizzie touched her as if they were familiar, as if they'd known each other for years. She touched her the way one touched a lover, with sure hands, hands that knew their way without direction and felt at home on naked skin. Every touch was confident but soft, delicate, slow, nothing like the rapid heartbeat Fiona could feel thumping steadily against her own.

It shook her, that tiny revelation of how nervous Lizzie actually was beneath the surface, how excited she might be by an embrace that felt both tremendous and treacherous. She couldn't help but wonder if the same potent heat rolling through her body also coursed through Lizzie's, comforting her as effectively as it devoured her. Was Lizzie clenching her thighs? That thought was enough to rattle her, to yank her out of her drowsy reverie and into electric awareness.

She became acutely aware of every point of contact, every pop of static on her skin as Lizzie's fuzzy sweater lay against her, and every seductive scratch across her scalp. How exposed she was. How exposed *they* were. Her senses lit up like the Christmas tree downstairs, and suddenly she was more anxious than she was comfortable. She opened her eyes and stared intently over Lizzie's shoulder at the open bathroom door. It stood before her like a one-way mirror, bright on their side and shadowed on the other, the unlit bedroom beyond. She knew no one stood watching, but her body thrummed with the feeling of being observed, the uneasiness of possibly being caught, any second now, doing something she shouldn't be. She squirmed in Lizzie's arms, unable to tame the growing nerves or temper her sudden embarrassment, her discomfort. Her arousal.

"I'm naked," she blurted, then immediately bit her tongue and tamped down the urge to smack herself on the forehead.

Lizzie's sweet laugh was more a purr than a melody. "Almost," she said, turning her nose in toward Fiona's neck. The tip rubbed up and down, back and forth, every puff of warm breath against her skin the best kind of torture. "And trust me, I'm *extremely* aware of how almost naked you are."

Every word was sex, rocking its way down Fiona's body and back up, driving her toward the edge. She was on the precipice of doing something she knew she shouldn't do, something that could send up in flames the best friendship she'd ever had. But when Lizzie pulled back from the embrace and looked at her, eyes determined and wanting, tongue flicking out to wet her lips, Fiona was ready to burn her life to the ground just to meet her halfway. Just to taste her, if even for only a moment.

That moment passed in a hard blink and a cleared throat, in the sudden withdrawal of Lizzie's warm, soft body and hooded eyes. "You should get dressed," she said so quietly that Fiona almost missed the words. "The others are probably back by now."

She stood, her hand slowly untangling itself from Fiona's hair, and crossed to the bedroom. She paused in the door frame for a moment but didn't look back. "See you down there."

"Wait."

Lizzie halted again, but Fiona wasn't sure what she wanted to say. She didn't know why she had called Lizzie back, didn't have a clue. Every feeling she had stuck to her insides and refused to budge, refused to be pressed into words, so, after a moment, she shrugged and said the first thing that popped into her mind. "How did your grandpa lose his toes?"

"Really?" Lizzie's boisterous laugh bounced about the small room as she leaned one shoulder against the doorframe. "That's what's on your mind?"

Fiona tried not to blush. "It's probably better if we don't talk about what's actually on my mind." The smirk that settled on Lizzie's lips was so smug that Fiona scoffed at her. "Are you going to tell me about the toes or not?"

"Okay, but I'm warning you, you're about to trade in what I'm guessing is a pretty damned good image in your head for a horrifying one. You realize that, right?"

"A dose of horrifying would probably do me some good right now."

"Wow." That smug expression reappeared, making Fiona burn anew. "Must be a *really* good image floating around in there, huh?"

"Lizzie."

"Mhm?"

"Are you always like this?"

"Like what? A holy terror? Yes, my mother's been calling me one since I was at least four."

"Tell me about the toes."

"He mowed them off."

Fiona blinked. Her mouth worked wordlessly for a moment. "Um, he did what?"

"He *mowed* them off." Lizzie rocked back and forth against the doorframe on the ball of her shoulder. "It was one of those older push mowers. Not like the ones now that have the self-propelling thing, but like the old-school ones that you basically have to put all your body weight behind to push. Do you even know what I'm talking about? I mean, there's nothing in LA but dirt, and the people who do have grass all hire gardeners and stuff to do it for them."

"I know what a lawn mower is, Lizzie."

"Are you sure? Because I'm talking about a machine, not a person."

"I'm going to throw this hot chocolate at you."

"Have you ever even mown a lawn before?"

"No. I've also never performed surgery. Doesn't mean I don't know what a scalpel is, does it?"

"Uh-huh. And what about grass? Did you ever witness actual grass before you moved to Missouri?"

"Oh yeah. California's got tons of grass. There's a pot dispensary on every corner. Just look for the stores with the green plus signs on the windows."

"Ha! Well, the story goes that he was out mowing with one of those big, old push mowers, and when he dragged it back to start another lane, he pulled it right over his foot."

"What about his shoes?"

"He wasn't wearing any."

"He wasn't wearing any *shoes*?"

"It's Arkansas, Fiona. People do all kinds of shit here with no shoes on. Mom and Dad don't even lock the doors at night. They leave the car keys in the ignition half the time. It's a lot more relaxed out here in the country than it is in the city."

"But while you're *mowing*?"

"Yeah, admittedly, that was pretty dumb, but nobody ever said it was smart."

"So, he just chopped them off with the mower?"

"Oh yeah. The mower ate them right up like weeds. Spit them back out like weeds, too, shredded to hell." Fiona's mouth hung open as she listened, the new image in her head just as horrifying as Lizzie had promised it would be. "Grandma tried to collect all the little pieces, too. She threw them in one of the old ice coolers and lugged the thing to the emergency room with Grandpa, who, by the way, insisted on finishing the yard before going."

"Okay, now you're screwing with me." Fiona ran her hands down her chilled legs, then gripped her bare toes. They ached despite still being firmly attached. "You can't be serious."

"No, I'm dead serious. Grandma actually lugged a cooler full of grassy, severed body parts to the hospital just so Grandpa could get his toes put back on, but the doctor said the pieces were too mangled to reattach. He said Grandpa could do physical therapy, but of course he didn't want to do it because he didn't want to have to pay for it, so Grandma settled for giving him a stern lecture about wearing shoes when he mowed. Then, I guess, she just took him home with, you know, significantly fewer toes than he'd started the day with."

Fiona's silent, astonished gaping gave way to a loud, ringing laugh. "Holy shit." She laughed so hard her belly hurt. "That's insane."

"Just wait," Lizzie said. "There'll be plenty more stories before the weekend's over." She popped off the doorframe and tapped the door. "Now, hurry up and get dressed. We've got gingerbread houses to build."

Almost as soon as the words left her lips, she was gone, and all Fiona could do was sit and stare at the place she'd only just been, a goofy grin still stuck on her lips.

It lasted only seconds before the ridiculousness of the story melted away and all that had come before began to leak in again. It amazed Fiona how surreal it all suddenly seemed, as if it had never actually happened or had perhaps only occurred in a dream. It was as if Lizzie had never come, never touched her, never been there at all. All that remained of her, the only proof of her presence, was the scent of apricots and the untouched mug of hot chocolate on the floor.

The scent around her faded as Fiona disturbed the air, grabbing the mug. It was cool to the touch, the contents inside now as cold as Fiona's mostly bare body. She sipped it anyway and grimaced, then made herself get up and dressed. As each article of clothing slid on, she couldn't help wondering what might have happened if she'd remained bare, if she'd stayed in Lizzie's arms. What would have happened if they'd closed the door and locked it, if they'd had just a bit more time together on that chilly bathroom floor? What would have happened if she hadn't been so afraid?

Chapter 6

WHEN FIONA ARRIVED DOWNSTAIRS, FRESHLY dressed in a thick pair of sweatpants and a Saint Louis University sweatshirt, it was like walking onto the set of a Food Network competition show. The large dining room table had been divided into elaborately stocked stations, each already occupied. Charlie Sr. and Rosie sat at the head of the table with Charlie on their right, surrounded by his daughters. They climbed all over him, passing candies back and forth and occasionally sneaking them into their mouths. Beside him sat Sophie, and next to her, the only empty seat at the table. It sat between her and Michael, waiting for Fiona. Brian and Grace occupied the stations on the other side of the table, along with Lizzie and Jessie. Everyone was present except Grandma Sophia, who Fiona guessed was still lounging in her chair in the living room, likely asleep.

Candies of every shape, shade, and size filled the bowls and boxes that lined the length of the table. There were gumdrops and peppermint sticks, licorice ropes and crushed peanut brittle. Silver and gold candy-coated chocolates shined under the dining-room lights, their pearlescent sheens making them appear as precious gems waiting to be discovered. Jelly beans, gummy bears, and candied popcorn added bursts of bright color, and Fiona could already imagine putting them to use. They could be Christmas lights strung along the frame of her and Michael's gingerbread house. And the white-chocolate Kit-Kat bars could be the wooden planks of a picket fence. Ideas presented themselves with each new candy bowl she explored.

"Come on, Fi," Michael said. "Everyone else's already got a jump-start on us."

Fiona claimed the empty seat beside him. "Okay, I knew this was going to be good, but this is next level."

"Yeah, Mom goes all out," he said. "She even used to bake all the gingerbread herself, but it got to be a bit much after a while, so we switched to the kits. We still get all the good toppings, though."

Decorating bags filled with different-colored icing and assorted design tips were set up at each station. There were tips for piping out flowers, straight lines, angled lines, stars, balls, and squiggles. White royal icing had been prepared to glue the gingerbread siding together, and there was buttercream for embellishments. It seemed not a single thing hadn't been thought of or prepared. Everything a person could hope to have in order to build their dream gingerbread house was right there, right at their fingertips.

"There's only one craft store in town," Sophie said. "It's a little mom-and-pop shop, but really well stocked, and you can practically see the owner's mouth watering every Christmas when we walk in." She grabbed a peppermint stick from their station and placed it at her own. "This competition probably pays his December rent every year."

"Hey." Michael reached over Fiona and swatted Sophie's hand. He tried to snatch back the peppermint stick but couldn't reach it. "You've got your own peppermint sticks. Put it back."

"I need an extra."

"There are extras down by Mom."

"Oh, good. So, you can go down there and get an extra one to make up for the one I just took. No big deal, right?"

Fiona nudged Michael with her shoulder. "One less peppermint stick isn't going to kill us. I mean, we could make a whole gingerbread penthouse with all this stuff."

"It's been done already." He cut a glance Sophie's way. "Christmas 2012."

Sophie smirked at him. "My trophy hot chocolate that year was divine."

"Are all your competition trophies food-and-drink related?"

"Pretty much," she said. "We like our treats."

"Okay. How about this?" Michael shoved a napkin Fiona's way, on which he'd drawn his gingerbread architectural plan in crayon. "Stop trying to look, Sophie." He flung an arm around Fiona so he could block the paper from the other side and hunkered over the table. "What do you think?"

The three-story shack in the drawing leaned oddly to one side, had a snowman in the front yard, and was surrounded by a short fence. "Why is it crooked?"

"My hand slipped."

"I mean," Fiona said, choking back a laugh, "it honestly just looks like a shack. A leaning, three-story shack."

"All right. Fine." He tossed the napkin aside and watched it float to the floor. "I was trying to actually make a plan since you just want to sit here and talk to everyone, but since nothing I make is good enough, *you* design the stupid thing."

"Oh, honey, don't be such a sourpuss," Rosie said. "It's supposed to be fun."

"I *am* having fun, Mom," Michael said through gritted teeth.

Fiona leaned into him. "I'm sorry. It's great. I love the way it leans to one side and looks like it's about to topple. It's sheer art. Truly."

"God, you're a butthead."

The laugh Fiona loosed on him made Michael roll his eyes, but he smiled as he did it, so she knew he wasn't mad. "Come on," she said. "Let's get to work on this thing. Look, Brian's already made his gingerbread man a hot tub."

Michael's head shot up. "What?!" The peppermint-bark hot tub was filled with blue icing and topped with white cotton-candy steam. A small gingerbread man with a satisfied licorice smile stuck out of the top of the icing water. Beside him, on the lip of the hot tub's frame, set a tiny bottle of beer molded out of fondant. "Are you serious right now?"

"Hey." Brian rolled out another tiny piece of fondant, preparing to sculpt it. "Grace is the brains behind the operation. I'm just the very skilled hands."

Grace worked on an elaborate napkin sketch with one hand and slid a peppermint to her twin with the other. "Smash that up when you're done with the fondant."

"I honestly don't even know why you're surprised." Lizzie held two pieces of gingerbread siding together, waiting for her icing to harden like glue. "After that carnival she designed in '09? You remember that? It was the Christmas after I graduated high school. I don't think anyone's ever going to beat that one."

Fiona's brows shot toward her hairline. "An entire carnival?"

"Oh yeah." Lizzie nodded. "There was a Ferris wheel and everything."

"That *turned*," Sophie added. "I was so mad too because that was the year I made the livestock barn."

"Oh, Soph, come on," Grace said. "That barn was never going to win."

"It was *good*!"

Jessie chimed in from her station next to Lizzie's. "Um, no, Sophie. That cow you made looked like a deformed dog." She focused on piping something onto one side of a piece of gingerbread, tongue stuck out between her teeth as she worked. She paused for a second and looked up. "With, like, psoriasis or something."

The intense concentration around the table broke with a wave of laughter that rolled down the length of the table, making its way from person to person. They all shook with it, Fiona included. She tried to imagine such a thing and couldn't. The best she could muster up was something similar to a cat she had attempted to mold out of Play-Doh when she was in elementary school. That creation had been the sad stuff of nightmares.

"Oh, shut it," Sophie said, throwing a gumdrop across the table. "What do you know? You were five."

"I was ten."

"I was talking about your mental age."

"Listen." Rosie pointed around at her children. "You've all made something as ugly as sin at one point or another." She elbowed her husband. "Remember that little haunted house Lizzie made when she was—what was she, hon?—six or seven? Oh, Fiona, you should've seen it. She tried to use peanut butter instead of icing to glue the pieces together, Lord knows why; so her little house just starts collapsing left and right." She stopped and held her belly while she giggled. "So, she makes a little ribbon out of yellow fondant and wraps it around the whole pitiful thing."

"It was caution tape," Grandma Sophia said, wobbling into the room with her gnarled cane in one hand, an empty coffee mug in the other, and Otis tucked under her arm. His legs and head hung as if he'd given up on life, or at least on struggling to get away.

"Exactly!" Lizzie said. "Thank you, Grandma. It was genius."

"It sure was," she said as she plopped into a cushy chair in the corner by the back door. She tucked Otis into the space between her thigh and the chair arm, then pulled a cigarette from behind her ear and stuck it into her mouth. A cool draft blew in as she cracked open the door and lit up. "Rosie, hon, the pot's empty."

"Michael, put a pot of coffee on for Grandma, will you?"

"Yup." He popped up, no hesitation, and grabbed Grandma Sophia's empty mug. He kissed the top of her head. "You want cream, Grandma?"

"No, black's fine, hon," she said and patted his arm. "Well, a little whiskey, if there's any."

He laughed. "All right. Be right back."

As the croak and wheeze of brewing coffee filtered in from the kitchen, Rosie launched into another tale. Fiona leaned back in her chair and listened, realizing that she felt more relaxed than she had in a long time. The gingerbread-house-building competition was much tamer than the snowball fight had been, less cutthroat and more mellow. The energy around the table flowed with ease, light and airy and pleasant. Fiona was content to sit within it, soaking in the feeling of a big, full family who, for at least this one weekend out of the year, had not a worry in the world beyond being together and making the most of that time. She didn't care who won the competition and nabbed the prize. She was glad to simply be a part of it and suddenly found herself wishing she could be there under different circumstances.

Across the table, Lizzie was engaged in a quiet conversation with Jessie. She said something, nudged Jessie, who nudged her back, then started laughing. They kept it low, snickering like two kids with a secret, but Lizzie's smile was loud, stretched wide, showing all her front teeth. The skin around her eyes wrinkled the slightest bit, and Fiona found she couldn't look away.

Lizzie must have felt her staring. She looked up right at that moment and caught Fiona's eyes. Her smile didn't fade. It softened, a smile for someone she knew well, someone she cared for. Fiona wasn't sure she deserved it, wasn't sure she'd earned it in such a short time, but she was grateful for it all the same.

"Hey." Michael's hand on her arm jarred her from thought. She hadn't even realized he'd returned. "You know you actually have to help, right? Otherwise, I'm not giving you any of my hot chocolate when I win."

"Sorry. " Her consciousness flooded with guilt. "I was just, um, listening to your mom's stories."

"Yeah, that's Mom's tactic." Michael threw a hot-tamale candy down the table and laughed when it landed and nestled into Rosie's thick ginger curls. She didn't even seem to notice it, too focused on smacking her husband's hands away from a piping tip he was trying to screw onto a decorating bag. Michael raised his voice. "She likes to tell old family stories to try and distract us so we mess up. Ain't that right, Mom?"

Rosie stuck her tongue out at him. "Hush."

Fiona went to work, helping Michael create his three-story gingerbread shack—or as he referred to it, his "masterpiece." The gingerbread pieces didn't all fit perfectly together, but he'd made it work well enough. The actual tower, at least, wasn't leaning to the left as the one in the drawing had been, and Fiona was impressed by the fact that Michael had managed to create a crooked little window at the top. A hole had been cut into the gingerbread and lined with a pretzel-stick frame.

All that remained to do was the exterior decorating. Currently, it sat bare as bones, just an ugly, plain brown with white oozing out at the seams. Michael didn't seem concerned with it, however. He was instead focused on the yard surrounding the tower, where he had created an admittedly awesome ice-skating rink of crushed blue-and-white peppermints.

"That's cool." Fiona poked one of the mounds of miniature marshmallows surrounding the rink. Smashed together, they looked like little hills of snow.

"Thanks." Michael passed her one of the big tubs of fondant. "Here. You can start on the fence."

"So, Fiona, how about you tell us a bit more about yourself," Rosie said as Fiona began rolling out pieces of fondant. "You said you grew up in Los Angeles? Lizzie just loves it out there. Do you miss it?"

"Definitely." Fiona bit off a piece of the fondant she was sculpting, much to Michael's obvious chagrin. "Especially the weather. People always say it's so hot in LA, but it's nothing compared to St. Louis. It's a drier heat in LA. In Missouri, summer is like walking around in a hot bowl of soup."

"It's not any better down here," Rosie said. "What about your family? I'm sure you miss them, too."

"Yes. Right." Fiona snorted and shook her head at herself. "Of course. I miss my parents all the time."

"Do you get out to see them often?"

"Not as often as I'd like. It's been a couple of years now since the last time I flew out. I've just been swamped with school."

"What do your parents do?"

"Well, my mom's an attorney. She mostly deals with people's wills and estates. And my dad's a professor. He teaches Mandarin and also works in student recruitment."

"Yeah," Michael said, "He's been trying to get Fi to transfer back to LA since—"

"Since I left LA." Fiona laughed. "He's still holding a grudge against me for not applying at the university he works at."

"I don't think any of ours would want one of their parents as a teacher, either." Rosie chuckled. "I can't imagine many kids who would."

"Probably not." Fiona grinned. "No, I just really wanted to get out of LA, actually. Until I left for college, I'd only ever been to two other states, and they're both so close to California that it's like it doesn't even count. So, I figured a little adventure was in order. SLU has a great master's program for nurse practitioners, too, and it's right in the middle of the country. So, why not go for it, right? Plus, there are some really great children's hospitals in St. Louis, and I'd like to work primarily in pediatrics."

"Oh! Do you like children? Michael just *loves* kids, don't you, hon? How many kids do you think you'd want, Fiona?"

"Yikes," Lizzie said under her breath, and Fiona couldn't help but agree. She hadn't missed the sudden twinkle in Rosie's eyes, and she wasn't about to go anywhere near *that* particular topic. She looked at Michael, who was now as pink as a bottle of Pepto Bismol, and bugged her eyes out at him. *Help!*

"Mom, come on," he whined. "Are we playing twenty questions, or what?"

"What? I'm just trying to get to know her, son. That's what you want, isn't it? Why else would you bring a girl down to meet your family?"

"Clearly not to help me win the gingerbread competition."

Fiona patted his back. "That sad shack was never going to win whether I helped or not."

He huffed like an annoyed child and leaned into her embrace, abandoning his sad creation entirely. "*Such* a butthead."

"Aw." She kneaded his shoulder. "You're such a sore loser. It's cute." As he grumbled at her, she laughed and glanced around the table. The other McElroys were scrambling to finish their own gingerbread creations. Except for Lizzie. When Fiona's gaze landed on her, she found Lizzie staring right back. Watching her. Tracing her lips, skating down her chest, lingering on the hand still massaging Michael's shoulder. Fiona felt that gaze like a probe, digging for information, seeking answers they already had. Searching, perhaps, like she, for a way for things to be different.

That's when it hit her. Looking at Lizzie, all her insides suddenly felt like putty, and Fiona realized exactly what she wanted. Those different circumstances she wished for, being surrounded by a family she already felt so much a part of—those longings were because of her, because of Lizzie. As much as she wished it weren't the case, it was. Fiona didn't want to be there *pretending* to be somebody's special someone. She wanted to actually *be* a McElroy's special someone. Just not Michael's.

Chapter 7

THE CLICK OF THE DOOR closing behind her was a relief. Fiona leaned against the wood and closed her eyes. "There are too many cute girls in this fucking house," she muttered to herself. It was only then that she noticed the sound of water running. She opened her eyes, gaze drawn toward the closed bathroom door. In a few short steps and the turn of a knob, she was on the other side of it.

Michael stood in front of the toilet with his fly open. The sound hadn't been water running at all but Michael relieving himself. He nearly missed the bowl, however, when Fiona flung herself into the room.

"What the hell, Fi?"

"I'm so glad you're in here." She dropped to the floor and lay her back against the door.

"Um, I'm trying to pee here, in case you hadn't noticed."

"So?"

"*So.*"

"So, just *pee*. It's not like I can see anything, and even if I could, big deal. I've seen your junk before."

"What? No, you haven't."

"Uh, yes, I have."

He shuffled around the toilet to put his back to her. "When?"

"Junior year. When you ate half that plate of brownies I made before you realized they had pot in them."

He was silent for a moment. "I can't finish." He bounced on his feet a bit, then came the sound of his zipper. "And I don't remember that. Well, vaguely."

"You remember." The faucet squeaked as he flicked on the water and quickly washed his hands. "Plus, we've talked about it like a million times. You know that's one of my favorite stories to tell."

"I don't know why. It's stupid."

"It was hilarious. You were so freaked out."

Instead of drying his hands on the towel hanging beside him, he turned and shook his arms over Fiona's head so that all the water lingering on his skin rained down on her from above. "Are you done, Fi?"

"I will never forget you shuffling into the living room with your pants around your ankles, holding your little penis like it was some precious little bird you found with a broken wing."

Michael's face flushed red. "Please stop using the word 'little?'"

"Oh, stop being such a guy. You know what I meant." She tugged on his pant leg until he lowered onto the floor beside her. "It was cute." Her hand shot up as soon as the words were out. "It was cute how *worried* you were, *not* your penis, so don't even try to make a joke. Your penis wasn't cute."

"Rude."

"Sorry, not sorry."

"It could have been something serious."

"It was a freckle. I mean, admittedly, it was a pretty big freckle, but still just a freckle. No different from the five million other freckles you have on the rest of your body."

"Then how come I never noticed it before?"

"Maybe it was a new freckle."

"Can you just *get* new freckles?"

"Yes." Fiona patted his knee. "People get new freckles all the time, especially fair-skinned people, and especially if they're out in the sun a lot. So, just stop tanning naked, and you'll be fine."

"As if I've ever tanned a day in my life."

"True. You're like the white crayon, if the white crayon was covered in reddish-brown spots."

He laughed. "So, why are we hiding in the bathroom?"

"Because I desperately need to get out of here." The back of her head rolled against the hard door as she looked at him. "No offense, but there are just too many McElroys in this house." She refrained from telling him that it was one McElroy in particular that was plaguing her, the one she couldn't stop bumping into, the one whose smile drove her mad.

"No argument there."

"I need a break." *From your sister, who I can't stop thinking about kissing. Help.*

"Welcome to my childhood, kid."

"Are you aware that your grandma has, like, a designated chair in every room of the house?"

"Yeah. That's how we make sure she's included, even if she doesn't actually participate in any of the activities anymore."

"She just migrates from chair to chair?"

"She used to do some of the stuff with us when we were little, but now she pretty much just sits, sleeps, smokes, and drinks coffee all day. She's extra chill."

"I aspire to someday be that chill," Fiona said, nodding, "minus the smoking and the casual racism, of course. Totally down with the coffee, though." She sighed. "Also, your brother hasn't stopped bragging about winning the gingerbread competition last night, even though Grace was the one who designed the whole thing. I swear it's like he's being extra loud just to make up for the fact that Grace is so quiet. Again, no offense."

"None taken. Brian likes the sound of his own voice."

"And he's recreated his 'trophy' hot chocolate, like, three times now just so he can carry it around, waving it in front of everyone as if we're supposed to be jealous of him."

"Are you?"

"A little."

"Thought so."

"And also—"

"There's more?"

"Your sister."

"Which sister?"

"Sophie."

"What about her?"

"She keeps trying to make conversation with me about how you and I ended up together and how we feel about each other and stuff, and I can only pretend to be hetero for so long, so I don't even know what to say anymore. But, also, she's really pretty and really nice, so it's like, I *want* to answer her just to, I don't know, make her happy or whatever, so then I just end up stressed and gay. And, yes, I know I'm talking really fast right now. I can't help it, because you keep leaving me alone with your family, and I'm overwhelmed."

"You've got a thing for Sophie?"

"No. God, Michael." *Please don't ask me the same question about Lizzie.* "But, I mean…would that be a problem if I did?"

"Oh my God!" He sat straight up, rigid as a board, and looked at her, stricken. "You've got a thing for Sophie!"

"You didn't answer my question."

"You didn't answer mine."

"Why are you being so weird?"

"Because you're acting like you've got a thing for my *sister*."

Nausea stirred in Fiona's gut, and her nerves started to twitch. Clearly, it *would* be a problem. She chewed her bottom lip until a chunk of skin pulled loose. "Relax," she said, wishing she could take her own advice. "I don't have a thing for Sophie."

"You swear?"

"Yes, I swear. But look, pretty girls are still pretty girls, whether I'm into them or not, and I can't help it if their prettiness affects me."

Michael eyeballed her, as if trying to ferret out the truth. After a moment, though, he shrugged and leaned against her. "So, basically your problem is that Brian is annoying because he's super full of himself, Grace is annoying because she's super quiet, and Sophie is annoying because she's super pretty and is actually trying to get to know you?"

"Yes. Exactly. Well, no, technically I never said Grace was annoying. I like her nose ring."

"So she gets a pass because she has a piercing?"

"And because she doesn't ask me any questions."

"Wow. I'd hate to know what you think of my mom, since questions are her main form of communication."

"Listen, I have anxiety."

"I'm aware."

"I'm having anxiety right now."

"I'm aware of that, too." He clapped his hands against his thighs and hopped to his feet. "All right. Come on, then." His hands were as cold as Fiona's butt against the floor, but she took them and let him pull her up. "We're busting out of this joint."

"Yes!" She followed him out of the bathroom. "Wait. Where are we going?"

"Eh, we'll figure something out." He grabbed his car keys off the dresser and led her toward the door. "Let's go."

<hr/>

The empty hallway teased them as they peeked around the door frame. "Coast is clear," Michael said, but Fiona had a foreboding feeling.

"Too easy."

"It's an empty hallway. Guards aren't going to jump out of the walls."

"Look, this many McElroys in one house and you're telling me there's even *one* empty hallway?" She shook her head. "I don't buy it."

"You've seen too many crime movies." He tugged her hand, and together they crept down the hallway like two cartoon villains, all tiptoes and high knees. "No one's going to—"

"Hey, guys."

They sprang up from their crouched positions and froze, stiff as statues. "See," Fiona said out the side of her mouth. "I told you it was too easy."

"You jinxed us."

Sophie stood at the end of the hall, blocking their path and staring at them as if they'd lost their minds. "Wow, and here I thought Michael would never find anyone as weird as him, but so wrong. So wrong I was."

"Yeah, thanks Yoda," Michael said, "but we've got important business to attend to, so if you could just move aside."

"Uh-huh. Important business." She eyed the keys in Michael's hand, then stepped out of the way. "Sure thing, weirdos. But whatever you're doing, make sure you're back in time for presents tonight."

"Presents?" Fiona almost tripped over Michael's foot as they raced down the hall, then she nearly tripped again over her own. Her firm grip on Michael's hand thankfully kept her upright. "It's only Christmas Eve."

"Yeah, we do Secret Santa on Christmas Eve," he said. "We'd all be broke as hell if we tried to buy for each other every year, so we decided to do Secret Santa so we only have to buy a present for one sibling each year. Then, we all pitch in together for something for Mom and Dad."

"Oh, that's nice."

"Yeah, but we still do presents Christmas morning, too, all the ones for Charlie's girls, and then whatever Mom and Dad got each of us. We've been telling them for a while now that they don't have to get us anything anymore, but they always do anyway. Well, except Jessie. She still thinks she needs a hundred presents to unwrap every year." They slid to a halt at the top of the stairs, glanced cautiously around, then began their descent at a snail's pace. Every few seconds, they peeked over the bannister to make sure no one was waiting at the bottom to interrogate them about their daring escape. "Wait."

Fiona stilled at his back, hand still clasped in his. "What is it?"

"I heard something."

"Heard what?"

"Talking."

"I didn't hear anything."

"Well, *I* did, so just trust me and wait."

"Why are you guys creeping around the house like you just stole something?"

"Oh, holy shit!" Fiona jumped so hard she nearly slipped off the stair she was standing on. She grabbed Michael's shirt with her free hand and clung for dear life.

Lizzie appeared at the bottom of the stairs as if she had just teleported into the room. Her wide hips were hugged tightly by a pair of well-worn jeans, and the tank top she had on accentuated every curve, from her full, plump breasts to the curve of her soft belly. Fiona ached at the sight and buried her face in Michael's back. "Oh God, Michael," she groaned. "Why do McElroys just keep popping out of nowhere?"

"Wait. *Did* you guys just steal something? Or are we just having some kind of weird stairway get-together?"

"No," Michael said. "This is not a get-together. No one is getting together."

"So, then, you stole something. Ooh, what is it? Something of Brian's? Please tell me you stole something from Brian."

"Shut up, Lizzie. God. We didn't steal anything. We're just trying to get the hell out of here, so go away and pretend you didn't see us."

"What? You guys are making a break for it? No way."

"What's it to you?" Michael, pulling Fiona along, legged it right by his sister. Fiona caught a whiff of her as they passed, the scent of wood smoke and apricots that she was becoming much too familiar with. She squeezed Michael's hand involuntarily, and he seemed to take it as a sign that they should hurry.

They hit the first-floor landing just as Lizzie said, "Oh nothing. It's just that I may or may not have a hot tip concerning our darling mother and where she may or may not be right now, which may or may not affect your ability to successfully make the aforementioned break."

Michael stopped, whirled them both around, and narrowed his eyes at Lizzie. "Where is she?"

"Oh, if only you knew, right?"

"Lizzie. Seriously. We're trying to get out of here for a few hours, and I don't want to have to deal with Mom asking a million questions or stopping us to tell a story I've already heard a thousand times or guilting us about abandoning the family until it's too late to go out and do anything. So, do me a favor for once and spit it out."

"What's in it for me?"

Michael looked at Fiona, who shrugged and turned to Lizzie. "What do you want?"

Lizzie smiled. One red-brown eyebrow ticked toward her hairline as she sauntered down the steps toward Fiona. "Oh, I think you know exactly what I want."

The force with which Fiona's stomach bottomed out nearly made her lose her balance. It was just like the one and only time she'd gone bungee jumping, just before she left for college. The second she'd jumped, her stomach had gone screaming into her knees, and all she could think was that the rope wasn't going to catch, she was going to hit the ground with a splat, and everyone watching would glimpse her insides. She felt that way now. It was as if all the things she had hidden inside had been gutted out of her and put on display.

But then Lizzie laughed. "Take me with you. Duh."

"All right. You can come with us," Michael said, "but only you and only because—"

"I'm your favorite sibling."

"Eh, I was going to say because you've got valuable information to trade, but I mean, I *guess* you're up there on my list of favorites." He squeezed Fiona's hand. "What do you think? Is it cool if Liz comes, too?"

What am I supposed to do? Fiona thought, resisting the urge to roll her eyes. *Say no because she's the reason I need to escape in the first place?*

Fiona forced a smile and nodded, unable to say anything at all. She was afraid of what might come out if she actually opened her mouth. Neither Michael nor Lizzie seemed to notice or care that the smile was fake. They bounded toward the door like happy dogs on their way out for a walk. Fiona made herself follow, certain her blessed few hours of escape and relief had just been transformed into an even more unbearable form of torture than what she had already endured.

Chapter 8

"So, where are we going?" Lizzie shimmied her way up between Michael and Fiona. Each of her arms brushed theirs as she leaned as far forward as she could manage. "Also, I hate sitting in the backseat."

Michael glanced sideways at her from behind the steering wheel. "Does it even count as sitting in the backseat when you've already crawled halfway onto the console?"

"How else am I supposed to know what's going on?"

"You could try using your ears."

"From a comfortable distance," Fiona added. Her stomach hadn't settled once since she'd climbed into the car.

Lizzie looked at her. "What? Am I too close?"

Yes.

"Does it bother you?"

Yes.

"You're fine," Fiona said, leaning away from her. She leaned so far to her right that she was practically on top of the passenger-side door. The cool glass of the window soothed her burning cheek.

"Some people like their personal bubbles, Liz," Michael said. "You should know this considering you're always complaining about people getting in yours."

"Only people I don't know, and I'm pretty sure that's everyone, Michael. No one wants a stranger rubbing up against them in line at the Panda Express."

"True, but to be fair, you've only known Fiona for a few days now, so you're still basically strangers."

"Huh." Fiona could feel Lizzie's eyes on her and looked over. They shared one short but heated stare, then Lizzie laughed and shook her head. "Nope. The way I see it, we stopped being strangers the second we ended up in bed together."

Heat flooded Fiona's body from her head right down to her toes. She simmered against the window, half-expecting it to fog at her touch. She was so close to boiling, and she was certain Lizzie knew this. At this point, it couldn't be coincidences anymore. It couldn't just be unfortunate but innocent word choices. It was deliberate. Lizzie was fucking with her.

"You mean when you attacked her?" Michael steered them onto a larger road, one with actual cars and businesses. Nearer the McElroy home, there had been nothing but land filled with various junk and livestock, of course, but mostly just acres upon acres of land. Thankfully, it didn't take them long to reach the rest of civilization.

"Attack is a strong word."

"But appropriate," Fiona said and readjusted herself against the window.

"You know my sister doesn't bite, right?" Michael leaned forward to look at Fiona. "You're gonna push yourself out the door if you keep trying to get away."

"Is it my perfume?" Lizzie flashed a smug grin her way. It was all Fiona needed to know that Lizzie was a troublemaker and likely had been all her life. She was enjoying this. "Because it's not *mine*, I swear. It's some crap old-lady perfume Mom bought me. She loves those little Avon perfumes. She sprayed it at me, but I could've sworn I dodged it in time. Do I smell like I'm headed to a Bingo tournament?"

Fiona tried not to give her the satisfaction of a laugh, but it bubbled up and out before she could stop it. "You smell like apricots, actually," she said, then silently cursed herself. Her body had apparently decided to respond to Lizzie regardless of her insistence on resisting.

"Oh, that's just my conditioner. Hey!" Fiona looked up, startled, but Lizzie was focused on the windshield, not her. They had just pulled into the parking lot of a small theater. Its marquee was yellowed, and some letters appeared to be missing. There were only two other cars in the parking lot. "Are we going to a movie?"

"Yup," Michael said at the same time that Fiona shouted, "No!"

The car lurched to a hard stop, jarring everyone inside, and Michael and Lizzie both whirled to face Fiona. They wore expressions so similar that, in that moment they could pass for the third set of McElroy twins. Their ginger eyebrows arched high above their eyes, both sets surprised and pinned on her. Fiona cleared her throat, unsure of what to say to explain or cover her outburst. She'd tried not to react, but the protest had simply jumped out of her.

A dark cinema. A cute girl. An undeniable attraction. What could possibly go wrong?

"Um, I just meant…is this theater really open on Christmas Eve?" She took a subtle, deep breath through her nose. *Rein it in, Fiona.* "Wow. That's crazy."

Michael and Lizzie looked at each other, then burst out laughing. "You scared the hell out of me," Michael said. "I thought I was about to hit something I couldn't see."

The laugh Fiona conjured was more a flutter of nerves than anything. "Yeah, I… Sorry."

"S'okay." Michael let off the brake and pulled the car into one of the many empty parking spaces. The engine clicked off, but Fiona was certain she could still feel its rumble in her stomach, in her bones. "Ready?"

"Are you sure we have time? Don't we have to be back soon for Secret Santa?"

"Nah, we've got plenty of time. Come on."

He hopped out of the car, Lizzie following. As soon as their doors closed, Fiona took a precious moment to steel herself. "Fuck, fuck, fuck, fuck, fuck," she muttered under her breath in rapid-fire rhythm. "Okay. Suck it up and go."

She threw herself out of the car, concerned she'd barricade herself inside if given too much time to fret. Word vomit spewed the minute her feet hit the asphalt. "Is there even anything playing that we'd want to see? What's even going to be in theaters on Christmas Eve? Some lame romantic comedy?"

"What's it matter?" Michael twirled his car keys around his fingers. "You're the one who wanted to get out of the house so badly. Who cares if it's lame? At least there's popcorn."

"Not even popcorn will save us if it's a bad Christmas movie."

"A bad *animated* Christmas movie, probably." Lizzie bopped into the space between Fiona and Michael and slung an arm through each of theirs. "Michael's favorite." She grinned and knocked her hip against his. "Does Fiona know you watch *Shrek the Halls* every Christmas?" She looked at Fiona. "*Every* Christmas."

"Unfortunately, I'm aware." Fiona tried to keep her voice even, but every step toward the theater felt like a step through quicksand. She was being dragged toward her inevitable doom. She could feel it. "And *Casper's Haunted Christmas*, too."

"Okay, first off, *Shrek the Halls* is amazing, and only someone with a true heart of coal would say otherwise," Michael said, "and second, *Fiona,* you like *Casper's Haunted Christmas*, so I don't know why you're trying to act like you don't in front of Lizzie."

"I get it," Lizzie said. "I'd try to hide that embarrassing truth from me, too."

"It's better than watching *A Christmas Story* every year."

"Hey." Her hands rose in a show of surrender, tugging Michael's and Fiona's elbows along with them. "I totally agree with you. Talk to Brian. He's the one who insists on watching it every Christmas."

"On loop."

"Or at least until Mom makes him turn it off so Jessie'll stop threatening to take a hammer to the VCR."

"Your parents still have a VCR?" Fiona endeavored to bury herself in the conversation so she wouldn't have to think about the doom. The dark-room doom. The dark-room, cute-girl doom. The hands-touching-in-the-popcorn-bowl-in-the-dark-room-with-the-cute-girl doom. *Oh God. Stop.*

"Uh, yeah, of course," Lizzie said as they bypassed the ticket window sporting a handwritten *Buy tickets inside* sign. "They still have Dad's old Atari system."

Inside, they were greeted by a dingy, well-worn red carpet, a half-asleep employee leaning on a service desk, and the overwhelming smell of buttered popcorn. "And Dad's old Stereo 8 player," Michael said, stomping the snow off his boots.

Fiona wiped her own feet on a small black rug just inside the door. It sat atop the red carpet, looking terribly out of place. "What's a Stereo 8 player?"

"You know. Like 8-track tapes. Those big clunky tapes they had before cassettes."

"Oh yeah. I know what you're talking about now. Wow. Do they still work?"

"If the seven-thousand-year-long intro to Boston's 'Foreplay/Long Time' blaring from the barn every time Dad goes out there is any indication, then yes," Lizzie said. She released their arms so she could dig a wad of cash out of her jeans pocket, then squinted up at the digital red lettering of the day's showtimes. "Okay. What are we seeing? It's on me."

Michael and Fiona both grabbed Lizzie's fistful of bills and pushed it away. "No," they said in unison.

"It's only fair. I mean, I *did* force y'all to let me come, so I owe you."

"Not sixty bucks!"

"Fiona, it's Arkansas, not LA," Lizzie said. "Tickets aren't twenty bucks a pop here."

"Still."

"Still, you're not paying for either of us." Michael swatted Lizzie's hand back down when she attempted to slide her wad of cash to the zombie behind the desk. "I'll cover my own ticket, and Fi's with me, so I'll cover hers, too."

"And because *you* actually do owe me," Fiona said with a laugh.

Lizzie looked between the two of them. "For what?"

"Uh…" Michael glanced at Fiona, panic in his eyes. He couldn't exactly say that he owed her for pretending to be his girlfriend. "For, um…"

Fiona tried to help. "For an incredible—"

"Orgasm!" His face ripened in seconds, the reddest tomato face Fiona had ever seen, and his hand balled into a fist as if he was resisting the urge to slap himself in the mouth.

"I mean, I was going to say an incredible Christmas weekend," Fiona said, smacking her lips together awkwardly, "but, uh, sure, yeah. An incredible orgasm. Yup. That's what you owe me for. That incredible… orgasm…that I gave you…"

Lizzie's lips pursed, clearly holding back a laugh. "Right," she said. "An incredible orgasm. Sure."

"Can we just buy the fucking tickets already?" Michael asked with a huff. He yanked his weathered leather wallet from his back pocket, wiggled free his debit card, and practically threw it at Lizzie. His eyes glued themselves to the floor as he wandered a little way off from them, unwilling to exist any longer in the awkward tension he'd created.

"Congrats on the incredible orgasm," the heavy-lidded theater employee mumbled, waving Michael off with a tired hand and a dreamy smile. That's when Fiona realized that the kid wasn't half-asleep at all. He was high. Or, well, maybe he was both. He turned back to Lizzie, who stood ahead of Fiona, shoving cash back into her pocket and sliding over Michael's debit card. "You guys seeing the Christmas movie?"

"Is it good?"

The employee, whose nametag read *Jonas*, shrugged. "Haven't screened it, but probably not. It's the only ticket we sold today, though."

Lizzie looked back at Fiona, eyebrows raised. "What do you think?"

"Can we not?"

"Michael'll be crushed, but then I guess you could always just cheer him up with another incredible orgasm, huh?"

Jonas chuckled behind the desk, propping his lazy, heavy head up on his hand. "Heh. Nice." He grinned at Fiona in a way that made her physically uncomfortable, as if he was wishing he could hit her up for his own incredible orgasm.

Fiona didn't give her the satisfaction of answering, nor did she give Jonas the satisfaction of returning his smile. "What about *Autumn Falls*? That's a slasher flick, right?"

"I think so."

"Works for me." Fiona blurted the words, then took off to catch up with Michael, leaving Lizzie to finish the transaction. Once at his side, she took one look at him and said, "A fucking incredible *orgasm*, Michael? Really?"

Red still marred his face in big, uneven splotches. He looked like a miserable baby with a fever. "I know."

"Do you, though? *Do* you?"

"I hate myself right now."

"I hate you right now, too."

"I deserve it."

"Yeah, you do."

"I'll buy us some Milk Duds."

"Yeah, you will."

"'Kay. Come on." He tangled his hand with hers and pulled her toward the concessions stand.

Long, thick branches crept over one another, weaving and tangling between trees so the canopy overhead effectively blocked out the moon. The forest was as dark as pitch, and the rustling of leaves in the breeze accounted for the only sound outside her short, shaky breaths. She pressed her back to the rugged bark of the nearest tree trunk and silently slid to the ground. Bloodied, bare knees were pulled to her heaving chest, and she wrapped her arms around them, trembling.

The snap of a twig.

Her terrified eyes widened. With quaking, dirty hands, she cupped her mouth so tight that the skin of her cheeks strained around her fingers. Her eyes shut hard. Tears spilled through her lashes.

Another snap! The shuffling of brush underfoot.

"Mhm. That's what you get for breathing so loud," Lizzie said, staring up at the scared girl on the movie screen. She shoveled a handful of popcorn into her mouth and spoke around it. "Of course he fucking found you. You're out here wheezing like a dying cow."

"Liz."

She leaned forward, past Fiona, to look at her brother. "What?"

"Stop talking out loud."

"We're the only people in here." She waved a hand out over the seats in front of her. Not a single one was occupied beyond the three they'd taken at the very top of the cinema. "Who am I bothering?"

"*Me.*"

"Whatever." With a huff, she sat back in her seat and chomped on another handful of popcorn. One kernel soared past Fiona's face, barely missing her, and smacked Michael in the cheek. "It's not like you don't already know what's going to happen."

"No, I don't," he snapped, "and I'd rather find out from the movie than from you."

"Good. I'm busy eating my popcorn anyway." Another piece flew his way, catching him on the shoulder. "My *delicious* popcorn."

"If it's so delicious, then stop throwing it at me and shut up and eat it already."

"It *is* delicious." Lizzie crunched a piece between her teeth loud enough to rival the movie's volume. "It's incredible, really. Like an *incredible orgasm*, but you know, in food form."

Michael growled and stood up. "I'm going to the bathroom."

"Oh. Really? I thought you were really into the movie. You sure you can handle missing even a minute of it?"

"Never should have let you come," he grumbled as he clambered past their knees and made his way toward the stairs.

Fiona grinned as she threw a Milk Dud into her mouth and dug another out of the box. She, too, hated when people talked in the theater, but the movie was boring. Every scene was predictable, every death over-the-top, and none of the characters were even fractionally likeable. Plus, she liked to bask in the glow of Michael's embarrassment. He was the king of creating situations he later wished he hadn't, and no matter how many times Fiona had gotten onto him about taking a moment to think before he spoke, he still hadn't learned.

"So, now that he's gone..."

And, apparently, neither had she. *Shit.*

All the joy and humor she'd just been reveling in stopped on a dime, shriveled, then died a crumbly death. Caramel plopped off one tooth and stuck to another as her jaw hung wordlessly open. Melted chocolate coated her fingers, still pinched around a now firmly squashed Milk Dud, and the pulpy, quivering organ in her chest that couldn't choose between honor and desire decided it was as good a time as any to pick up the pace. It raced like the now dead girl's shallow, scared breaths had on screen just moments earlier. It raced like the clumsy, fast footsteps of the male character through the woods, the one they all knew would die just as horrible a death as his brother had at the start of the film.

It raced in time with the rapid tap of Lizzie's heel to the floor. "Fiona?"

"Huh? What?"

"I said you're avoiding me."

"What?" Fiona hadn't heard a thing. Her blood was rushing too loudly in her ears. "You did? I didn't. I'm not. What? No. I'm not avoiding you."

"You are." Lizzie shook her bucket of popcorn around, then dug free another handful. "You think I didn't see your face when Michael said I could come with you guys? You looked like someone just killed your cat."

"I don't have a cat."

"You're a lesbian, and you don't have a cat?"

Fiona choked so hard on the Milk Dud she'd just swallowed that she dropped the box. It hit the floor, spilling candy around her feet, and all she could do was cough and splutter and wheeze.

"Pretending to choke isn't going to get you out of this conversation, you know."

The chunk of caramel stuck in her throat refused to budge, and for a moment, Fiona was certain she was going to die. She clawed at her throat with one hand and grabbed Lizzie's arm with the other, burrowing her nails in to get the point across. She wasn't fucking joking.

"Oh! Oh my God. You're serious. You're actually serious." Lizzie tossed her popcorn bucket into the chair beside her and jumped to her feet. Her hands hovered around and in front of Fiona as if attempting to cast a spell. "Oh my God. Wait."

Fiona wanted to scream that she couldn't wait. Her lungs weren't going to wait patiently for air. They would either catch a breath in the next few minutes or die an empty, crackly, chocolate-coated-caramel-flavored death. "Heimlich." She barely managed to squeak the word out around the Milk Dud, but it was enough to spur Lizzie into action.

The velvet-covered, cushioned seat popped up with a creak and groan as Fiona was wrenched free of it. She stumbled as Lizzie spun her around to put Fiona's back to her chest. "Okay," Lizzie muttered at her ear and wrapped her arms around her middle. "Okay. Okay. I can do this. I don't know how to do this, but I'm just going to do it."

Just do it! Fiona screamed inside her head, fumbling with Lizzie's hands. She tried to help her form proper fists and place them in the correct position, but she was rapidly growing dizzy and the longer the Milk Dud remained in her throat, the more it hurt. Every tortured swallow resulted in another round of helpless gagging and coughing.

"Okay. Here we go. Here we go, Fiona." Lizzie slammed her joined fists into Fiona's gut so hard that she lifted her off her feet. Nothing happened beyond a grunt, a cough, and a wheeze. Fiona kicked her feet as Lizzie held her in the air. Her eyes burned with tears. "Shit. Shit. Okay. Again. I'm gonna do it again." Lizzie set her back on her feet and repositioned herself. "Here we go. Please don't die, Fiona. Please don't die. We haven't even kissed yet." Her hands, knotted firmly together, rammed inward, and Fiona shot off her feet again with the force of the blow.

The Milk Dud flew out, a melty, delicious cannonball that likely stuck wherever it landed. Fiona collapsed against Lizzie's chest. The breath she took was one of a corpse spasming back to life, so loud and obnoxious that it drowned out the screeching violins of the movie still playing before them. Her feet dropped gently back to the floor as Lizzie lowered her down, holding her from behind.

She eased into her own seat and pulled Fiona with her, down into her lap, where they both sat panting, not saying a word. Fiona took breath after breath, slower with each inhale until she calmed enough to relax, and lay her arms over Lizzie's, still wrapped around her middle. A sheen of sweat coated Lizzie's palms, but Fiona didn't care. She laced their fingers and gripped tightly.

"Thank you," she said, leaning back to rest their heads together.

"Please don't thank me." Lizzie laughed. "I'm the one who put your life in danger." Her laugh was tired, astonished, the kind one offers up when something is too much to process, too much to analyze. It was infectious. Fiona lay against her, letting herself be held without thought or worry or guilt, and delighted in the sound gurgling up her still-sore throat.

"I lied," she said, trailing her thumb over the back of Lizzie's hand. Back and forth. Back and forth. Soothing. "I do have a cat."

The quiet laugh they shared cracked wide open, became an eruption shaking everything in their vicinity. The entire cinema seemed to tremble with them as they held tight to one another and dissolved into giggles. Fiona wiped tears from her eyes and sighed, then slid off Lizzie's lap and back into her own seat. "Lizzie."

"Yeah?"

"This is a disaster."

They stared at one another in the dark, neither saying a word. Fiona wasn't sure there was anything more they could say. It was as simple as the words she'd already spoken, and it was as complicated. Lizzie finally opened her mouth to reply, but Michael appearing at the bottom of the stairs caught Fiona's attention. She stiffened in her seat, alerting Lizzie, and the two went back to staring at the screen as if they'd never stopped.

"Geez," Lizzie said as he squeezed by them to reach Fiona's other side. "Think you were gone long enough? What'd you do? Fall in the toilet?"

"Yeah, well, Mom called me when I was on my way back in," he said. "She figured out we were gone, so I had to stand outside the door for ten minutes listening to her cry about how the whole family never gets to be together anymore, and when we do, one of us is always trying to run off and get out of it."

"Oh, Christ."

"She's apparently never going to forgive you and Jessie for going to Taco Bell."

"That was three years ago."

"Yeah, but you guys were gone for, like, two hours."

"Yeah, because we were *high*. I was trying to give Jessie time to come down so Mom wouldn't know. She kept calling herself Lady Gaga and singing the rah-rah part of 'Bad Romance' over and over. Mom would've known something was up."

"Well, now she's mad at us."

"Great."

"Yeah." He took a sip of the Sprite he'd left behind and relaxed into his seat. "So, what'd I miss?"

"Uh." Fiona and Lizzie looked at each other, panicked, but then Lizzie simply shrugged and said, "Some more people died." The answer evoked a snort and an eye roll, but Michael didn't press for more details, and they carried out the rest of the movie in silence.

When the credits rolled, they collected their trash and headed for the door. Near the end of their lane, Michael stopped and let out a loud howl of disgust.

Fiona turned back. "What is it?"

"I think I stepped on someone's gum or something."

"Gross."

Once outside the cinema, he propped his leg up so they could inspect the bottom of his shoe. Embedded in the grooves were the dirty remains of a half-eaten Milk Dud.

From the couch to the recliners to the floor around the fireplace, the McElroys' living room was crowded with redheads. Everyone had already gathered for Secret Santa by the time Fiona, Michael, and Lizzie returned. The instant they walked into the room, they were hit with an expression so disapproving Fiona found she couldn't stomach looking Rosie in the eyes.

"Well, well, if it isn't the little rebels," Rosie said from her place on the couch. She pursed her lips at them. "Come running back home for presents, I see."

Lizzie removed her coat and hat and lay them across a small table in the corner. "No one was rebelling, Mom. We just went to a movie."

"Because we apparently aren't entertaining enough here." Rosie sniffed and ran a hand through little Maddi's hair. The girl was asleep in her lap. "Put your coat up in the closet, Lizzie. You know better than to let it drip on the table."

"But it's not even wet. It's not snowing anymore."

"In the closet, please." She pointed at Fiona and Michael. "The same goes for you two."

They moseyed back around the corner together, into the foyer, and discarded their coats in the closet by the front door. "Mom's in a mood," Lizzie said as she hooked the last of their coats onto the rack.

"I told you," Michael said. "I don't know why she's making a big deal about it. Sophie and them were at the store for over an hour yesterday, and she didn't act mad at them about it."

"They were out doing *her* bidding, so it's okay."

"Think a hot chocolate'll do the trick?"

"Eh. It's worth a try. You wanna make it, or should I?"

"You can. I've gotta run out to the car to get your present."

"Oh, you got my name this year?"

"Yeah, but don't get excited. I was a little low on funds after getting my tires changed and pitching in for Mom and Dad's present, and I didn't want to ask them to help me pay for yours."

"Come on. You know I don't care about that."

"It's a book."

Lizzie stared at him, deadpan. "Really? You just had to go and ruin the surprise like that? You couldn't have waited fifteen minutes for me to actually open it?"

"You just said you didn't care."

"About it being cheap! Not about you ruining my surprise."

Fiona leaned against the foyer wall and listened to the quiet, rapid exchange, smiling. "Hey, Michael," she said before they could spiral any further. "I think I'm just going to head upstairs and skip the whole Secret Santa thing, if that's all right."

"Are you okay?"

"Yeah, I'm fine." She placed a hand on his upper arm and squeezed. "I'm just tired." The frown dragging his lips down told her he wasn't buying it. "And I wanted to call my parents before it gets too late."

"But they're two hours behind us. You've got time."

"Just let her go, Mike. It's Christmas Eve. She wants to call her parents. Besides, it's Secret Santa. So, it's just going to be us giving each other our gifts. If I was her, I definitely wouldn't want to sit around watching everyone but me get to open a present."

He looked at Lizzie, then back at Fiona. "Okay. Yeah, I guess. But you're sure you're okay?"

"Of course. I'm fine. Why wouldn't I be?"

"All right. Well, tell your mom I said hi."

"I will."

"'Kay, I'm running out to the car." He gave Lizzie's shoulder a light shove. "Get started on the hot chocolate."

"Will do." She waited for him to sprint out the front door, then zeroed in on Fiona. "Are you *really* okay?"

Fiona smiled, soft and genuine. She could feel it becoming a habit, the way Lizzie made her smile. "I'm okay. I promise."

"You don't have any more Milk Duds, do you? I don't trust you to eat them alone. They aren't safe."

"Fresh out."

"Good. All right. I won't keep you." She leaned toward Fiona as if to touch her, embrace her, *something*, but apparently second-guessed herself. Her expression was all brows furrowed and lips quavering around a timid, unsure smile. She shrugged. "Good night, then."

"Good night." Fiona parroted back the words but didn't make for the stairs. Instead, she reached out, took Lizzie's hand, and drew her closer. "Come here." She didn't like that look of doubt, so alien on Lizzie's usually confident face. Fiona wanted to ease whatever it was that bubbled under the surface, wanted to answer questions she knew she couldn't. Still, she tried. She tried with her body, with her warmth, with the grip of her fingers on Lizzie's back. The smell of apricots filtered in as she buried her nose in Lizzie's hair and whispered to her again before letting her go. This time, it was real. "Good night."

"Night."

As Fiona made her way up the stairs, she heard Lizzie sigh and head for the living room. She barely made it in before Rosie's voice floated out, starting in on her daughter again. "Well, where'd they run off to now?"

"Michael's getting his Secret Santa gift from his car, and Fiona went to bed."

"Bed? It's barely eight o'clock."

"So? Jessie's asleep on the floor right in front of you."

"You probably ran her off with that stink eye you were giving them, Mom," Brian said, "looking like you were about to whip out your belt and bend them all over your knee one by one."

Rosie sounded genuinely distraught by the idea. "No. Oh no, Lizzie, honey. That's not what she thought, is it? Oh, my goodness. I'm not *really* upset. She doesn't have to go off to bed. I just—"

The voice, distorted by distance, died to a murmur as Fiona reached the top of the stairs and headed down the hallway. She made it to the bedroom, stepped calmly inside, and closed the door behind her. Instantly, her calm composure crumbled. She slapped her hands to her face and groaned. The theater fiasco played on loop in her head, more memorable than the film they'd seen. Requiring the Heimlich maneuver from the girl she secretly wanted to date because she was too gay to properly chew and swallow a Milk Dud easily took the top slot on her ever-growing list of "Reasons I Can't Be in Public." The whole ordeal had, however, landed her in said girl's lap, so, admittedly, it could have been worse.

She face-planted on the bed, lying horizontally across the mattress, and tried not to think about the warm, soft press of Lizzie's body. Enveloping her. Holding her like something precious. The thoughts came anyway. They bombarded. Fiona could still feel the sweat on Lizzie's fingertips as their hands skated over one another, grabbed, and held on tight. Their quiet, exhausted amusement danced around in her ears, a phantom of sound, and made her smile against the bedspread. She curled in on herself as the feelings overwhelmed her, those of want and wonder, and lifted her head just enough to glance over her shoulder at the door.

She had time. Michael was downstairs with his family. They were opening presents. That would take a while, she was sure. She definitely had time.

Her shoes hit the floor with two light thuds, followed by the plop of her phone against her pillow. She got her jeans unbuttoned and halfway down her hips before she even made it into the bathroom. The door clicked behind her. She locked it for good measure.

"I can't believe I'm doing this," she muttered to herself, but the urge was immense. It demanded she ease it, feed it, relieve it. Everything she'd experienced over the last three days, everything she felt, had balled itself into a massive knot of tension. It sat heavy at the base of her spine, making every move achy and agitated. She needed release.

She caught the edge of the sink with one hand, steadying herself, as the other wriggled down her unfastened pants and into her underwear. Lizzie's laugh played like a melody, as if recorded and set to repeat, echoing about Fiona's head. The memory of her fingers squeezing Fiona's sides, gripping Fiona's hands, turned her skin electric. Her fingertips met moisture on the first touch.

Just a bit of relief, she told herself. That's all she wanted, something to clear the haze from her mind, calm the erratic beat of her heart. It would only take a few minutes, a few good, hard strokes and one perfect, scandalous image in her head.

No one needed to know it was Lizzie's name she bit down on when she tipped herself over the edge.

Chapter 9

Exhaustion racked Fiona's body, but she couldn't sleep. The moon shined through the white bedroom curtains like a knife slicing through paper, and Michael's snoring rumbled louder than usual. She couldn't stand it any longer, so she tossed the covers off herself, donned Michael's far-too-big house shoes, and shuffled out of the room.

The hallway was dark and empty, like something out of a ghost story. Fiona crossed her arms over her chest and hoped there wasn't some creepy, haunted history lurking in the walls of the McElroy manor. Surely, she'd have heard about it by now. Rosie was keen on telling every family story she could think of. That wouldn't be one to skip out on. Thankfully, it didn't take long to reach the stairs, and Fiona ran down as fast as she could without tripping over the house shoes swallowing her small feet.

Downstairs, a fire crackled in the living-room fireplace, its orange glow bouncing about the room and over the twinkling gold lights of the large Christmas tree. The festive aroma of burning pine permeated the air and paired perfectly with the smell of cinnamon wafting off the scented pine cones decorating the tree. Fiona was hooked. Every element worked perfectly together to soothe her. She found herself hypnotized, staring into the fire.

"It's nice, right?"

Fiona practically jumped out of her skin as a head of bushy red hair and a white, toothy grin popped up over back of the couch. Her hand shot to her chest. "Jesus Christ, Lizzie! Do you make a habit out of scaring the shit out of people?"

"It's more like a career, actually." She waved Fiona over to the couch and pulled back the wooly blanket wrapped around her legs.

Fiona looked from the blanket to the striped, pajama shorts hugging freckled thighs to Lizzie's amused, beautiful face. "You want me to get under that?"

"No, I'm giving you a peepshow of my pasty white legs." She shook the blanket impatiently when Fiona didn't move. "Sit the hell down already."

Not a good idea. Romantic fire, Christmas tree lights, and a cozy blanket for two? That's a recipe for temptation if I've ever seen one.

But the longer Lizzie looked at her, huffing and shaking her blanket like an impatient old woman, the more inclined Fiona felt to oblige her. Lizzie was just too *Lizzie* to deny. In only three days, she'd grown into someone precious to Fiona, someone important. Every time they spoke, it felt more and more familiar, as if they'd known each other for years. Lizzie breezed through awkwardness with ease and pulled everyone, especially Fiona, right along with her, right into comfort. It was as if one mistaken tackle on a cold winter morning had tethered them to one another, woven together the loose strands neither knew they had. Now all Fiona could feel was the tugging. She wanted to be closer.

She started to sit, but Lizzie quickly held up a hand to stop her. "Wait," she said. "Don't sit on Otis." She pointed toward a thick pillow beside her. Yanked aside, it revealed the chubby orange ball Fiona had only seen a few times, occupying the kitchen counter or being lugged around by Grandma Sophia. Now he wore a Christmas sweater with bells sewn into it and glared at her until she covered him back up. She made sure to sit as far from the pillow as she could, though that meant squeezing right into Lizzie's personal space.

"Finally." Lizzie curled the blanket over Fiona. "My arm was getting tired."

"Are you always this dramatic?"

"You've met my family. Are you really that surprised?"

Fiona glanced back at the pillow once more. "He's not going to pop out and claw my face off, is he?"

"Nah. He mostly just hates everyone with his eyes."

"I can relate."

"Same." Lizzie lay her head back against the couch. "So, do you want to make boring small talk and pretend like what happened in the theater never actually happened?"

Fiona pursed her lips. "I would have liked to do that without acknowledging it at all."

"Too late." She grinned and poked Fiona's shoulder. "So, you and Michael met in Calculus class. Sounds boring."

"It pretty much was, yeah."

"I thought about being a nurse once, but unlike Michael, I pretty much loathe all things math-related."

"It's not for everyone."

"I think it's not for most people."

"Probably." Their legs rubbed briefly together. "You're a film student, right?"

"Yeah. Figured I'd try that whole struggling-Hollywood-wannabe thing for a while since I wasn't doing anything around here."

"How's that going for you?"

"Totally fine. I eat dollar tacos from the food truck by the grocery store and film mundane things with a cheap camera I bought at Target and argue with my mom when she tries to send me rent money through Western Union." She shoved her feet under Fiona's thigh, startling her. "Sorry. My toes are freezing."

Their gazes met, the reflection of flames dancing in the dark pupils of Lizzie's different-colored eyes. Fiona melted into the back of the couch. "You're just one of those people, aren't you?"

"One of what people?" Lizzie wiggled her toes, tickling the bottom of Fiona's thigh. "Annoying people? People who talk too much? Beautiful people with charming personalities?"

"One of those people who makes everyone feel comfortable. Like you know them even when you don't."

"Maybe you just like me."

Tingles erupted along Fiona's spine, then rushed out over her limbs until she buzzed with the feeling. She didn't think when she responded. She just leaned closer and watched as Lizzie did the same. "Maybe I do."

"Well, at least we're finally being honest."

"We shouldn't be."

"I don't see why not," Lizzie said, voice dropping to a whisper.

Fiona's gaze shifted to Lizzie's mouth a second before Lizzie's hand peeked up from under the cover to touch her face. Fiona closed her eyes and took a deep breath. "Are you going to kiss me?"

Lizzie's thumb brushed Fiona's bottom lip, then ran along its length. "Do you *want* me to kiss you?"

When Fiona opened her eyes again, Lizzie's gaze was locked on hers, and it was no longer playful. It was bright and intense and beautiful and *close*, and it left Fiona breathless. She nodded against Lizzie's hand and gave in to everything bubbling up inside her, everything she'd been trying so hard to rein in and tamp down, everything she so desperately desired. "Right now," she said, "that's pretty much all I want."

The first touch of their lips was a soft zap of friction. It was brief but electric, and Lizzie wasted no time. When Fiona opened her mouth to her, they both took shaky breaths and began again, melting into each other just as they'd melted into the couch. The deeper the kiss, the more they pulled at one another, hands gripping at each other. It was the slowest sort of frenzy, wild but measured, silent but eager. They couldn't get close enough, until Lizzie shifted onto her knees, crawled onto Fiona's lap, and straddled her.

"Is this okay?" she whispered against Fiona's lips, to which Fiona could only offer a guttural moan from the back of her throat. Lizzie laughed, the sound a hot puff of air between them. "I'll take that as a yes."

Fiona tucked her hands under the hem of Lizzie's shirt, fingers cold against her skin, and sighed into their kiss. "You're so warm."

Leaning back, Lizzie pulled her shirt over her head, exposing a gray bra barely covering her large breasts and a tiny ribcage tattoo of a rainbow-colored sparrow. "Is that like the medium place between ugly and hot?"

It took Fiona a minute to catch up with her, a little dizzy with arousal, then she rolled her eyes.

"Oh, come on," Lizzie said. "You think I'm charming."

Fiona traced over the sparrow with her thumb. "That's beautiful," she said, and Lizzie hummed. "I didn't know you were...When I came here, I wasn't expecting..." She stuttered over the words. "I mean, Michael never told me you were gay."

"That's because Michael doesn't know." She brushed a few wild hairs off Fiona's face. "I think, considering he's told the whole family that you're his girlfriend, though, the better question would be: Does he know *you* are?"

Reality blasted through the haze of desire like a sharp slap to the face. Fiona blinked. "Oh *God*. Michael's going to kill me."

"I was kidding, Fiona. Relax."

Leaning in, Lizzie claimed her lips again—once, twice—and Fiona nearly fell into her rhythm once more. She forced in a breath and leaned back, putting the scantest bit of space between them. "Wait," she puffed out. "Wait, Lizzie. We need to wait."

Lizzie immediately ceased chasing Fiona's lips and sat back. "Are you okay?"

"I just... I'm confused." Fiona took another hard breath and looked up at her. "I mean, all this time, all this *whatever* this is between us, you knew. I know you knew. I mean, I didn't at first, but then the things you said in the bathroom. Then, the movies. You've been teasing me." She ran her hands up and down Lizzie's bare sides, lingering, pressing, rubbing. It was automatic, as if her body intended to continue, even if her mind had smacked into a massive roadblock. "How did you know it wasn't real between Michael and me? Or maybe you thought it *was* real, but you were just okay with making moves on your brother's girlfriend? If that's the case, that's seriously shady, but if it's—"

Lizzie suddenly grabbed Fiona's hands and stilled them, effectively silencing her. "Okay, look. We can either have this conversation, or we can carry on with the touching, because I can't focus well enough to do both. If you're going to keep touching me like this, then we're going to do the touching. If not, we can talk. So, which is it going to be?"

Fiona bit her lip, ensnared by Lizzie's intense gaze. It seared. When she didn't move or say anything, Lizzie slid off her with a huff and grabbed her shirt. "All right. Fine. Talking it is." She put her shirt back on, resituated the blanket over the two of them, and dug her frigid toes under Fiona's thigh once more. "Yes, I knew you guys weren't really a thing. If you really *were* Michael's girlfriend, then, yeah, I would have felt bad about the way I feel about you and wouldn't have tried anything. But you're not really a thing, so I don't feel bad about it in the slightest."

"Okay, but *how*? How did you figure it out?"

"Well, first of all, I know my brother."

"What does that mean?"

Lizzie looked at her for a long moment as if pondering whether or not she should elaborate. She clearly decided she shouldn't when she skipped right onto her next point. "Then there was the way you looked at me when we first met—"

"Oh, you mean when you tackled me in bed?"

"The way you looked at me when we *first met*," Lizzie said with a smile, "was all I really needed. I felt that look in places no one should feel a look from their brother's supposed girlfriend. Then, when I landed on you in the snow."

"When you tackled me in the snow."

"When I *landed on you* in the snow, I thought you might kiss me. The way you looked at me, touched me. I thought it was going to happen right then and there, that you were just going to lean up and kiss me right in front of my entire family, which, you know, was terrifying since I'm not out to any of them yet, but at the same time, I was like, well, hey, that's one way to do it, right?"

Fiona laughed and ran a hand down Lizzie's shin under the blanket. "Would you have wanted me to?"

Lizzie licked her lips but didn't answer. Her eyes sparkled in the firelight. A smile still teased her lips. "Then the closet…"

Heat flushed Fiona's chest and cheeks, making the living-room fire suddenly feel oppressive. "Yeah," she whispered, breath leaving her in one long, heavy stream. "The closet."

"I swear to God all I wanted to do was close the door and lock us in there together." She leaned her head against the back of the couch. "But you…" She reached out, brushed Fiona's cheek with her fingertips, then twirled a strand of dark hair around her index finger. "You weren't ready."

The Lizzie-related lump Fiona had grown accustomed to coming and going worked its way back into her throat and stuck there. This time, it hurt, like a piece of jagged potato chip caught in her esophagus. It felt as if at any moment it might tear her open and pour all her secrets into the tense space between them. The thought petrified her. At the same time, it tempted her. It teased her. There was a part of her that wanted to spill, wanted to crack wide open and let Lizzie see everything she kept so well hidden inside, let her explore.

"You have no idea how ready I was," Fiona whispered. "You have no idea."

Lizzie's smile was gentle, affectionate, *mature*. There was something about it that felt young and old at the same time. Hot yet tempered. She had a way of making Fiona feel calm even amidst the storm brewing inside and between them, even as she stirred the storm with her own hands, her own words, her own unique effect. Fiona found her presence as soothing as it was tormenting, as comforting as it was dismantling. She wanted to fold herself into Lizzie's arms as much as she wanted to pin those arms down and show her *exactly* how ready she had been, how ready she was right at this moment. She wanted to be near her just as much as she wanted to run away, and no one had ever made her feel that way before.

The trembling breath Lizzie took told Fiona she wasn't the only one tormented by such things, as confused and thrilled and terrified and wanting. "But then in the bathroom," she said. "You looked so—"

"Scared?" Fiona nodded. "Yeah, I was. I am."

"Because you want me." It wasn't a question. It was a hard, hot fact, so hot Fiona could feel it melting her from the inside. She shivered despite the heat, and when Lizzie moved toward her again, the shivering turned to a tremble. She vibrated under Lizzie's wandering hand as it worked its way up from her wrist to her shoulder. "And you think it's not okay, but it is." Her hand disappeared under the blanket again, one finger sliding down the tank-top-covered valley between Fiona's breasts, down to her belly button. "It's okay to want me."

Fiona caught Lizzie's hand just as it reached the top of her shorts. She held it tight, unmoving for a moment, then slowly pushed it away. "I think I need some air," she said, tossing the blanket aside and standing.

"It's snowing."

"Even better." Fiona rounded the couch and shot for the foyer, then the front door. She was out of the house in seconds, breath puffing out around her. She gulped down the frozen air as fast as she could and tried to let it soothe. It didn't. The longer she stood there, the taste of Lizzie still lingering on her lips, the worse she felt. Guilt pooled in her gut and refused to budge, sloshing against her insides every time she rocked on her heels or shivered. It quarreled with the want, with the need, with the sharp spear of loneliness that had been eviscerating her for some time.

She was supposed to be there for Michael. He was her best friend. Sneaking around with his little sister behind his back? God, as good as it felt, it sounded awful, even inside her head, and the few times she'd tested the water with Michael, his reaction had left much to be desired. It was the whole reason she'd warned herself off in the first place, but the more Lizzie talked, the more she realized she hadn't been avoiding anything at all. She'd been developing her relationship with Lizzie in little moments, little interactions, little sparks and bursts of heat that drove the growing fire between them higher and hotter. She hadn't avoided anything. She'd reveled in it, in Lizzie, in thinking about her and learning about her. Wanting her. And she wanted desperately to believe that it was okay to feel that way, just as Lizzie said, but the clench in her stomach said otherwise.

She couldn't stop picturing Michael's expression were he to find out, couldn't stop imagining a reaction of hurt and anger. Fiona covered her face, now chilled. She couldn't take the cold much longer, but she managed a few more seconds, a few more breaths. A few more moments to loathe herself.

When she returned to the living room, the fire was out and Lizzie was gone, and Fiona was left with nothing but the soft, golden glint of the Christmas tree.

Chapter 10

CHRISTMAS DAY IN THE MCELROY house started before dawn. The sounds of children squealing, bacon sizzling, and siblings teasing one another drifted up from downstairs and stirred Fiona from sleep. She cracked one eye open, afraid to let the snow-reflected sun pierce her precious pupils. But she quickly realized the sun hadn't yet risen. The sky outside her temporary bedroom's window was a murky gray-blue curling around the fuzzy edges of an encroaching flood of orange—the early merging of night and day.

Fiona sat up in bed, realizing she was alone, and stretched. The clock on the bedside table read 6:23, an ungodly time to be awake when there were no classes or work demanding her presence. She grumbled to herself as she glanced around the room, briefly taking in high school pictures of a young, shaggy-haired Jack McElroy with friends and sports posters she knew nothing about.

"Hey." Lizzie stood in the open door in dark jeans and a red T-shirt with the words *Jingle Balls* printed across the front. A steaming cup of coffee sat clutched between her fingers.

"Oh." Fiona tried to smooth her hair down with one hand as she pulled the covers up over her chest with the other. She'd stripped off her sports bra at some point in the middle of the night, because it had been uncomfortable under her tank top, and now she felt exposed. She knew her nipples well enough to know they liked to stand up and say hello first thing in the morning, especially when there were pretty girls standing in front of her looking...well, *pretty*. "Hi."

"Merry Christmas."

"Nice shirt."

"I like to be festive."

Fiona laughed. "I see that. Seems like a shirt more suited for Brian, though."

"Funny you should say that." Lizzie moved into the room, quietly closing the door behind her, and sat on the edge of the bed. "Because I took it from his room this morning." She passed the coffee to Fiona. "It's from Mom. Mike told her to let you sleep, but she gets antsy when everyone isn't up by the time she finishes the bacon."

"Thanks." She let the cup hover just under her nose and breathed in the comforting nutty scent of the coffee. "I guess I'll get dressed and head down in a minute, then."

"Sure." Lizzie nodded but didn't move from the bed. "Look, Fiona, I wanted to talk to you about last night. Well, about this whole weekend, really." Her neck and cheeks flushed an orangey-pink color that somehow made her even prettier, and Fiona melted. Maybe it was because she had only just woken up, or maybe it was that strange, quiet magic of the morning before dawn. She didn't know, but whatever it was, it sapped away all her worries, all her resistance, and left nothing but the raw affection that had been brewing for days.

Fiona set her coffee on the bedside table and inched herself toward Lizzie. "Don't," she said, placing a hand on top of Lizzie's. "Don't apologize."

Their fingers wove together. "I wasn't planning on it."

"Oh." Fiona chuckled. "What were you going to say, then?"

"I was going to ask if you were done freaking out about us so we could plan our next secret Christmas rendezvous." She squeezed Fiona's hand. "I was thinking the kitchen counter this time. Ooh, or the laundry room. Do you like a little rumble with your tumble?"

Fiona snorted and pushed Lizzie away, nearly knocking her off the bed but catching her at the last second. "You're—"

"Adorable," Lizzie supplied, flashing her mischievous grin.

With a sigh, Fiona relaxed and pulled Lizzie a little closer. "I was going to say you're a pain, but I guess two things can be true." Another gentle tug and their noses bumped. Once. Twice.

"I have a confession to make," Lizzie whispered against her lips. "All the things I said last night about how I knew you and Michael weren't really together…"

"Yeah?"

"They were all true, but I didn't really need any of that to tell."

"Oh no?"

Lizzie stifled a laugh and nudged her nose against Fiona's again. "You don't really need any signs when Michael has two different pictures of you on his Instagram with the hashtag *when your best friend is a lesbian*."

Fiona's body stiffened. She pulled back just enough to look hard at Lizzie's face. "Are you serious?" The laugh Lizzie had been choking back burst free as she nodded, and Fiona collapsed against her. Her forehead smacked against Lizzie's shoulder as she groaned.

"Guess he forgot about that." Lizzie ran a hand through Fiona's bed head. Her fingers snagged on a tangle, then smoothed it out. "Good thing no one else in the family cares about Instagram. Well, except Jessie, but she doesn't even follow Michael."

"How do you not think to check something like that when you ask a lesbian to pretend to be your straight girlfriend?" She burrowed into Lizzie's neck, scooting closer and closer until she was practically in her lap. "God, you smell good." She nosed up the length of her neck, unable to help herself. The warm skin there was too inviting. She pressed her lips to Lizzie's throat and was rewarded with a vibrating, pleasant hum.

"You're friendly in the morning, aren't you?"

Fiona pulled back, and her breath caught somewhere in her chest. Her stomach clenched. Lizzie was so close, so open to her, so goddamned beautiful. One of her hands rested casually on Fiona's thigh over the covers, comfortable and familiar, and everything about it felt right. It felt good. Fiona's heart seemed eager to escape, hammering away at her insides as she curled a hand into the front of Lizzie's shirt and drew her in. Then, finally, relief. Their lips touched, and everything calmed. All the boiling world slowed to a simmer, and for just a moment, there was nothing but perfection—the perfect heat, the perfect touch, the perfect kiss, the perfect girl.

Then, the moment erupted, taking the perfect kiss and the simmering world right along with it. The gasp that shattered the stillness pulled Fiona's heart right up into her throat, and she choked on it. She couldn't move. Lizzie spun toward the door, but Fiona was frozen, staring at the back of Lizzie's head. This was what she had been afraid of—ruining things.

"Mom!" Lizzie's hand was still resting on Fiona's thigh. She quickly jerked it free.

Rosie stood in the now open door, one hand splayed across her chest as if she was trying to reach in and physically soothe her shocked heart. The other gripped the doorknob like a lifeline. Fiona hadn't even heard the door open. Apparently, neither had Lizzie. "Elizabeth Dawn," she said, breathless, "what in God's name is going on in here?"

Lizzie seemed lost for words. Her mouth moved without a sound, opening and closing as if she was trying to suck in air that simply wouldn't go down. Her beautifully unique eyes glossed over, an elegant sight that seemed out of place on such a playful, funny person. There was a shock of fear in them, one Fiona recognized all too well. She'd seen it in her own reflection when she was younger, when she had hovered around the edges of coming out but hadn't yet taken the dive. That fear, now alive on Lizzie's face, begged to be chased away. It was enough to jog Fiona from her frozen stupor. She grabbed Lizzie's hand and squeezed as tight as she could. "It's okay." Her voice barely worked. "It's okay."

Lizzie took a breath and nodded and faced her mother again. "Um," she said. "Well, Mom, I guess what's going on in here is exactly what it looks like." She swallowed as if she was trying to choke down vomit and took another breath. "I…"

"Hey, Mom. You guys get her up yet?" The sound of Michael's voice was like iced water spilling down Fiona's spine. "I'm telling you she sleeps like a rock sometimes." He appeared around the door frame a second later. His smile fell. "What's wrong?" He glanced from his mother to his sister, then down to Fiona's hand resting on top of Lizzie's. Fiona watched as he put the pieces together. His eyes blew wide.

"Oh, Michael, honey," Rosie said, reaching for him, but Michael shook his head.

"Give us a minute, Mom."

"Honey, I think I should sta—"

Her words were silenced by the door closing in her face. Michael had squeezed right past her and slammed it behind him, barely giving her a chance to move. "What the *hell*, Fiona?"

"I can explain," Fiona said, though she wasn't the least bit sure how. There wasn't really anything *to* explain. Michael had figured it out in seconds, hadn't he? All there was left to do was apologize. At the same time, an apology didn't seem right. It seemed like an admission of wrongdoing, and what she felt for Lizzie scared the hell out of her, but it didn't feel wrong. It was the circumstances that felt wrong, not the want. Not the passion. Not *them* and what they were becoming together.

"I think it's pretty self-explanatory," Michael said. "My *sister*, Fi?"

"I know. I know. I'm sorry, but I can't help how I feel. It's not like I was *trying* to—"

"Trying to what? Trying to fuck my sister?"

"I wasn't trying to 'fuck' anyone. In fact, I've been trying really hard not to feel anything at all."

"Well, clearly, you didn't try hard enough, because Mom obviously just caught you doing *something*. With my *sister*."

"I'm sorry. I didn't mean for any of this to happen. We didn't—"

"Oh don't. Don't say 'we' like you two are a thing now. Please don't." He ran his hands up his face and through his hair, paced for a few seconds, then turned back to her. "She's my *baby* sister, Fi."

Fiona felt her eyes begin to burn and sting with moisture. Her skin crawled. An awkward, inappropriate laugh sat in her throat like a bubble, waiting to pop. *Oh God. Don't laugh.* She hated the way her body responded to discomfort.

"Stop it, Mike." Lizzie's eyes were glossed, but no tears had fallen. Fiona could still see the nerves ticking, the fear making her muscles rigid and skin paler than usual. "I'm not a baby. I'm twenty-six. So, can we please stop with the fake outrage, already? I can't deal with it right now."

"Fake outrage? Who's faking? I'm serious, and don't think you're off the hook here either. You went after my girlfriend."

"Jesus Christ." Lizzie took a breath, blew it out toward her eyes. "She's not even really your girlfriend."

"That's not the point!"

"How is that not the point? That's exactly the point. She's not your girlfriend. She's not even into guys. And it's not like you really care anyway, since you don't like girls either."

"Wait, what?" Fiona looked up, shocked.

"*Or* guys," Lizzie continued, barreling right through the interruption. "*Or anyone*, for that matter. So, you can be mad that we hid it from you or whatever, but stop acting like it's because anyone here stole anyone else's girlfriend or whatever the hell. I've got a lot bigger issues on my plate right now than you being mad at me for no reason."

Michael's cheeks reddened. He shuffled in place for a moment, and when he spoke again, there wasn't a hint of anger in it. He was quiet, his voice now stopped in his throat as if reluctant, as if mortified. "I only ever said that once, Lizzie."

"But you still said it."

"I was drunk."

Lizzie wiped the building wetness from her eyes. "You're more honest when you're drunk." A heavy breath pushed up and out as she plopped back onto the mattress and patted the slim space between her and Fiona. All her fear seemed to leak away with each pat. Just the three of them, Fiona realized, was a balm for Lizzie, whether Michael was angry or not. It was the thought of facing her parents that scared Lizzie most. "Now, can you please stop being dramatic and help me figure out what we're going to say to Mom? Because I'm pretty sure she's pasted to the other side of the door, trying to figure out what's going on in here, and us saying 'April Fool's' about my tongue down your girlfriend's throat isn't going to work on Christmas Day."

"Ugh, God." He shoved her over and sat down between them. "Can you not?"

Fiona wriggled out from under the blanket and on top of it. She wrapped an arm around his back and rubbed circles between his shoulder blades. "Hey," she whispered, but he didn't answer. He wouldn't even look at her. "You never told me you might be asexual. Or aromantic? Both?" He didn't say anything, just shrugged and kept his eyes on the floor. "Why didn't you talk to me about it?"

He leaned his head against hers. "I'm still figuring it out, I guess."

"That's okay. I think we all are." She rested her chin on his shoulder. "Are you mad at me?"

"Yes." He sighed. "No." He slipped his hand into hers and laced their fingers together. "Well, maybe a little. It's just, you know she's my sister, right?"

Fiona smiled. "She's cute."

"I am," Lizzie said from his other side. "Cut her some slack."

Fiona smacked a kiss to his cheek. "You're still my favorite McElroy, though."

"For now," Lizzie said, grabbing Fiona's other hand from Michael's back and knitting their fingers together.

Michael and Fiona lay back, Fiona's arm stuck under his back and each hand tangled with another. The three of them lay on the bed together, staring up at the ceiling in silence. It was strange but easy, nice, and for a moment, Fiona didn't even care that they'd been exposed. It was Christmas morning, and she was happy with her beautiful boy and her beautiful girl, and for that one blip in time, that could be all there was in the world. She was happy.

"So, this is nice and all, you guys," Lizzie said after a while, "and I'm glad no one's really mad at anyone, but seriously. What the fuck are we gonna tell Mom?"

ᴣᴄᴏᴖᴇᴏᴇᴏᴥ

Fiona feared the door opening. In only a few minutes, the room had become their own little bubble, their safe haven, a place where they didn't have to explain anything to anyone or even contemplate what they were feeling and why. They could just be, be together, be themselves, and not think. But Fiona kept imagining Rosie shuffling impatiently just outside, an angry fire in her eyes, or perhaps just a shock of confusion. When Michael flung the door open, however, they found not only Rosie but the entire McElroy clan, save Lily, Madison, Jessie, and Grandma Sophia, lingering in the hall.

"Vultures," Michael said, shaking his head. "Should've known." He looked at Rosie. "Did you really have to tell them everything? You couldn't have waited for me?"

Sophie and Grace, at least, had the decency to look ashamed. Brian, on the other hand, defended her. "What'd you expect, Mike? She was worried about you. We all are."

"Well, don't be. I'm fine."

"Yeah, right." Brian leaned past him and looked at Fiona and Lizzie sitting on the edge of the bed. Fiona had donned a sweatshirt over her tank top, but she still felt exposed. His gaze was cutting, then it fixed on his sister. "Tell me you didn't actually do what Mom said you did." He noticed their hands then, their fingers tangled together. "You've got to be kidding me. Are you serious right now, Lizzie? He's your *brother*, and you're not even gay!"

Lizzie didn't bother answering. She didn't even look him in the eyes. "Mom," she said, focusing instead on the woman now filling up the door frame, "can I talk to you? Alone?"

"Sure thing, pumpkin," Charlie Sr. said, though his wife's face communicated that she wasn't entirely sure she was ready to have the conversation Lizzie planned on having. "Let's go, knuckleheads. All of you. Get." He shuffled his adult children away from the door and down the hall, but Brian hung back.

"Come on, man." Clearly, he wasn't convinced that Michael was fine. After all, how could anyone be fine after catching their significant other cheating on them with their sister of all people? He clapped Michael on the shoulder and nodded his head toward the hall. "Let's get out of here. We can take some beers out to the barn. It's early, but who cares? I'll grab the space heater from the closet."

"Thanks, but I'm okay." He patted Brian's back. "I need to stay here."

"No, you need to drink. Trust me. That's the only thing that's going to fix this shit-show."

"Brian."

"Just calling it like it is, Mom."

"Really, I'm okay," Michael said with a light laugh. "Really. I promise. It's not what you guys think. Just go on. I'll catch up with you later."

"You sure?"

"Yeah. I'm sure."

"All right, but I'll be downstairs if you change your mind."

His footsteps thudded heavily in the hallway as he left, both Rosie and Michael watching him go. Michael turned toward his mother. They didn't say anything to one another; they simply stared. Rosie seemed to have caved in on herself, transforming into something so much less than the larger-than-life, full-of-heart woman Fiona had come to know. Now she stood with her arms wrapped around herself, chin tilted toward her chest, and eyes tormented by something that looked like a cross between anger and hurt. Or maybe, Fiona thought, she was simply confused. It would be understandable. The situation she'd walked in on would confuse anyone.

After a moment, Rosie took a deep, audible breath, as if preparing herself. Her chest puffed out, her spine straightened, and she steeled herself the way mothers had been steeling themselves for centuries—for bad news, terrifying news, confusing news, surprising news, wonderful news. Mothers had to be prepared for anything where their kids were concerned, especially when they had as many kids as Rosie McElroy did. So, she hardened up her exterior and took a step ahead of Michael into the room. He walked in after her and closed the door, shutting the four of them in together.

"I thought you wanted to talk alone," Rosie said, glancing between Lizzie and Michael. She avoided looking at Fiona, a fact which stung, but Fiona understood. She was a potential enemy, a thorn amongst Rosie's darling little roses, someone she believed had hurt one of her babies, betrayed them. As far as Rosie was concerned, Fiona was the source of the mess fouling up her perfect Christmas morning, and there was simply no forgiving that.

"She meant the four of us." Michael crossed to the bed to fill the empty space beside Fiona. She was grateful for his presence, his warmth, because the longer she sat there waiting in the tense, thick air of a quiet room that seemed to be holding its breath, the more uncomfortable she became. Michael motioned toward the chair in front of Jack's old desk in the corner. "Maybe you should sit down, Mom."

"I think I'd rather stand." All the joy and humor Fiona had come to associate with Rosie had left her voice. She sounded as stiff as she appeared.

"So you can escape if you don't like what I have to say?" Lizzie tried for humor, but it fell flat. It fell hard, like a water balloon hitting concrete, only what spilled out instead was all the awkwardness they'd been trying to hold in. It flooded the room and stunk up the air, and Fiona's skin began to crawl again. It itched and writhed, and all she wanted to do was bolt.

I shouldn't be here, she thought. *Not in this room or in this house, in this entire state.* She hung her head, not wanting to draw any attention to herself. *I never should have come here.*

"Mom, please just sit down," Michael said. "I think it'll make everyone more comfortable."

With a huff, Rosie grabbed the desk chair and dragged it over in front of the bed. The moment she sat, facing them, Fiona was struck with the urge to confess to something. She didn't know what, because there wasn't a person in the room who wasn't already entirely aware of what had transpired. There was just something so very motherly about Rosie's posture and expression, something that reached in and latched onto Fiona's inner child and reminded her of all the times she'd sat, as a kid, in front of her own mother, preparing for a lecture or a scolding or for the "opportunity" to admit whatever wrong she'd done and face the consequences. Lizzie and Michael must have felt the same, because they shriveled beside her until Fiona imagined the three of them appeared like moping dogs who'd gotten into something they shouldn't have.

"Well?" Rosie said after a pregnant pause. She looked expectantly at her kids. "Someone's going to have to start talking. Michael? Elizabeth? One of you had better explain, because I'll be perfectly honest, I'm just about as confused as a fart in a fan factory, and I don't know which of you I ought to be comforting and which I ought to be lecturing. So, let's be out with it, one of you."

Fiona's lips rolled inward as an untimely laugh suddenly pushed its way up her throat. She tried to hold it in, but one glance Michael's way then Lizzie's, and it burst forth. The three of them laughed together, and Fiona was relieved to see a smile starting at the corners of Rosie's mouth as well. Clearly, she was trying to make her children a little more comfortable, even if she, herself, was anything but.

"Okay." Lizzie shook out her arms, took a huge, animated breath, and blew it out as loudly as she could. "Let's get serious." She slipped her hand back into Fiona's and squeezed. "Mom."

"Elizabeth."

"Stop calling me Elizabeth." Her shoulders caved a bit. "It makes me feel like you're scolding me, and I really can't feel like this is a bad thing right now. Okay? I've wanted to talk to you about this for a long time, and I haven't been able to bring myself to do it, because I've been afraid that this is how it would go. That I'd tell you and you would be disappointed in me or mad and scold me the way you did when I was a kid."

"Well." Rosie's voice trembled a bit. Her eyes watered. "I can't know how to react until you tell me. I don't know what else I can do."

"I'm gay."

Fiona blinked, a bit startled by the confession, not because she didn't know it was coming but because of the way it was expressed. All that buildup and Lizzie had just spat it out as if it was a piece of fuzz trapped on her tongue. A moment earlier, it had been locked up tight in Lizzie's throat, a sticky, painful secret she'd been choking on for years, and the next, it hit the air with a blunt splat.

"I'm sorry," Lizzie said immediately after, gripping Fiona's hand so hard that it hurt. "I mean, no." She whined and rolled her eyes at herself. "I'm not *sorry*, I mean not for being gay, but I'm sorry for the way I just sort of word-vomited it at you. I meant to have a little more finesse, but I guess… *Anyway*." She cleared her throat. "So, yeah, well, there it is. I'm gay, Mom."

"Yes, you said." Rosie's voice was quiet, so quiet it danced around the edges of a whisper. Her eyes were on her hands in her lap, and at that moment, she and Lizzie seemed nearly identical. Fiona looked between the two of them, their body shapes and sizes, their hunkered postures, their bowed heads. Rosie appeared to be the mirror image of Lizzie, just aged up a couple of decades.

Silence took up residence between them, so thick and uncomfortable it made Fiona feel she couldn't properly breathe. Her chest was tight. Her stomach writhed, and she was torn between running for the door and wrapping her arms around Lizzie to comfort her. She desperately wished she could do both. Or rather, she wished she could take Lizzie out of there, Lizzie and Michael, somewhere where they could rediscover that safe, comfortable place they'd been in before. Somewhere free of this tension, this torment, this bubbling confusion making the air nearly effervescent. She couldn't take it much longer, and she knew if her own skin was crawling, Lizzie's must be on the verge of cracking open.

Nerves upon nerves upon nerves, multiplying with each second the silence persisted, yet no one said a thing. No one moved. Fiona ached to dispel the tension herself, but it wasn't her place. She couldn't be the one to stir up the settling dust. Lizzie would have to do that for herself.

"Mom, come on." *Or* Michael could do it for her. He let go of Fiona's hand, leaving a stain of sweat behind, and wiped his palm on his pant leg. "You have to say something."

Rosie looked up at him, sheer torture written across her features. She appeared as helpless as Fiona imagined Lizzie felt. "What do you want me to say?"

"I don't want you to say anything to me. Talk to Lizzie. Tell her what you're thinking. Tell her how you feel. Tell her you love her and that this is okay, because you do and it is." He paused, staring intently at her. "It is. Right?"

"Is that what you thought? What you were afraid of?" She looked to Lizzie, who kept her head down and refused to meet her gaze. "That I wouldn't love you anymore?" A sniffle sounded from beneath the waterfall of hair hiding Lizzie's face. "Oh, Elizabeth. Look at me." Lizzie didn't move but to cup a hand over her mouth and sniffle once more, but that seemed to be all Rosie needed. She dropped from her chair to kneel on the floor in front of her daughter. Her hands settled atop Lizzie's knees, thumbs rubbing back and forth. "Honey, look at me."

A tug on Fiona's arm drew her gaze away, and she was grateful. She felt as if she was peering in on something she shouldn't be, a private moment she was never meant to be part of. Michael motioned for her to follow him. She carefully wriggled her hand from Lizzie's, giving it one last squeeze, and followed Michael to the bathroom. They didn't close the door but stood just inside the frame, close enough to jump in for comfort but far enough to give Rosie and Lizzie a little bit of privacy.

Michael looked at Fiona as they leaned against opposite sides of the door frame. His eyes were bloodshot, as if he'd strained to keep them dry. He'd always hated to cry. Fiona reached over and took his hand. Their fingers looped loosely together and hung in the space between them. Fiona closed her eyes and rested her head back against the door frame. Together, they listened to Rosie's soft, murmuring voice.

"You know I could never love you any less, Elizabeth. Never, not for anything. You're my sweet girl. You've always been my sweet girl, and you always will be. You understand me?" When Lizzie didn't respond, and the silence began to creep in again, Fiona opened her eyes to see what was happening. Rosie remained on the floor, but one hand had released Lizzie's knee to tuck away her waterfall of hair. "Honey, please. Will you look at me?"

Lizzie finally looked up, tossing her hair back with a flick of her head. She blew a rush of air up toward her wet eyes. The sigh she let out bordered on a growl. "I *hate* crying," she said, now staring at the ceiling instead of her lap.

The quiet laugh Rosie released comforted Fiona from a distance. She hoped it served to soothe Lizzie as well. "I know."

"So then why couldn't you have just said all that right away instead of letting me sit here in this dumb silence, afraid you were about to disown me?"

Rosie's laugh, this time, jumped free, loud and wet. She wiped her eyes with one hand then grabbed onto Lizzie's knees again. "Oh sweetheart. I'm sorry. I just, I guess I was a little taken by surprise."

"Really?" Lizzie's body sagged, the tension in her back giving way. "You walked in on me kissing a girl, and you were surprised when I said I was gay?"

"Well, I never claimed to be the brightest crayon in the box, now did I?"

Lizzie snorted and placed her hands atop Rosie's, who turned hers up so they could clutch onto one another. They looked at each other and started laughing, low and slow at first, but it quickly evolved into something loud and untamed. It was as if the absence of tension triggered all that pent-up adrenaline their nerves had produced, and all they could do was tremble and laugh and *be*.

The sound filled the room, lighting it up brighter than the early morning sun now beaming through the windows. Fiona looked from the two currently in stitches to the man across from her and found him looking back. A smile pushed at his lips, pushed and pushed until he was on the verge of laughing himself. His wide grin was infectious, and Fiona found herself smiling back at him, relief and joy rushing through her.

When they, too, erupted in laughter, Rosie pulled away from Lizzie and pointed their way. "Now, you two," she said. "Get in here." Fiona's laugh died an instant death. She choked it back with a painful swallow and glanced from Michael to Lizzie. "Come on, now. I'm not going to bite you."

Michael led Fiona back into the room where they reclaimed their places at Lizzie's side, and Rosie grunted her way back into her chair. She rubbed her knees and sighed. "Now," she said again, "I'll admit I didn't respond the best way, but it wasn't because of what you told me, Elizabeth."

"Mom."

"Fine. Okay. *Lizzie*." She rolled her eyes. "You know, you have such a beautiful name. I don't know why you hate it so much."

"I don't hate it. I just associate you saying it with me getting in trouble. It's not my fault it's a trauma trigger, woman. Blame yourself."

"Oh, you." Rosie waved a hand at her. "Don't make it out like you ever got anything more than a swat of a towel to your behind or, God forbid, no dessert for a night. No one beat you."

"No dessert *is* traumatizing when you have to sit and watch nine other people eating it around you, and you get none. If that's not torture, I don't know what is."

Fiona's stomach rumbled at the mention of dessert, and though she hoped it wouldn't make a sound, it yawned and groaned and drew everyone's eyes to her. "Sorry," she said. "I guess my stomach is ready for breakfast."

"We ought to get down there and get to eating it," Rosie said. "Hopefully the oven's keeping it all warm, but I'll have to nuke the biscuits, I'm sure." She sent a smile Fiona's way. It helped alleviate some of Fiona's nerves.

Things seemed civil enough, at least, for now. She hoped she was reading the woman the right way and that everything could remain with her as it had been—good, comforting, like family. Fiona wanted so much to be a part of this family in whatever way they'd allow her, *if* they'd allow her. She hoped that not *really* being Michael's girlfriend wouldn't prevent that from happening.

"But first, you two need to explain what's going on here with the two of you." Rosie cocked her head at her son.

"Right," Michael said. "That. Uh, so I may have lied a little bit about Fiona being my girlfriend."

Lizzie leaned forward and bugged her eyes out at him. "A *little* bit?"

"Okay. I lied a lot of bit."

Rosie shook her head. "Why on earth would you even lie about something like that, Michael?"

"Honestly?" he began.

Fiona tensed again, convinced, for a moment, that they were about to go through the motions of another sexuality-based confession. But it didn't come. "I just got tired of you and Grandma and everyone always teasing me about not having a girlfriend and needing to find someone to settle down with." Fiona didn't blame him for not telling Rosie about possibly being asexual, not because it was something he should hide, but because he wasn't terribly sure of it yet himself. He wasn't ready, not the way Lizzie was and had been for some time. He needed to find his own time, his own way. "I think maybe you guys don't even realize how much you do it, but it started to feel like I couldn't ever come home or even talk to you on the phone without it coming up. It just got exhausting."

"Oh, Michael." Rosie patted his knee. "We do that to all you kids. It doesn't mean you have to get a girlfriend. It's just that we want you to be happy, and so many of you are away from home. It breaks my heart to think you might be lonely."

"I know, Mom, but you never do it to Brian or Jack the way you do me, and maybe it's because Brian has the business with Charlie and Jack's got the Marines, but I'm doing stuff, too. I'm working and going to school and trying to make a life for myself, and it just feels like that's not enough for you guys sometimes." He shrugged. "So I asked Fiona to pretend to be my girlfriend for Christmas. I just thought if you guys thought I had someone like that, you'd drop it for once. Just once, you know?"

Rosie glanced Fiona's way. "Well, you must be a good friend to go to all that trouble."

"Oh, the best," Fiona said with a smile, hoping it would land well. It did, drawing a chuckle from Rosie. "Except for the whole falling-for-his-sister part."

Lizzie bumped her shoulder. "Totally understandable."

"All my babies are beautiful," Rosie said, and Fiona nodded.

"Yes, they are."

Rosie clapped her hands to her knees and stood. "All right, kiddos. Let's go. Time to face the music before the food sits too long."

"So, you're okay, then?" Lizzie asked, drawing her back. "Mom?"

"Okay? Of course. What do you mean?"

"With me being gay."

Rosie shooed Fiona and Michael over so she could sit beside her daughter. She drew Lizzie to her side and held her close. "I'll admit it's not something I understand very well. You know, I didn't grow up around people who were openly that way, and I was always taught it wasn't right." She patted the side of Lizzie's head and kissed her hair. "But I figure it's as simple as this: You're my baby, and you finding love and being happy can't be wrong, now can it? Hmm? Because that's all I really want. That's all I want for any of you, is for you to be happy and safe. That's what matters. Understand? I'm going to be in your corner, always, no matter what."

Lizzie smiled, a genuine toothy smile that made her appear so much more like herself, like the Lizzie Fiona had come to know and care for. An airy, feel-good smile. She was free.

Chapter 11

"ARE WE READY FOR THIS?" Michael stood just outside the bedroom door, staring down the hall after his mother. "You know Mom going down first is only going to help so much. It's still going to be awkward as hell."

"I think that's an understatement," Fiona said.

"I think, maybe, I need a minute."

She looked up at Lizzie at the same time Michael did. He frowned. "You okay?"

Lizzie stood between them, hands knotted together in front of her stomach. She chewed on the inside of her cheek, hollowing out one side of her face. "Yeah, I just, I need a minute."

"Okay, I'll stay with you. You want me to stay with you?"

"No, it's fine, Mike. Go ahead. I'll just take a minute then be down after you."

He turned toward Fiona, looking worried, so she encouraged him on. "She's fine. I've got her. Go ahead. We'll see you down there."

"Okay." He moved to stand in front of his sister. One big hand cupped the back of her head and pulled her toward him until her cheek lay against his chest. He kissed the top of her head. "I'm just gonna be downstairs if you need me." Over Lizzie's head, he pinned Fiona with a hard, pleading stare. Fiona gave him a small smile. She'd heard him loud and clear. She would take care of Lizzie. And with that, Michael planted one more kiss on the top of Lizzie's head and left.

For a long moment after he was gone, Fiona and Lizzie didn't stir. They remained stuck in their positions, Fiona on the bed and Lizzie standing in the middle of the room with her back to her. Fiona didn't want to push or bother her. Lizzie had said she needed a minute, and Fiona didn't want to deny her that, but she also wanted to make sure Lizzie was truly okay. Before she could ask, though, Lizzie finally shook up the stillness, crossing to the door and closing it, shutting them in together. She lay her forehead against the door, hand still poised on the doorknob.

Fiona stood. "Lizzie?"

All she heard in response was the click of the lock being pressed in. Then Lizzie turned, and something sparked inside Fiona. The look in Lizzie's eyes was pure heat, unexpected, terrifying, thrilling. Her tongue darted out, slid along her bottom lip, and when she spoke, her voice rasped as if strained.

"Come here."

Those two little words were a lasso, thrown with expert precision. They wrapped around Fiona and tugged, hard, nearly pulling her to her knees. She felt weak. "Are you okay?" She swallowed and forced her feet to remain rooted to the floor.

"Come here."

"Maybe we should talk."

"Or we could *not* talk, and you could come here."

"What about breakfast?"

"Okay, fine." Her shirt landed silently in a crumpled pile on the floor. "I'll come to you then." Gray bra on display again, she crossed the room in five short steps and reached for Fiona's hands. She didn't have an ounce of hesitation in her when she placed them directly on her barely covered breasts. "Do I need to be any more obvious?"

Fiona stared at her hands covering Lizzie's breasts. Her fingers spread of their own accord and squeezed, their natural reaction to the wonder that was a beautiful woman's body. She didn't speak, couldn't speak. Her tongue had shriveled to a prune. Her throat was dry land and scorching heat. Her brain might have even short-circuited for a moment, because all she could do was stand and stare and squeeze.

"Well, you're squeezing them, so that's a good sign." Lizzie snapped her fingers in the small space between them. "Fiona."

The choked sound that escaped Fiona's throat embarrassed her. She clamped her thighs together and looked up. "Huh?"

"Is this the first time you've ever seen boobs? Because it gets better. Just wait. There are nipples in there and everything."

The humor shook Fiona out of her stupor, and she laughed. "Shut up." She pulled her hands away. "Of course I've seen boobs before."

"Well, you seemed pretty mesmerized there for a second."

"I guess I just didn't expect you to whip them out like that and, you know, hand them to me."

"Seems to work for guys. Figured I'd give it a try."

Fiona snorted. "Never take sexual cues from guys."

"Good point."

"But feel free to put my hands on your boobs any time you like."

"So, are we done, then? With the hesitation? Because I'm ready. If you're ready, if you want to do this, I'm ready."

"Your entire family is downstairs waiting for us."

"I really don't care." She reached back and popped the clasp on her bra. It opened, and Fiona's eyes shot straight down. She watched as Lizzie slid the straps off her arms and tossed the scrap of material to the side. Her plump, heavy breasts sat beautifully on display, large pink nipples standing at attention as if eager to be tended to. Lizzie was just as freckled under her clothes as she was everywhere else, and just as beautiful.

"God, your body is amazing."

"Thank you." Lizzie smiled, and despite having just boldly stripped her top bare, it was a shy smile, shyer than Fiona was used to seeing on her face. Still, she held her head high when she propped her hands on her hips and said, "I'd like to see yours, too."

Fiona was caught in that place between awkward and aroused. She was wet and wanting, could already feel her underwear sticking to her, but she couldn't stop thinking about the last time she'd let herself go with Lizzie. Rosie's stricken face, her standing in the open doorway. She glanced nervously past Lizzie to the closed door.

"I locked it. Don't worry."

"You're sure?"

"I'm sure."

"Maybe you should check it."

"It's locked, Fiona. Trust me."

"Have you ever done this before?"

"What?" Lizzie moved closer and placed her hands on Fiona's shoulders. They skirted down her arms then under to her sides. "Secretly had sex with a girl in my brother's room while the rest of my family was downstairs?" Her fingers curled under the hem of Fiona's sweatshirt and tank top and played across her stomach. Fiona closed her eyes and reveled in the touch, the way it made her itch with want. She trembled under each tickling, teasing dip of a finger beneath the waistband of her shorts. "Oddly enough, yes, I have."

Fiona's eyes shot open. "Seriously?"

"Seriously, though it wasn't Jack's room. It was Charlie's."

"I feel like I shouldn't find that as hot as I do."

Lizzie laughed out loud, hooked a hand around the back of Fiona's head, and jerked her in. The sound of her laugh vibrated against Fiona's teeth as they came together in a hard, hilarious, wonderful kiss. It was playful and eager, messy, and the push-pull of it nearly knocked Fiona off her feet. She stumbled backward, the backs of her knees hitting the edge of the bed, and caught herself with one hand on the mattress.

"Lay down," Lizzie said and undid the button on her jeans. "I want to sit on your face."

Fiona nearly swallowed her tongue, though she wasn't sure why she found it so shocking. Lizzie had been bold and blunt since the moment they met. No reason for that to change in the bedroom. She stripped off her sweatshirt and tank top, so she was as bare as Lizzie, then dropped onto the edge of the bed and reached for Lizzie's jeans. She grabbed the waistband to help yank them down over her wide, perfect hips. "I've been told it's a good place to sit."

Lizzie grinned and pushed Fiona down on her back. "That's what I was counting on." Her jeans flopped off her legs with a kick of one bare foot, leaving her in nothing but a pair of plain black cotton panties. Fiona couldn't stop staring. Every inch of her, from her freckled, dimpled thighs to her ridiculously tiny feet, begged to be touched, kissed, adored. When her underwear hit the floor, Fiona took a deep breath. Her stomach was in knots, tension balling up wherever it could. Her entire body felt like a trigger waiting to be pulled.

The mattress sunk under her as Lizzie crawled on top of her, knees first straddling Fiona's hips, then higher. Higher still. Her exposed slit swiped over Fiona's quivering stomach, and Fiona's breath shot from her lungs as she felt it. Lizzie was soaked.

"Oh God," Lizzie choked out, nearly stopping right there. She shuddered over top of Fiona then moved further up. She stopped over Fiona's chest, hovering, and lowered herself onto the valley between Fiona's small breasts. She rocked her cunt against Fiona's chest, slicking her skin with the evidence of her desire, and Fiona dug her short nails into her thighs. "You have no idea how much I've wanted to do this."

"I think I have some idea," Fiona said between shallow breaths. "Come up here. I want to taste you."

Lizzie planted one knee on each side of Fiona's head and looked down at her. She bit her lip and cocked a brow. "Well, this is an enticing view."

"I know what you mean," Fiona said, though the words left her as barely more than a whisper. Her throat felt tight again. She stared up at Lizzie from between her legs, arms wrapped firmly around her thighs. She took in the sight of her, hovering overhead. Her freckled thighs and soft belly, her breasts heaving with each breath. Thick hair frizzed out around her face as she grinned down at Fiona, and her pupils were so big that her eyes appeared nearly the same color for once—a deep, dark ocean blue. She was stunning. "You ready for this?"

Lizzie answered by lowering herself onto Fiona's mouth. She stifled her own cry as soon as Fiona's eager tongue swiped up the length of her, then found its way inside. Her hand dropped onto the mattress above Fiona's head and dug into the comforter as she rocked against Fiona's mouth. "Oh fuck, Fiona," she whispered. "Oh fuck."

Fiona had never wanted to take her time more than she did in that moment. She wanted to taste every inch of Lizzie, drink her down until she was bone dry and spent, but she knew they didn't have much time. They were pressing their luck as it was. She reached around Lizzie's thighs and spread her lips with her fingers, took a deep breath through her nose, the scent of arousal dizzying her in the best way, and licked up the length of her again. When she wrapped her lips around Lizzie's clit and sucked, one eager, vicious pull, Lizzie's thighs closed around her ears like a vice. The entire world disappeared into muffled thumps inside her head, only the wet sounds of Lizzie's pleasure amplified in her ears.

Warm, soft flesh rippled and dipped and sank around her fingers, like taffy molding and folding around Fiona's hungry grip. She couldn't stop her hips from bucking up as Lizzie grew wild on top of her, riding her face with abandon. Her own clit was throbbing. She could feel her liquid want dripping down the back of one thigh, and all she could do was hold onto Lizzie as if she might fall off the edge of the earth otherwise. It served her well as Lizzie took the hint, leaning back to balance on one hand. The other shot down Fiona's pajama shorts and straight to the source of her agony.

She cried out against Lizzie's soaked flesh as two fingers sank into her and curled, an overwhelming, intoxicating hit to her senses. A high, a relief, all mixed into one skilled stroke. She nearly came on the spot. It wouldn't take long, and Lizzie was already close. Fiona could tell by the way her thighs were shaking, the way her inner walls clamped down around Fiona's tongue as if trying to hold onto it. She was close, and the closer she drew, the more Fiona's body ached to follow.

"Come with me," Lizzie said, the words muffled but clear enough. "I want you to come with me."

Fiona didn't dare free her mouth to answer. Her body would have to answer for her. She pulled Lizzie's clit into her mouth again and sucked hard. One pull, two.

Lizzie followed her rhythm with her strokes and curls, fucking Fiona as intently as she was being fucked. When she rolled over the edge and hit her climax with a breathless growled curse, Fiona rolled into her own orgasm right after her. Her hips rocketed off the bed, one hand shooting down to wrap around Lizzie's wrist. She held it tight, pressing Lizzie's hand as hard against her clit as she could while sucking her into her mouth. Together, they froze at the apex of pleasure, nothing but dizzying, trembling perfection for one incredible moment in time, then slowly, slowly, they rocked back down to earth.

Fiona wiped her mouth on the inside of Lizzie's right thigh and then planted a kiss there. She helped her slide off of her, shuddering as Lizzie pulled out of her in the process. When they collapsed on the bed, side by side, to catch their breath, Lizzie reached over and patted Fiona's thigh. "Fiona?"

The tart taste of her coated Fiona's mouth. She licked her lips, savoring it, and turned her head on the mattress. "Yeah?"

Lizzie tangled their hands together. "Do you have any idea how hot you are?"

"I do have a mirror in my apartment."

The laugh Lizzie set free was shaky and beautiful. She rolled over and threw a naked leg over Fiona's hips. "That was the second-best bit of cardio I've had in a while."

Fiona frowned and pinched her thigh. "Second best?"

"Tuesday-morning Zumba classes with Miguel in Lake Balboa Park." She kissed Fiona's bare shoulder. "He's just so enthusiastic."

They laughed into a kiss, slow and soft. Fiona nuzzled her nose against Lizzie's and rubbed up and down the length of her now-chilled thigh. "That was definitely the fastest I've ever gone from a first kiss to oral."

"Time crunches will do that for you." Lizzie kissed her again. "We'll take our time later. I promise." Another kiss. "And if you're interested, I even have a new toy in my suitcase I've been dying to try."

They wrapped fully around each other, as close as they could get, and were content to simply hold one another for a moment. "Sounds perfect," Fiona said, burying her face in the crook of Lizzie's neck, in her mess of red hair. Apricots. The scent was quickly becoming a favorite.

"I'm looking forward to getting you out of your pants next time."

"You aren't the only one." Fiona wiggled her hips a bit. "Being this wet and clothed is grossly uncomfortable."

"Trust me. I know," Lizzie said. "I've been walking around like that for days now thanks to you."

Fiona squeezed her tighter. "As if you haven't been gleefully torturing me since I got here."

"I'll confess to that." She sucked Fiona's bottom lip into her mouth and bit down on it gently. Just a nip that made Fiona's thighs ache. "But I won't apologize." She let go of Fiona's hand just long enough to swipe the hair from her face. "You're too beautiful, and I wanted you." Her fingers trailed down Fiona's cheek, down her neck, and rested just above her left breast. "I want you."

The ache, this time, blossomed in her chest. Her heart swelled at the words, and she found she wanted nothing more than to bask in all the new, wild, and wonderful effects this woman so easily had on her.

Lizzie kissed her again, slowly and soundly. "We should get down there."

The annoyed sigh that dragged its way up from the depths of Fiona's soul made them both laugh. She buried her face in Lizzie's neck and hair and savored the feeling of having someone in her arms, of being held in return with such care and want. It had been such a terribly long time. "Just one more minute."

"Yeah." Lizzie tangled her fingers in Fiona's hair and scratched gently at her scalp. "One more minute."

Chapter 12

"Wait."

Lizzie stopped Fiona just outside the dining room. Inside, the family spoke loudly, animatedly. Strong opinions with sharp edges tossed about from one end of the table to the next. Lizzie and Fiona pressed themselves to the wall as Lizzie held a finger to her lips. She wanted to hear what they were saying.

"...and she can't expect us not to be confused."

"What is there to be confused about?" Michael's voice took center stage. "She's gay, Brian. There's nothing confusing about that."

"There's nothing confusing about that? Are you serious? Two hours ago, Fiona was *your* girlfriend, and now she's what? *Lizzie's* girlfriend? Are you seriously gonna sit here and try to say that's not confusing as hell?"

Lizzie looked at Fiona and whispered, *"Are you my girlfriend?"*

Fiona shrugged. She didn't have a clue. It had only been a few days of flirtation, and they'd only just had their first kiss the night before, their first *anything*. It was too soon to be thinking about labels.

"I told you, it was all pretend," Michael said. "Fiona was never my girlfriend. She's just my friend."

"That doesn't make it any less confusing, Mike. It just makes you an ass."

"Okay." Sophie's soft voice cut in. "Stop. We're not going to start calling each other names. Michael had his reasons to do what he did, and Lizzie had her reasons not to tell us until now."

"She hasn't actually told *us* anything." Jessie's voice was sharp, serious. It lacked its usual dry, playful tone. She sounded more upset than anything.

"She didn't want us to know. If she did, she would've told us herself. Instead, Mom told everyone for her, and now we know something we weren't even supposed to know yet."

Brian scoffed at her. "What's it matter who told who?"

"It matters because it's *Lizzie's* business. If you had something you wanted to keep secret until you were ready to tell, you'd be pissed if one of us found out accidentally and told everyone, so stop acting like it's okay that you're all sitting here talking about something we shouldn't even know about yet. She should've gotten to tell us herself when she was ready, on her terms. That's how coming out is supposed to work."

"Oh, and you're the expert on coming out now? Why's that? Because you're on the Internet day and night? You're up to date on all the new terms and rules we're supposed to know?"

"Brian, that's enough." Charlie Sr.'s voice surprised Fiona. It was severe, all discipline with no wiggle room. It clearly surprised Lizzie, too, because she looked at Fiona with her eyebrows raised.

"I'm just saying. I don't know why everyone's getting all pissy at me. I'm not the one who ruined Christmas."

"No one's ruined Christmas."

"I don't know, Dad. Feels pretty ruined to me."

"Now, Brian, I said that's enough. I've just about had it up to here." Charlie Sr.'s voice hit a volume high. "When Lizzie's ready to come down, she'll come down, and we'll talk about all this then. Until then, quiet, all of you, and finish your breakfast. The girls'll be ready to open presents as soon as Charlie brings them in from outside."

"She's not coming down, her or Fiona," Brian dared to argue. "Michael's been down here twenty minutes, and neither of them's come down yet. They're hiding out, because they don't want to face us."

"Well, can you blame them?" Michael asked. "You haven't shut up about it since I got down here, so no wonder they don't want to come down."

"I just think they owe us an explanation. Hell, for all we know, they've been carrying on behind all our backs since the day they both got here, but instead of coming down here and owning up to it, they're just gonna hide out up there all day."

"Probably because they don't want to have to deal with shit like this," Jessie snapped. The sound of a fork clattering against a plate echoed out from the kitchen.

"Jessica Lynn!"

"No, Mom, I'm done. I don't even want to open presents." Her slapping footsteps crossed the dining room, making their way toward where Fiona and Lizzie stood hiding. She stepped just beyond them. "You know, gay or not, Lizzie's our sister. The least you guys could do is not talk about her behind her back like you do everyone else in this stupid town. Especially you, Brian, since we all know you're screwing a married woman, so you've got no place to talk. The rest of you, I don't even know."

Fiona stood stiff as a board, watching Lizzie's expressions run the range of emotions. Humor. Hurt. Disappointment. Surprise. Pride. There was so much to unpack in what they knew, what they didn't know, what had happened, and what was yet to come. There was so much to address, so many people to talk to, deal with, face. Fiona didn't envy Lizzie at all, and for the first time since arriving at the McElroy home, she was actually grateful she didn't have siblings. Clearly, from one issue to the next, you never knew what you were going to get.

Jessie shot out of the dining room like a streak of lightning and immediately stumbled over her own feet at the sight of them hiding behind the wall. Shock riddled her features for a moment, then her eyes began to water. And to think Fiona had suspected she wasn't even human. But when Lizzie grabbed Jessie and pulled her into a hug, Jessie cried real human tears and squeezed her sister like she was a life raft.

"I'm sorry," she said as Lizzie rubbed her back and petted her hair. "I'm sorry."

"You don't have anything to be sorry for."

"I'm sorry for *them*." She huffed as if annoyed that her body had dared to experience emotions and pulled back. She wiped her eyes with the back of her hand and motioned toward the dining room. "They're being assholes."

"Eh, just Brian," Lizzie said and wiped away a streak of moisture Jessie had missed. "And he's always been an asshole."

"Grandma said some things, too."

"Yeah, well, where do you think Brian gets it from?"

Jessie let out a wet laugh and held her sister's hand. "Are you okay?" She glanced at Fiona. "Are you guys okay?"

The urge to hug her hit Fiona hard, but she restrained herself. Jessie looked like she wanted to vomit just from having to endure feelings and an extended conversation. Instead, she nodded, while Lizzie stroked Jessie's arm and said, "Yeah, we're fine."

"Really?"

"Really."

"You want to get out of here? I can steal Mike's keys, maybe. His car is closest to the road."

"I wish, kid," Lizzie said with a laugh. "I think I've got to stay and face the music, though."

"You want me to go in with you?" Her face made it clear that she wanted anything in the world *but* to go back in there. "Because I will if you want me to, even though I already stormed out and everything."

"Nah, you go ahead. Go hide in your room. I know you hate emotions."

She nodded, her face pinched into an expression that made her look constipated. "I really do."

"Go on then. Hide for the both of us." Lizzie ran her hands through her hair and let out a heavy breath. "But I'm definitely going to need to smoke a bowl when this is over. You still have my stash?"

"Of course."

"See? This is why I love you."

"Yeah, you, too." She hesitated. "Are you sure you're okay?"

"I'm fine. I promise." She put a hand on Jessie's shoulder. "I really appreciate you standing up for me in there."

"You're welcome, but, like, I know I said I was done, but I really did want that last biscuit, so if you could steal me one, that'd be great."

Lizzie snorted. "You got it."

"'Kay. Cool. Thanks." She glanced at Fiona again. "Don't hurt my sister. Okay? Because I actually like you, which is seriously rare, so really, don't ruin it."

"I wouldn't dream of it." Fiona suppressed a laugh when Jessie rolled her eyes and walked off, headed for the stairs. She clearly intended to do exactly as Lizzie had said: hide in her room and wait for all the emotional turmoil to pass. *If* it passed at all.

Fiona and Lizzie entered the dining room holding hands. It was a daring display that inspired such a grimace on Grandma Sophia's face that Fiona was briefly concerned she might be having a stroke. "Well," she said and set her coffee down. Her eyes remained fixed on their hands, and the smoking cigarette in her mouth bounced between her lips as she spoke. "I was waiting to hear it straight from the horse's mouth, but I guess we've got our answer now, don't we?" She shook her head. "You see, son? Why I told you not to let her go off out there?"

"Mom."

"No. Now, I told you it was a bad idea and look." She sneered at Charlie Sr., lip curled up in a show of either disgust or disappointment. Fiona didn't know which, though she imagined it to be both. "It's just the way it was with Dot and Pat McGowan's boy. You know their boy, Johnny, moved out to California a few years back, and it wasn't two months 'fore he was calling her and Pat up, saying he'd decided he was a woman on the inside. I tell you, Dottie like to had a coronary, bless her heart, and Pat wasn't much better. Swore that boy off soon as he got off the phone. I told Dottie, I said, 'You need to bring Johnny home straight away, get him ironed out right again.' But did she? And now, look, he's running around California in a skirt and popping off at the mouth about the president on that Facebook. She showed me. Charlie, I'm telling you, you need to get a handle on this right now, 'fore it gets out of hand."

"I'm not gay because I moved to California, Grandma," Lizzie said, barely containing an eye roll.

"Well."

"I've known since I was twelve."

"Yeah, right," Brian said. "And we're just now finding out about it? Please."

"Yeah, did you ever consider that *this* might be why? Because I was afraid of how you guys would react? Because I was. I still am, but I'm tired of hiding it."

"You mean you found someone to fool around with." Brian cut a glance Fiona's way.

"Why are you being such an ass about this?" Lizzie asked him, point-blank. "It's only you who's giving me shit about it. I mean, I expected Grandma to have a problem with it, but you're acting like I've personally offended you. What is your problem, Brian? What have you got against gay people?"

"Nothing!" He snapped at her. "I ain't got nothing against gay people. I've got something against liars."

He shoved his chair back, the wood scraping on the floor, and stomped past them out of the room. Lizzie took a second to steady herself, squeezing Fiona's hand as hard as Fiona could handle. She then held her head high, looked around the table, and said, "Does anyone else have a problem with me being gay?"

"I certainly don't," Grace said, surprising everyone by speaking up at all. She dropped her napkin onto her plate and stood. When she wrapped Lizzie up in a hug, Lizzie closed her eyes and let out a slow breath.

Another chair scraped the floor, and in seconds, Sophie's arms were around Grace and Lizzie both, holding them tight. "I don't either. I never could. I love you."

Fiona released Lizzie's hand and edged out of the way, giving them space as Michael, eyes red and watery, surrounded his three sisters with his long, lanky arms. He lay his head on top of Lizzie's and didn't say a word. He didn't need to. When Charlie Sr.'s chair squeaked back, the sea of siblings parted, and Lizzie stood like a small, spooked animal, facing her father.

He opened his arms to her, wide. A cry that shot straight to Fiona's heart echoed around the room as Lizzie covered her mouth with one hand and walked into his waiting embrace. He held her close, one hand on her back, the other buried in her hair. He kissed the top of her head, then dropped down by her ear. Whatever words he said were whispered so quietly that no one in the room except Lizzie heard, but Fiona could tell by their body language that they were soft words, gentle words, words to soothe and reassure.

The needling sensation of eyes on her drew her attention toward one of the two women still occupying seats around the table. Rosie openly watched her with a smile. It wasn't as warm as the others she'd received throughout her time with the family, but it was there. It was open to growth, and that was enough for Fiona. She returned the timid expression just as she heard Sophie say, "This is definitely the most interesting Christmas we've had in a while."

The McElroy huddle broke into loud laughter, Sophie, Grace, and Lizzie each wiping their eyes free of tears. "You're welcome," Lizzie said, holding her dad in a side hug as the others shuffled awkwardly in place.

"All right," Charlie Sr. said. "What are we all standing around for? We've got presents to open. Someone call in Charlie and the girls."

"Uh, son," Grandma Sophia butted in. "We're not done with this. Not by a mile."

"Yes, we are, Mom." He barely spared her a glance. "Lizzie's said what she needed to say, and that's that. We're not going to talk about it anymore."

"No, that's certainly *not* that. It's not right, and you know it. I didn't raise you to let your kids behave this way."

"Grandma, please," Lizzie tried, but the old woman waved her off.

"Now, Lizzie, you know I love you, hon, but this ain't right. Being out there's got you mixed up, and then this one comes along, and..." She waved a hand toward Fiona. "You need help, hon. You need to come home and let us get you taken care of, so you can get your head screwed on right again."

The slam of Rosie's hand to the table vibrated through the room. "That's enough!" She pointed sharply at her husband. "*That's* your baby, Sophia. You raised your baby, all your babies, but now you're done. Elizabeth is *my* baby, mine, and I'll see to her how I see fit. And that's the end of it." The napkin she'd balled up in her lap opened with a flutter, and she folded it neatly and carefully as she spoke. Not once did she look at any of them. "Now, you can either accept that, and you can sit there and drink your coffee and spend Christmas with your family, or Charlie can take you home. Either way, I won't hear another word of it."

She glanced up, only once, and sent a cutting look Grandma Sophia's way. "And *this one's* name is Fiona," she added, tilting her head toward Fiona, "and she's been nothing but kind and patient with all of us since she got here, so you can just hush up about her, too. Hear?" She didn't wait for an answer and was already on her feet. "It's time we *all* evolved a little." Without a second glance, she barreled toward the door. "Let's go, kids. The girls won't wait all day."

As she passed by her children, she ran a hand down the back of Lizzie's hair, a simple, fleeting touch Fiona knew meant so much, then hustled out of the room.

Michael found his way to Fiona's side as the rest of the family filed out, one by one. He wound their hands together and led her into the hall, leaving only Charlie Sr. and Grandma Sophia behind to have whatever harsh discussion Fiona imagined was in store. In the long, picture-strewn hallway by the den, Michael stopped and drew Fiona to his side. "Well, that was interesting," he said and rested his back against the only part of the wall he could find not adorned in frames.

"Yeah. Your mom is fierce."

"She has her moments. That's for sure."

"You think she can? Evolve, I mean. Your grandma?"

"Probably not." He sounded truly disappointed in the fact, and Fiona understood. It was hell to love someone who couldn't love you back, not for who you were but rather for who they wished you could be. It wasn't any kind of love to envy. She could only imagine what was going through his mind in that moment, perhaps the realization that he would likely be met with the same reception from his grandma should he ever choose to come out as asexual. The thought devastated Fiona. "I hope so, though," he said and knocked his hip against her side. "You okay, kid?"

"I'm good." She lay her head against his arm. "Thanks for standing up for her. Lizzie."

"Always." He stared down at her, and she could tell he was trying to figure out where she stood in that moment, with him, with the family, with Lizzie, with herself even. He always looked at her that way when he wanted to know how she was feeling or what she was thinking but didn't want to ask. She expected him to anyway, because that's just the way he was. He could rarely leave anything alone. Instead, he bumped her again and quietly said, "We don't have to stay."

"What do you mean? You want to leave?"

"We could head back early."

"But it's your family's Christmas."

He shrugged. "We have one every year, and this wouldn't be the first I've missed. I don't need to be here for presents. I'd rather know you were somewhere where you felt comfortable, and I don't think you do here, not anymore anyway. That's probably not going to change anytime soon."

"Michael."

"I'm not blaming you or anything," he said quickly. "It's okay. You have every right to feel uncomfortable, and I'm sure it'll pass once everything dies down and gets back to normal, but there's really just no sense in us staying here when things are like this. You know what I mean? It's family drama. You shouldn't have to be caught up in the middle of it."

"I think I might have caused it."

"Don't think that. Really." He grabbed her hand and held it tight. "Lizzie would've eventually come out on her own. You were just kind of her tipping point, I guess."

"Sometimes, we need a little push."

"Yeah."

"You could have told me, you know. About you."

"I know."

"Do you, really?"

"Fiona." He turned fully toward her and looked her right in the eyes. "You're my favorite person in the whole world. Trust me, the minute I'm ready to have an actual, *sober* conversation about it, you'll be the first person I call." His arms slinked around her middle and folded her in against him. "Come here." They stood that way for a long time, just hugging alone in an empty hallway. "Whatever you want to do, we'll do. And if that means you want to get out of here, then I'm ready to go."

It was one of those moments, the kind in which she was hit with a sudden rush of immense affection. The kind in which she realized, fully, just how much Michael McElroy meant to her. She clutched the soft, fuzzy material of his sweater a little tighter. "As good as that sounds, going home and crashing on your couch—"

"With a pizza."

"—*with* a pizza." She tossed her head back. "Holy God, that sounds amazing."

"So, we're going then?"

Fiona stepped back and ran her hands down her tired face, then planted them on her hips. "I don't want to leave Lizzie here." She looked back toward the far end of the hall. "Do you think we could take her with us?"

"Back to St. Louis?"

"If she wants to, of course. I mean, we won't take her against her will or anything, but if she wants to go, then I think we should invite her to come stay with us for a while. She could stay at your place or mine. Or both. Whatever."

"You think she'd want to after everything? I won't be surprised if she's already on a plane back to LA by the time we get to the living room. Grandma was really pissing me off."

"I think coming out is hard," Fiona said. "Someone is pretty much always bound to piss someone off. But I know if I were her, I'd need to get away, too. Sometimes, it's just better to do that with people who love you."

His eyes bulged. "You *love* her?"

"You know what I mean."

"I know." He laughed and looped an arm around her neck. "Come on. Let's go find her."

They expected to find Lizzie in the living room. Instead, they found her halfway up the stairs in a shouting match with Brian, who stood at the top, yelling down at her.

"I just think it's messed up." His face was as red as a ripe cherry. "And I'm entitled to my opinion."

"You're also entitled to silence, but I don't see you seizing that right any time soon," Lizzie said. "I didn't tell you because I didn't tell *anyone*. It wasn't you specifically, so stop being such a baby about it, for Christ's sake."

"But you were the first person I told that April was still married to her ex."

"Oh, please. Grace was the first person you told."

"She doesn't count."

"I'm sure she'd appreciate you saying so."

"You know what I mean." He walked down a step, then another. His voice softened a bit as he took a breath and blew it out in one loud, heavy rush. "She's my twin. Telling her is like telling my reflection. But you were the first person I told after her, because I thought that's what you and me did—tell each other things. But I feel like I'm the last person to find out about you."

"Brian, you literally found out at the same time as everyone else."

"Bullshit." He nodded his chin toward the bottom of the stairs where Fiona and Michael stood watching the scene unfold. "You're telling me you didn't tell Michael first? How else would he know to bring your girlfriend here for you?"

"Are you serious right now?" Lizzie stomped up the stairs. As soon as she reached Brian's side, she smacked him on the back of the head. "You big idiot."

"Ow!" He rubbed the back of his head. "What?"

"I never even met Fiona before Michael brought her here."

"Yeah, right."

"I swear!" She widened her eyes at the two of them, expectant. "Guys."

"It's true, man," Michael said. "I didn't know about Lizzie. It's a total coincidence that they, you know, fell for each other or whatever. I swear I thought Fiona would be the only lesbian here."

"Fiona also thought Fiona would be the only lesbian here," Fiona said, raising a hand.

"See? I didn't lie to you."

Brian looked at Lizzie like a scolded puppy. "Well, you still didn't tell me."

"And now you know, so can you please just get over it already? I'm not Mom. I'm not going to coddle you." He caught himself on the wall as she shoved him. "This is *my* day to be a big baby, not yours. Okay? If anyone's going to throw a fit about being mistreated, it's going to be me. So, how about you just agree to whine about it later and give me a hug now?"

His childish grumbling as he shuffled into Lizzie's arms made Fiona laugh. She looked at Michael. "Is there ever a dull day in your house?"

"Not a one."

"Why aren't you guys in the living room?" Lizzie headed back downstairs, Brian following right behind her. "Mom's probably about ready to explode. She's been trying to get everyone in there since the dining room."

"I think she gave up," Michael said. "She was just sitting in the recliner, staring at the tree, when we walked through."

"Oh hell. She's shut down."

"What does that mean?" Fiona asked as the other three chuckled. "Is she okay?"

"Yeah, she'll be fine," Michael said. "She just does that sometimes. I think she just hits maximum *mom*-ing for a day. Like, she just hits a limit and goes into statue mode."

"Eight kids'll do that to you," Brian said, passing by them. "I'll round everyone up."

Lizzie started to follow after him but stopped when Michael grabbed her arm. When she turned to look at him, her usual sweet, teasing smile was in place but appeared more practiced than genuine. Fiona could see in her body how tired she was, how heavy the day was weighing on her. As far as coming-out affairs went, Grandma Sophia hadn't been kind, but the whole affair could've been much worse. Fiona figured that was just the nature of the thing, though—the immensity of releasing a secret that had been packed and pressed so tightly inside for so many years. Her own coming out had been an exhausting affair. She still felt tired just thinking about it. She imagined the same was true for Lizzie and likely would be for a while yet to come.

"Hey," Lizzie said softly, rubbing Michael's hand where it lay on her arm. "Everything okay?"

"Yeah, everything's fine with us. We were more concerned about you. Fiona was thinking maybe you might—"

"Want to get out of here," Fiona finished. She pointed between herself and Michael. "With us."

Lizzie's smile grew a bit. "Another shitty horror movie?"

"A little farther than the movie theater, actually." Michael scratched the back of his head, then stuffed his hands into the pockets of his jeans. "Back to St. Louis."

Her brows ticked up. "You're leaving early?"

"Only if you'll come with us. You weren't supposed to go back to LA for another week anyway, right?"

"That's right, though I was considering amending that plan. You know, given everything."

Fiona stepped closer and took Lizzie's hand. "Come back with us. We'll gorge ourselves on pizza and beer and *Game of Thrones*."

"You can crash on my couch," Michael said, to which Lizzie scoffed.

"I'm not sleeping on your couch. I'll sleep in the bed."

"No. You kick in your sleep."

"I don't do that anymore."

"Yes, you do."

"We haven't shared a bed in, like, six years. Not since that shitty motel outside New Orleans."

"And you kicked the whole night."

"Well, a little kick never killed anybody, Michael. Geez."

"Said the person doing the kicking."

"The person doing the kicking can sleep in *my* bed," Fiona said. "I've got no problem sharing."

Lizzie pursed her lips as if attempting to hide a smile. "Hm. Let me think about it."

"All right." Michael smacked his lips as if he suddenly had a bad taste in his mouth. "You do that. Without me. I'm gonna go tell Mom we're heading back early."

Once he was gone, Lizzie swung toward Fiona and looped her arms around her waist. She pulled her in so that their chests met and kissed her chin. Then her cheek. Her lips. "So," she said quietly, "sharing a bed already, huh? That's not moving too fast?"

"My head was literally between your legs just a few hours ago."

"Mm." Lizzie hummed, a delicious sound that made Fiona's stomach flutter. "Yes, it was." She swiped a strand of hair behind Fiona's ear. "Definitely one of my fonder Christmas memories."

"Not the fondest?"

"Ask me again tomorrow." She grinned. "The day's not over yet."

Fiona laughed out loud and pressed the sound to Lizzie's lips. It vibrated between them, warm and wonderful, and all the tension of the day seeped out and away.

Chapter 13

LEAVING THE MCELROY HOME PROVED to be as awkward for Fiona as her arrival. The events of the weekend hung in the air like a thick fog. The entire family, with the merciful exception of Grandma Sophia, who elected to remain in her chair in the living room, had gathered on the large front porch to say goodbye. Fiona stood among them with her suitcase handle in one hand and the tinfoil-covered remainder of her prize pie in the other. The smile she wore felt as oversized and uncomfortable as the puffy marshmallow coat Rosie had insisted she take with her.

"Are you *sure* you want to go back early?" Rosie's hands skated up and down Michael's arms. "I think you should stay."

"It's fine, Mom. It's just one day. We aren't missing anything."

"I'll be the judge of that."

"Really." He drew her into a hug and patted her back. "It's better that we go ahead and go."

"Oh, hon. No one here's going to make a stink, really. I'll make sure of it."

"Mom," Lizzie said, shoving Michael out of the way to hug her, "we're going." She slung one arm around Rosie's neck and smacked a kiss on her cheek. "Stink or no stink, so you'll just have to let us."

"Well." She cupped Lizzie's cheek, then gave it a quick pinch. "That doesn't mean I have to like it."

"All right." Charlie Sr. massaged his wife's shoulders, then gently moved her aside. "Let's let the rest of us get our hugs in so the kids can get on the road. It'll be dark before you know it."

"It's not even lunch yet, Dad."

"Come here." He held Lizzie close, resting his cheek on the top of her head. "You don't get into any trouble while you're up there, hear?"

"Nope. I plan to get into as much trouble as I possibly can."

He chuckled. "Little devil."

"Always." Lizzie turned toward the rest of the family, all hovering around like a flock of pigeons waiting for crumbs, and opened her arms wide. "Who's next?"

One by one, the McElroy family said their goodbyes. They hugged on Michael and Lizzie as if the two were headed off for war. Fiona wondered if it was always this way or if this Christmas's shocking revelations had anything to do with it. As they went about it all, Rosie slipped out of the crowd and right into Fiona's orbit.

"Oh," Fiona said. "Mrs. McElroy."

"Oh, now, hon, we don't have to go back to that." She held her hands just in front of her, just over her stomach with her fingers locked together as if she was unsure of what to do with them. It clearly wasn't in her nature to keep her hands to herself. She was a toucher, a patter, a hugger, but the ease between them seemed to have been soured. Rosie's smile wasn't as big or as bright and even seemed a bit timid. "I don't want you to think I'm angry with you, because I'm not."

"Are you sure?"

"Well, I've got no reason to be, do I? It was Michael's half-cocked plan, after all." She untangled her hands and reached out but seemed to think better of it just before she touched. Her hand retracted. "You're still someone special to Michael, whether you're dating him or not, and I suppose now you're pretty special to Lizzie, too."

Fiona tightened her hold on her suitcase and pie. She shifted from foot to foot, unsure of what to do or say. "They're special to me, too. Both of them."

"I hope so."

"They are."

"Good." A long pause followed, filled only by the chatter of the others moving and talking around them. "Well, I guess I'll say Merry Christmas, then." She reached out again and, this time, followed through. Her hand landed on Fiona's upper arm, a gentle weight, and gave a soothing squeeze.

"Merry Christmas," Fiona said with a smile that felt more sad than good. "I'm glad I finally got to meet you. All of you."

"Hopefully, we'll get to see you again soon." Fiona expected the words to sound hollow, something said out of courtesy or expectation, but they didn't. They sounded and felt as genuine as Rosie's motherly touch.

"Do you really mean that?" Fiona asked before Rosie could walk away.

"Oh, hon." A bright smile showed all of Rosie's front teeth, a smile that so reminded Fiona of Lizzie. "One thing you'll learn about me is I rarely say things I don't mean." She squeezed Fiona's arm again. "Now, you take care of yourself, hear? And come back and see us."

Fiona grinned to herself as Rosie blended back into her pack of children. "Yes, ma'am." She watched them all smiling at one another, laughing and pushing each other's shoulders. Joking and saying goodbye over and over as they started conversation after conversation, never quite able to make a clean break. It was a beautiful kind of chaos Fiona was content to witness and grateful to be a part of.

"And when Jack calls, tell him to FaceTime me after, okay?" Lizzie told Charlie as she reached behind her to find Fiona, as if sensing Fiona's presence. Fiona released her suitcase handle and took her hand instead. "Promise me."

"I already promised I would, Liz." Charlie laughed and kissed her temple, pulling her into a one-armed hug and yanking Fiona in along with his sister. "Now, stop hounding me."

"It's a favorite pastime of mine."

"I know."

"Tell Sophie to tell you to tell Jack to call, though, because even if you forget, she'll remember."

"How do you know I won't forget to tell her to tell me to tell Jack, though?"

"Oh, damn, you're right. Soph!"

"Hey." Michael sidled up beside Fiona and took the handle of her suitcase. "You ready to go?"

"I've been ready for a while now."

"Yeah, saying goodbye is a marathon in this family. You kind of just have to drag yourself away at some point." He glanced to where her hand entangled with Lizzie's. It had become a tether. Lizzie held on but strained against it, shouting reminders at one sibling, then another. "Oh, good. You've already got hold of her. Just tug her, and she'll come."

Fiona snorted. "Okay." She gave Lizzie's hand a gentle tug and was surprised to see it worked. Lizzie shuffled backward as if being reeled in on a fishing line.

"Wait," she said, suddenly digging her heels into the porch. "Where's Jessie?"

"I'm in the car!"

Everyone seemed to jump at the same time, startled by the annoyed voice ringing out from behind them. Jessie sat in the passenger seat of Michael's car with a bright-blue beanie jammed down over her thick hair. The driver's side window was down, and she seemed to have been watching them all for a while.

"What are you doing?" Michael asked, only then realizing that his keys weren't in his pocket anymore. The car was running, its exhaust billowing out the back pipe and clouding up the cold air.

"What does it look like I'm doing? I'm going with you guys."

"Jessica Lynn, you can't just hop in a car and decide to drive to a different state!"

"I'm not driving. Michael is."

Michael laughed and looked at Rosie. "Is it all right if she stays with me for a couple days?"

"Well, I guess, but you'll have to drive her back down."

"Yeah, I will."

She called to Jessie. "What about your presents, hon?"

"Yeah, I opened mine while you guys were arguing about Mike and Lizzie leaving. Literally died over the Ray Bans." She popped on a brand-new pair of sunglasses despite the sky being mostly gray. "Thanks!"

"Spoiled rotten, I tell you." Defeated, Rosie waved at her youngest. "I guess you're too grown now to kiss your old mom goodbye, then."

"Yup. Bye, Mom." The window began its ascent, and Jessie slowly disappeared behind the glass. "Love ya!"

"She seems pretty alive to me considering she 'literally died' an hour ago," Brian said with a snort. "All right, guys. I'm going in. It's cold as all get-out. See you guys." He clapped Michael on the shoulder. "Safe trip."

"Yeah, thanks, man."

All but Brian stayed to watch them toss their bags into the car and climb in. Lizzie and Fiona piled into the back as Michael took the driver's seat. Rosie waved and waved as the car started up and crept out of the snow-covered driveway.

"Finally," Jessie said as Fiona clipped in her seatbelt and Lizzie skipped her seatbelt altogether. She lay down across Fiona's lap instead and stared up at her, an easy smile on her beautiful, freckled face.

"Finally," she repeated, reaching up to trace the length of Fiona's nose with the tip of her index finger. "Here we go."

Fiona grabbed her hand and kissed her palm. "Here we go."

"Ooh, Mike, you think Taco Bell is open?" Jessie asked. "I'm munching so hard right now."

"Oh my God," he said, "are you high?"

Lizzie laughed and stretched one hand toward the front seat. "Pass it."

"I brought the pipe, too," Jessie said as she passed back a skinny silver vape pen. "It's in my bag."

"Nice." Lizzie quickly took a drag. She trapped the smoke in her chest for one long moment before blowing it loudly back out. "Want?"

Fiona looked at the pen being danced around in front of her face. "I'll pass on the pot," she said, "but I could definitely go for Taco Bell."

"Deal."

"As long as you're buying."

Lizzie narrowed her eyes at her, then smiled. "Deal."

"Will you buy mine, too?" Michael asked.

"No."

"But you're buying Fiona's."

"That's because she owes me," Fiona said, and Jessie leaned into the space between the seats so she could look back at them.

"What for?"

"Oh my God," Michael said as he looked up and caught Fiona's eyes in the rearview mirror. "Please don't."

It was too late. A laugh began to build in her chest. With one glance down at Lizzie, Fiona lost all control. She cackled around the words as she and Lizzie simultaneously shouted, "An incredible orgasm!"

About KL Hughes

KL Hughes is an American author and screenwriter. Growing up in a small town, she spent much of her time inventing various ways to entertain herself and others. Whether through vocal performances or theatrical reenactments of books, movies, and actual events, Hughes showcased her extensive imagination and creativity at an early age.

Hughes later pursued and earned a bachelor of liberal arts degree in theatre arts and English literature. Her collegiate studies allowed her to develop and hone her skills in both creative writing and editing.

Working as a writer full-time, Hughes lives in California with her wife and two dogs. When not writing, she enjoys theatre and film, travel, visits to old cemeteries and haunted houses, putting on one-woman musicals for her wife, long walks and hikes, family time, and, of course, a good book.

Connect With KL Hughes
Twitter: @Chrmdpoet

Other Books from Ylva Publishing

www.ylva-publishing.com

Popcorn Love
KL Hughes

ISBN: 978-3-95533-265-5
Length: 347 pages (113,000 words)

Her love life lacking, wealthy fashion exec Elena Vega agrees to a string of blind dates set up by her best friend Vivian in exchange for Vivian finding a suitable babysitter for her son, Lucas. Free-spirited college student Allison Sawyer fits the bill perfectly.

The Art of Us
KL Hughes

ISBN: 978-3-95533-890-9
Length: 218 pages (79,500 words)

When Charlee met a leggy brunette with a valedictorian medal hanging from her rear-view mirror and an attitude as biting as a Boston winter, it was love. For four years, she and Alexandra were unbreakable…until they weren't. A chance meeting years later sweeps them up in a whirlwind of heart-rending history. Is it too late? Or should the past remain the past?

Under a Falling Star
Jae

ISBN: 978-3-95533-238-9
Length: 369 pages (91,000 words)

Falling stars are supposed to be a lucky sign, but not for Austen. The first assignment in her new job—decorating the Christmas tree in the lobby—results in a trip to the ER after Dee, the company's COO, gets hit by the star-shaped tree topper. There's an instant attraction between them, but Dee is determined not to act on it, especially since Austen has no idea that Dee is her boss.

Face It
(The Scissor Link Series – Book 2)
Georgette Kaplan

ISBN: 978-3-95533-976-0
Length: 198 pages (70,000 words)

Ten years ago, Elizabeth Smile had one sizzling night with her roommate that left her craving more. Now her friend has reappeared with an odd request: Will Elizabeth play her fake girlfriend for a family Christmas in Ohio? The deal comes with a suspicious sister with her own agenda and the digging up of Elizabeth's old feelings. A twisty lesbian romance about getting more than we bargain for.

The Wrong McElroy
© 2019 by KL Hughes

ISBN: 978-3-96324-263-2

Also available as e-book.

Published by Ylva Publishing, legal entity of Ylva Verlag, e.Kfr.

Ylva Verlag, e.Kfr.
Owner: Astrid Ohletz
Am Kirschgarten 2
65830 Kriftel
Germany

www.ylva-publishing.com

First edition: 2019

Credits
Edited by Michelle Aguilar and Amber Williams
Cover Design by KL Hughes
Print Layout by Streetlight Graphics

www.ingramcontent.com/pod-product-compliance
Lightning Source LLC
Chambersburg PA
CBHW032148020726
47496CB00003B/767